Greed

Greed

*A Tale of Power and Abuse
in Medicine*

Boudreaux

Copyright © 2010 by Boudreaux.

Library of Congress Control Number:		2010909633
ISBN:	Hardcover	978-1-4535-3039-9
	Softcover	978-1-4535-3038-2
	Ebook	978-1-4535-3040-5

All rights reserved. No part of this book may be reproduced or transmitted in any form or by any means, electronic or mechanical, including photocopying, recording, or by any information storage and retrieval system, without permission in writing from the copyright owner.

This is a work of fiction. Names, characters, places and incidents either are the product of the author's imagination or are used fictitiously, and any resemblance to any actual persons, living or dead, events, or locales is entirely coincidental.

This book was printed in the United States of America.

To order additional copies of this book, contact:
Xlibris Corporation
1-888-795-4274
www.Xlibris.com
Orders@Xlibris.com
82598

Contents

Introduction 7

Chapter One:	6 A.M. Monday Morning	9
Chapter Two:	The Daily Grind...	19
Chapter Three:	Doctor Jim Turner, My Partner	34
Chapter Four:	Sex and Shopping...	43
Chapter Five:	Dinner With the Deluna's	49
Chapter Six:	Tuesday Morning, 4 A.M. Call Day..................	62
Chapter Seven:	Getting My Niece a Job....................................	70
Chapter Eight:	Nap Time	78
Chapter Nine:	Trauma Time	85
Chapter Ten:	Time For a Break	94
Chapter Eleven:	Call is Nearly Done..	103
Chapter Twelve:	Free Time	115
Chapter Thirteen:	Booty Call	124
Chapter Fourteen:	6 A.M. Thursday-Call Day	127
Chapter Fifteen:	Lunch Time...	139
Chapter Sixteen:	Nap Time	146
Chapter Seventeen:	9 Cases to Go	152
Chapter Eighteen:	Call is Almost Done..	164
Chapter Nineteen:	My Weekend Starts	167

Conclusion 169

Introduction

The Operating Room is a world within a world. It is usually a world with no windows and none of the sounds normally found in a hospital. The OR is a world with specialized equipment and specialized people. These people usually consider themselves to be superior to other people in medicine. And they are! This is one of the last remaining arenas of medicine where instantaneous reaction to changes in a patient's condition still occurs. In other areas of medicine, the machinery of medicine has to be dealt with and move before action for the patient can occur.

For example, take 2 patients, both of whom need a unit of blood. One of them enters the Emergency Room, where they will have to be admitted, see a Doctor, get typed and crossmatched, and then finally get a unit of blood which will have to be run into them over 3 to 4 hours. Total time required = 5 to 6 hours, at a minimum. The second patient is in the OR and needs a unit of blood. They still have to be crossmatched, but after that, Anesthesia can infuse the blood in 15 minutes or less. Total time required = less than 1 hour. Lives can be saved or lost in the difference. There is always a need for safety and documentation, but the people in the Operating Room are used to doing it better and faster.

There is a power structure in medicine which is almost exclusively for the benefit of the Doctors who work in this world. This power structure has been created to maintain the power and protect the income of the Doctors. As expected, some Doctors use the power they have to abuse others and enrich themselves. These are domineering people who insist on maintaining absolute control. Then, on the other end of the spectrum, there are those Doctors who want to do their work as part of a team where everyone has a role and works together for the good of the patient. These Doctors are not interested in controlling others, but just want everyone on the team to do their job so that the end result can be achieved. They are mission oriented, instead of self oriented.

Unfortunately, some of the more famous Doctors spend most of their time and energy on medical politics and publishing to secure their positions and enrich themselves. They are usually found in teaching hospitals. In the smaller community hospitals of this country, Medical Doctors are like feudal lords in the power they wield. Some are absolute dictators. Some are good dictators, in fact, they are absolute angels, and some are bad. The vast majority are pretty good people, but every basket of apples has a few rotten ones somewhere.

This author has seen the good, the bad, and the ugly in medical practioners around the Operating Room. This includes both Surgeons and Anesthesiologists. The title Medical Doctor carries a lot of power and protection for its owner. It also tends to insure a better than average income for its owner. All types of people become Surgeons and Anesthesiologists. The vast majority are concerned foremost with the welfare of the patient. That is their game. That is their only game. Then, there are those few who are concerned primarily with control and what benefit is coming their way. These last ones are highly involved in hospital politics and control of everyone they deal with. They spend most of their time and energy on medical political intrigue. They have lost what the purpose of human life should be. They have it backwards. They love money and power, and use people.

It is one of the practitioners in this last group that this book is the focus of. He is a combination of several characters that I have worked with over the 2 decades that I have worked in the world of Anesthesia. These stories are based on firsthand experience.

Enjoy the ride.

Chapter One

6 A.M. Monday Morning

Beep! Beep! Beep! Beep! Goddamit! I mutter to myself as I roll over in bed to hit the off button on the alarm clock. I feel as if a mule has kicked me in the back of my head. Got to quit drinking so much at Sunday Night Supper Club, I think to myself. Then I glance over at my trophy wife, Shirley, who will wake up after I leave for work.

Work, hah! What a joke. Most of my day will be spent answering telephone calls about patients and playing video games on the computer (or zoning out pretending to play video games) so no one will notice the alcohol on my breath, if my breath mints don't cover it up. Another big part of my day is signing Anesthesia Records, over and over. Much of my job is repetitive and mind-numbingly boring.

My beautiful wife lying asleep there in bed looks like a scene from a movie. I'll never forget the first time I laid eyes on her beautiful ass. She was bent over, facing away from me, picking up a piece of paper she had dropped on the floor. When she stood back up, she was a stunning vision of beauty, even in a scrub suit. The smile she gave me when she looked at me then pretty well hooked me. I was married to my first wife, Judy, then.

Shirley even looks beautiful now, with tussled hair and no makeup. After I've gone to work, she'll slowly wake up and get herself together. Then she'll go to the gym to work out for an hour or hour and a half, and she'll meet up with some of her friends and then decide where to have lunch. Then will come her first big decision of the day, whether or not to go shopping with her girlfriends after they have lunch. What a tough life. I sure wish I had her lifestyle, I think to myself as I shuffle off to the kitchen. Talk about no stress. Most of my stress in life is at work, putting up with bullshit. After 20 years at this job though, I have pared the bullshit down to a bare minimum.

Thank God for automatic coffee makers. The smell of strong Columbian coffee hits my nose just before I reach the kitchen door. Man that smells good. That headache in the back of my skull is really pounding me hard. Pouring a big mug, I muse about what a great discovery coffee is. "Elixir of the Gods. Able to raise the dead," I say aloud as I reach for the bottle of brandy in the cabinet. I leave about an inch of room at the top of my coffee mug to allow for pouring in a little brandy. This stuff will ease my aching head, I think as I pour a shot into my mug. I am a little shaky, lifting the mug to my lips, but I really need this stuff.

Wow!! The first sip is a kicker, a major shock to the taste buds and brain. By the third sip, the pain in the base of my skull is beginning to ease up, just a little. I open the freezer door to get an ice cube out of the ice maker bin and put it into the mug of coffee and brandy so it will cool off and make it easier to drink more quickly. Now I can drink the mixture down in big gulps. Once the first mug is down, I am almost beginning to feel human. That pounding in the back of my skull is almost gone now. My brain is still not working well, but the fog is beginning to lift a little. Brandy and coffee will really help out with a bad hangover. Another ice cube, shot of brandy, and dose of coffee. The 2nd mug goes down much quicker than the first. I fix myself a 3rd mug, and it's time to be off to the bathroom for my morning ritual. Time for a shit, shave and shower, in that order. Much of my life is routine and ritual.

I shuffle slowly through the kitchen, gingerly sipping my special coffee, and head back to the bedroom. As I am walking through the bedroom, I glance over at Shirley. She hasn't moved one inch. It's like she is a statue, frozen in the position I last saw her in. I head into my closet, where I put my mug down on a little table and strip out of my pajamas. I fold them up and put them back in the dresser I got them out of last night, then I strip off my undies and socks and throw them into the dirty clothes hamper. Grabbing my mug of coffee, I finally make it into my bathroom. This is my bathroom and I walk over to sit on my throne to begin my morning ritual. There is nothing like drinking coffee with brandy while taking a crap first thing in the morning. It really cleans the rust out of the pipes.

After coming out of the bathroom all fresh and clean-shaven and dressed, 30 minutes after I entered it, I walk quickly through the bedroom and head back to the kitchen to refill my mug one more time. I look at the clock on the microwave oven as I fix one last mug of coffee plus one ice cube and a splash of brandy and notice it is 15 minutes to 7. It'll only take me 3 or 4 large gulps to finish off this last mug before I have to head to work. If I'm a few minutes late no one will say shit to me because I'm Doctor Jerry Deluna, Chief of Anesthesia. I don't have to punch a time clock and don't have a boss or supervisor to answer to. After being at the Hospital here 25 years, I am what is known as the old buffalo. I am the boss.

I reminisce about Jack Jamison, who was the old buffalo when I arrived in town, fresh out of my residency. I still had some fantasy about helping people get well and relieving misery, or some such nonsense. What a piece of work Jack was. He straightened me out about the real world of medicine in our after work drinking sessions. Boy could he put it away. Jack explained the relationship between Surgeons and Anesthesiologists in the real world versus the residency world. The man never took any shit off anybody. Jack had such a grip on the power conveyed by the title M.D. (Medical Doctor) and years of knowledge and experience that he was amazing to behold at times. The Nurses visibly trembled when he approached. He really knew how to crack the whip. His reputation as an asshole was well deserved. I bet the Nurses' blood pressure went up 20 points when they saw him coming.

I'll never forget the time he gave a paralyzing agent to a drug addict, high on angel dust, who was kicking everyone's ass. He just stood back as the guy slowly melted onto the floor, twitching and rapidly getting too weak to stand, move, or breathe. "You feel like fighting now?" Jack asked him, bending down and getting right in his face, knowing he could not possibly muster a response. "I'll give you some air and help you breath, but you better behave yourself when this stuff wears off or you won't be so lucky the next time," he said to the guy. The guy could not answer, but inside he was wide awake, feeling like he was dying and unable to do a thing about it. You never saw a more polite human being in you life after that experience. He realized that Jack could have let him die if he had wanted to, so he decided to change his game plan. Too bad you can't get away with stuff like that nowadays. Sometimes you just need to show the jackass who the boss is.

I take a big gulp and finish off my 3rd mug of coffee and brandy, boy this stuff is good. I believe it is bringing me back to life after all. Time to go to the bedroom to give Shirley a kiss on the cheek and tell her I love her. As I walk into the bedroom, I pause for a moment, admiring her half covered form; the blond hair, the lovely curve of her large breast poking out at me, tugging at me. Damn, but she is one hot looking woman. She still incites lust in me after 10 years of marriage. If only she wasn't so expensive, boy does she like to shop. Oh well, it's only money. Thank goodness I make a truck load of it. I lean over to give her a peck on the cheek and a pat on the rump. "Love you babe, call me later when you're up," I tell her. She moans and moves a little before murmuring "Love you," after which she sinks back into the pillow for some more rest.

There is 15 years difference in our ages, but this hasn't presented much of a problem in our relationship. She knows that she has my number. So do I. Thank goodness for me that she absolutely loves being the Doctor's wife, because I also love being with her. The Junior League, the Garden Club, the parties, the Hospital charity ball, and the Sunday night supper club; she eats it up. She possesses a good intellect and sense of humor; and she is so damn nice to look at.

I think that I am one lucky guy to have her. She likes to go out and socialize more than I do. Socializing and shopping are her reasons to live. I really don't mind being with her when we go out because she pays attention to me, and she looks so damn good. It's like being drug around in public by a model. You can't help but be proud when the woman on your arm is the best looking babe in the room. I feel like other guys are looking at us and thinking "That lucky bastard." That's why I don't mind going out in public with her. Besides, keeping up with her is some of the only exercise I get these days. We are out in public 3 or 4 times a week for dinner or some event or another.

It never fails to amaze me how much attention women require to be reassured and happy. They like to think that you are in touch with their feelings and devoted to them. This takes a lot of time and energy. Sometimes it's a lot crap to plow through to get to the sex. But you gotta do what you gotta do. Who gives a shit about feelings anyway, nobody gives a damn about mine. Oh well, at least she provides me with some glamour and prestige. Not to mention the great sex.

I walk back to the kitchen to turn off the coffee maker and head out to work. I guess I'm ready to face the world and deal with the mountain of bullshit I have to plow through every day. My cross to bear. Off to the garage I go and hop into my Mercedes SUV. Man, but this is one nice ride. It cost $90,000, but it commands respect, and after all, respect, power, and prestige are what I am all about these days. The money situation

I've had under control for some time. I open the door and ease into the glove soft leather seat, lean over to open the console to grab a breath mint to cover the smell of brandy on my breath, and pull the door shut with a heavy thunk. This thing is built like a tank, but what a luxurious tank. When you fire up the big V8 engine in this baby, you can't help but feel powerful. I hit the button to open up the garage door, put the transmission in reverse and back out of my fortress, into the real world.

Medical training is long, hard, and expensive, but Anesthesia is one of the best paying specialties in the game. Especially when you consider the low amount of effort required to make the money I do. Rarely do I ever do any work with a patient. 98% of my job is just signing papers and answering phone calls. I spend way more than half of my day sitting on my ass, making money. Money sure is nice to have because you certainly can buy prestige, and having prestige always makes you feel good.

When I first arrived in Ashburg, South Carolina, I had just finished my Anesthesia Residency. I was driving a 10 year old Toyota and had $80,000 in school loan and credit card debt. Now, 25 years later, I have $5 million in stocks, bonds, and mutual funds; I own $4 million worth of property outright, plus a 25% share in a $10 million professional office building where we rent out space to most of the other Doctors on staff. I make a little over $600,000 a year from working at the Hospital as an Anesthesiologist. Plus another $600,000 from rental income on the professional office building I own with 3 other Doctors, and other real estate and investment income. At this point in life, I am saving about ½ of my monthly income to live on for a while when I retire; so I won't have to touch my real retirement money for 3 or 4 years. I now live in a $1 million house and also have a $1 million beach house, both long paid off. Yeah, I'm doing alright now.

I was physically and mentally scarred from the 4 years of abuse heaped on me without mercy during my Anesthesia Residency. Residency is where Doctors just out of Medical School specialize in their particular field of interest for their career. Residencies typically take 4 to 6 years of training post graduation from Medical School. One Resident in my class couldn't take it and had a nervous breakdown, forcing him to resign. Another died in a car wreck on the way home after working 40 hours straight and having 2 patients code and die on him during his shift. Oh well, casualties of war. A patient who codes is one who has a respiratory or cardiac arrest, either of which can be fatal. You just thank God that this type of bad luck doesn't come your way and go on. Who knows how many near misses (nearly injuring or killing patients) I had during my Anesthesia training with those grueling stretches of work.

Those 120+ hour work weeks were hell; it took me over a year to get used to being at work only 50 to 60 hours per week. My life after Residency has been an exercise in making the most amount of money while expending the least amount of time and energy. Now, it is a very rare week when I am here a full 40 hours. I have played this game so well for so long now that I barely have to move or think to function successfully at work. Much of Anesthesia is repetitious and routine. This is good because most of the time I come to work now, I am either drunk or hung over.

During my Residency, there were many mornings that I was so exhausted; I honestly don't know how I made it back home safely to wife #1 (Judy). I swear that old Toyota just knew the way home by itself. It was only a 15 minute trip, but I don't recall anything about how I got home many days after putting in a 36 (or more) hour shift in the Hospital. Half of my Residency was spent working while under extreme sleep deprivation. I couldn't possibly know how many near misses I had with patients, or the quality of care I gave. I just constantly tried to do the best that I could under the circumstances.

Trying to cram in all the information I could while working insanely long hours was like being in a war, combat-zone type situation. The drive home after some of these marathons was a blur. My car just made it home by itself most days. I call it automatic driving. I guess when I was spending those marathon work sessions at the Hospital; many times I was doing automatic Doctoring.

During my Anesthesia Residency there were many times when my Attending Physician was such a nutcase, alcoholic, and/or incompetent that the only place in the world he could make a living and not be drummed out the profession was in a large teaching Hospital. They had the luxury of hiding behind many layers of Nurses and Residents who could take the blame for the dumb decisions and mistakes they made which resulted in bad patient outcomes. This type of thing only added another healthy dose of stress to an already highly stressful situation. You soon learned the moves you needed to make to in order to minimize your contact with these idiots, and so, decrease the chances of incurring their wrath. You had to maintain this throughout the entire 4 years of Anesthesia Residency.

These people could never survive the scrutiny involved in working in the real world, but have long successful careers in Academic

Hospitals. They could never function in the real world. You would never want them actually doing your Anesthesia. Hell, they probably couldn't actually do Anesthesia, only criticize you for how you did Anesthesia. Some of these M.D. professors are famous, demigods of the profession. They are considered authorities in their field because they are associated with research and they publish. They have their names all over the professional journals and Medical textbooks, taking credit for the research and writing skills of the bright, young overachiever Residents under them. Oh well, that's just how Doctors are trained, not only in this country, but around the world. This is exactly why Medicine is such a tightly knit fraternity. You have to claw your way through a river of shit, dodging all sorts of dangers and pitfalls, so you can come out on the other end, large and in charge.

Very few people nowadays are willing to give up 8 to 10 years (or more) of their life and endure that kind of abuse, even for the big payoff at the end. Four years of Medical School plus 4 years of Anesthesia Residency, in my case. Some Residencies take more than 4 years. Anesthesia pays off big, with money and power, for a minimum amount of effort. I felt mentally and physically crippled after 4 years of working 120 hours per week. The wimps going through it now are limited to an 80 hour work week in their Residencies, and still they whine about how tough it was, boo hoo.

Going from having no respect and being treated like you were lower than the housekeeping staff that emptied the garbage cans during your Residency to suddenly being king of the hill in a midsized community Hospital is quite a shock to the ego. Now, if someone doesn't show me the proper amount of respect, I just say a few words to the right Hospital Vice President and before you know it, the rug will be pulled right out from under their feet. They won't know what hit them. A list of their problems (minor peccadilloes become huge, insurmountable issues framed as direct threats to the patients' lives) at work will suddenly appear, along with a pink slip.

Sometimes they will be given the option of resigning immediately instead of getting terminated, because nowadays if you are fired from a Healthcare job for any reason, you will have a major problem trying to land another job in the same field. Many times it is the end of a career in which much time and money was invested to get the person to that point. The idiots in charge (Hospital Administrators and Departmental Managers) ignore the fact that the odds of working 20 years or more and not pissing someone off or not making a mistake somewhere are remote, at best. These people are bean counters, MHAs (Masters Degree in Hospital Administration) and MBAs (Masters Degree in Business Administration), who don't have a clue about what goes on in the clinical world of Healthcare. They especially don't have a clue about what goes on in the Operating Room, which is a world within a world. Working in Healthcare now is much like sliding down the edge of a razor blade and not getting cut, every day. It used to not be that way.

This is because of the 600 pound gorilla of Medicine, Medico-legal Liability, which adds 30-40% to the cost of Healthcare in the U.S., but nobody talks about it. The legal profession holds an ax over the neck of every Healthcare facility and worker, poised to drop at any time. This can happen even if no mistakes were ever made. For example, if a patient suddenly decides to commit suicide after finding out he has cancer, and jumps to his death in a Hospital stairwell, Lawyers will have little difficulty convincing a distraught family member that the Hospital didn't do enough to protect the patient from himself and they deserve to pay for it. This is especially true when the Lawyers are telling poor people how much money they stand to collect, usually more money than they have ever seen in their lives. There is no downside to this, because hiring the Lawyer and putting him to work for you costs you nothing out of pocket, but there is the possibility of a huge amount of money on the upside. It matters not to the Lawyer that they might destroy the career of a Doctor or Nurse who has helped tens of thousands of patients over the course of their career. It does not matter to the Lawyer that he might ruin the reputation of a hospital that helps thousands of people every year. It only matters to him that money will change hands and he will get a big cut of it. This is just one example out of thousands of ways that Lawyers suck money out of Healthcare as fast and as often as they can.

The Lawyers somehow fail to mention the fact that about ½ of this money will end up in their own pockets, instead, they emphasize that the lawsuit will cost the plaintiff nothing and they might make millions. Most people don't have any chance of making millions of dollars in their lifetime. Since there is virtually no downside and a possible huge windfall upside to the situation, guess what happens. Before you know it, a lawsuit is filed, a couple of heads roll (usually Nursing staff) and the Hospital is writing a big check, most of which ends up in the Lawyer's pocket. This is the scenario when the case is settled out of court, which the vast majority are, and nobody ever hears another thing about it.

Not only that, but if a newspaper gets a hold of the story and jumps on the bandwagon, it could end up costing the Hospital millions of dollars of lost revenue because of reputation damage when people read the story and choose to go down the road to another Hospital for their Medical care. No one in Healthcare these days wants to take a chance on a problem child employee, or anyone with a tainted work record because of this. After all, Hospitals try to minimize their risk of punishment from the legal profession, just like everyone else. Of course, eventually you won't be able to do anything without some risk. We fool ourselves into thinking that we still have some freedom to act and perform our functions as Healthcare professionals.

It does not matter that the chances of a human being not making a mistake during his or her entire career are ZERO. Never mind that there are so many facility, state, federal and insurance regulations that if you take any action involving patient care whatsoever, you will probably be in violation of one or more rules or regulations. In Healthcare, you can follow every rule and regulation, you can do everything right, and you can still have bad outcomes. And when bad outcomes happen, as they certainly will, the legal profession stands ready to make money change hands and collect their fee for making it happen. No other profession on planet earth is held to the standard of Healthcare in America. Yeah Lawyers! Soon, no one will be able to afford to have Healthcare in this country. Very few can actually afford it now.

So, if you mess with me, it will take you years to overcome the screwing I'll give you, if you ever get over it. Having power is sooo good. I have only had to do this (get someone fired) a few times in my 25 years at this Hospital to get the reputation of being someone dangerous. Word spreads quickly among the Hospital staff; don't mess with Doctor Jerry Deluna, he will get you fired and you won't be able to get another job. If he tells you to jump, you better say "Yes Sir," and ask "How high?" This system of employee abuse exists in one form or another at every Hospital in America, but more so in the smaller community Hospitals, where us M.D.'s are similar to feudal lords. In many Hospitals in this country, Nurses work in fear of Doctors, rather than coworkers of a team trying to provide care for the patients.

You have to be stoic at work and never let anyone know what you are feeling or thinking because they might discover the real you. The immature, petty, self-absorbed you. Doctors may be right, Doctors may be wrong, but they are never in doubt. This is precisely why I only hang out with a few other Doctors whom I have known for 20 years, plus a chosen few newcomers to the area who might someday be trusted to become members of the inner circle and take over when we retire. We are the only ones who understand us. I guess we'd be called the 'good old boy network' in layman's terms. These are the members of the Sunday Night Supper Club, which rotates every week to a different Doctor's house, until it makes the full circle and starts all over again. This cycle takes about 3 to 4 months of Sundays (depending on vacations) and makes for a small, but very tightly knit group of friends. We can only let our hair down and feel at ease to talk freely at these gatherings. Other than this, we have to remain guarded with what we say to others. I have led this type of life for so long that 99% of my interactions with people at work are repetitive, automatic responses which work just fine in my work setting and require almost no thought or energy to be expended.

Chapter Two

The Daily Grind

Anyway, I fire up the Mercedes' big V-8 engine, open the garage door, and back out into the turnaround so I can drive forward out of my driveway. It is 10 minutes to 7 A.M. and I will be at the Hospital in 12 minutes or less. I have made this drive thousands of times over the years. I hardly have to pay attention or even be conscious to make it (automatic driving). I ought to try to do the entire trip with my eyes closed one day, just to see if I can make it. At 7:00 A.M. I roll past the crossbar into the Doctor's parking deck right next to the Hospital building. The crossbar prevents any riffraff from entering this parking deck and puts you as close to the building as possible, minimizing the time and energy required to gain ingress to the building. Plus, you are parking next to other expensive cars, unless some new Doctor has just arrived in town driving an old Toyota.

I enter the building, walk down the long central hallway, and go to the Physician's Dressing Room, which I walk right through, then walk right through the Surgeon's Lounge out into the hallway of the Operating Room. This is where the assignment board is with all the surgeries and personnel posted. It takes me 2 minutes to make assignments for the Anesthesia personnel. Then, I turn around and reverse my path to go to the Physician's Dressing Room, where I'll put my street clothes into my locker in the Physician's Locker Room and put on the pajamas we call a scrub suit.

As I walk back through the Surgeon's Lounge, I take notice of the 2 small children that I thought I saw out of the corner of my eye when I came through in a hurry the first time. They are sitting quietly on a sofa with their book bags next to them, watching cartoons on the TV. They appear to be 6-10 years old. "How are you?" I ask them. "Fine sir," they reply with expressionless faces. "Who is your dad?" I ask. "Doctor Paul Bunch (General Surgeon), his office manager is supposed to pick us up in a few minutes to take us to school," they state matter of factly. "Where is your mom?" I ask. "She is in Ohio, visiting grandma," they say. "Oh, okay," I say back to them. I just turn and head to the dressing room, shaking my head.

It really gripes me when Surgeons drop their kids off in the Lounge, kind of like a holding area. I can't really complain about it though, because this is the Surgeon's Lounge after all. They have childcare responsibilities because their wives are off somewhere. Then, they have to come in to the Hospital unexpectedly to see about a patient or something. Their poor kids are left in the Surgeon's Lounge to wait for an office Nurse or office manager to take them to school or take care of them in the office until dad is freed up to resume his role as the responsible, caring father. Can't these Doctors hire a nanny?

I just can't understand these Doctors exposing their children to all the germs and disease that floats around a Hospital. This happens once or twice a month at this Hospital, Doctors bring their kids to the Hospital, to sit and wait in this Lounge until Dad is freed up or someone else comes to bring them where they are supposed to be. I wonder what the Hospital Administrator would say if he knew that this Lounge was being used by Doctors for a children's drop zone.

I am the last person in the Anesthesia Department to arrive at work, and the rest of the CRNAs (Certified Registered Nurse Anesthetists) and Anesthesiologists have been waiting for me to make work assignments. Making your own assignment at this Hospital could result in termination of employment, so no one touches this piece of turf until I arrive to do it. As the Chief of Anesthesia, it is my responsibility to make work assignments for myself and the rest of the department. The rest of the department being the other Anesthesiologists and the CRNAs who are with the patient throughout the entire surgical process, from arrival in the OR to dropping the patient off in the PACU (Post Anesthesia Care Unit) after surgery is done. This is the exact way that Anesthesia is provided for surgical patients in 2/3 of the Hospitals in this country.

When I am on vacation, or at an Anesthesia conference, I will designate Jim Turner, one of the other Anesthesiologists, and my second in command, to be in charge and perform this duty. It is 7:10 A.M. and half of the cases in our 12 operating rooms begin at 7:30 A.M., or else the OR (Operating Room) Nurses and CRNAs will be chastised for starting the cases late. I love to see them scramble off, grumbling to themselves, trying to get everything they need to start the cases on time. This starts their day off with a big stress load, but you just have to let them know who the boss is. If they don't like it, they can go find another job and move on, because I'm not going anywhere until I retire.

I choose the easiest and highest paying rooms for myself when making assignments. The other Operating Rooms are assigned to the other Anesthesiologists according to how close the rooms are to each other. This will save time when they go from OR to OR, starting cases and signing charts. My rooms are not chosen at random. I pick the rooms with the highest number of privately insured patients (because these pay the most), and then according to which cases are the easiest. After I am situated with the easiest and best paying cases, it doesn't really matter to me who gets what, just so everyone is occupied and working.

It takes us Anesthesiologists zero time to prepare for supervising the Operating Rooms that we are assigned to. We just drink coffee in the Surgeon's Lounge and wait around for the phone calls, telling us that they are ready for us in a particular OR. Then we go and assist with the induction of Anesthesia and, most importantly, sign the Anesthesia Record so that we may collect ½ the Anesthesia fees. The CRNAs however, have to get drugs and equipment to be able to do the Anesthesia for the surgeries. This doesn't take much time, and they are very efficient at their jobs. Therefore, a surgical case is almost never delayed because of someone in the Anesthesia Department.

Besides, the pressure to get the cases started on time really comes from the Surgeon anyway. If a Surgeon is held up 5 minutes after he has arrived and is ready to start, he will go to the Hospital Administrator and complain about the OR staff holding him up; which will make the surgical case begin even later. The fact that the patient is asleep, under Anesthesia and waiting for the Surgeon to begin their operation is seldom a concern in this situation. It is all about the power and feeding the ego of the Surgeon.

This Surgeon's complaint will then go to the Vice President in charge of Patient Services, who will go to the Vice President in charge of Nursing Services (the Director of Nursing), who will go the Nurse Supervisor in charge of Surgical Services (covering Same Day Surgery, Recovery Room—now frequently called the Post Anesthesia Care Unit, and the

OR), who will go to the Nurse Supervisor in charge of the Operating Room. This Nurse Supervisor will go to the Registered Nurse who runs the OR schedule (the board runner), who will go to the OR Nurse and CRNA responsible for getting this particular surgical case started on time. All this is done in order to find someone who may have faltered in the performance of their duties and upon which to place blame and punishment.

Finally, at the bottom of this waterfall of bullshit, the Nurse Supervisor in charge of the Operating Room will have a meeting with the OR Nurse and CRNA responsible for the case. She will chastise them, then write a report about the matter with corrective measures spelled out which will then be routed back up the chain of command. The offending personnel will have a smirch on their employment record, which usually results in a decrease in their annual raise, saving the Hospital money. Even after all this is done, everything will usually just go back to business as usual. Eventually, a copy of this report will end up in the Surgeon's mailbox where it will most likely end up in the trash after he reads the first line or two, just to make sure it isn't anything important affecting him personally.

In addition to all this, numerous committee meetings will be held, addressing delays in the OR. Causes will be identified and possible solutions proposed and discussed at length. All in all, thousands of hours will be spent dealing with this topic, and hundreds, if not thousands of pages of paper will be generated, documenting every move of this chess game. Keep in mind, this tremendous waste of time and money will take place even if the root cause was the Surgeon showing up late, in a bad mood, and being upset because the patient was not asleep and ready for him to begin operating on immediately. You can't legally put the patient to sleep until the Surgeon is at least in the parking lot of the Hospital. In my experience, Surgeons are the cause of delays in the OR about 90% of the time.

What will happen to a Surgeon who shows up late and causes a surgical case delay, or even a Surgeon who is habitually late for his scheduled cases one might wonder? Why absolutely nothing because the Surgeons are the ones that bring money into the Hospital. Waiting around, with the patient asleep under Anesthesia is expensive. This OR's time charge to the patient is $100 per minute, and we commonly wait 30 minutes or more for the Surgeon to show up. It's just added to the patient's Hospital bill. And people actually wonder why healthcare costs are spiraling out of control???

Needless to say, when making work assignments, I am going to give myself the OR rooms with the most privately insured patients and the easiest cases. After years of experience, I can do this nearly instantaneously after looking at the surgical schedule on the assignment board. This results in the maximum amount of revenue with the least amount of effort (remember my game?).

The other 3 Anesthesiologists in this department consist of a WASP (White Anglo-Saxon Protestant) named Jim Turner, who has been out of Residency training 5 years, and 2 J-1 Visa Anesthesiologists named Avi and Arnash from India (I can't begin to pronounce their last names). A J-1 Visa Doctor is one who is working in this country while trying to obtain U.S. citizenship, which usually takes 3 years (unless I drag my feet doing the paperwork). The advantage of this is that I get to pay them half what I make for this period of time while collecting full reimbursement for the cases they supervise.

I had to pay Jim 2/3 of what I make when he first got here and made him a full partner with full pay after 3 years. Now he makes the same amount of money as I do working in the OR. Of course, he had to pay me $100,000 for ½ the stock in my Anesthesia Corporation before he could become a full partner. And, when I retire in 3 years, he'll have to cough up another $100,000 for the rest of the stock in the corporation so he will be the sole stock holder. Education is expensive, and I have given Jim one hell of an education. Jim is my only partner and the only one in charge when I am gone; I never let Avi or Arnash be in charge of the Anesthesia assignments. Jim and I synchronize our time off so that one of us is always here to be in charge of the Anesthesia Department.

When Avi and Arnash obtain their green cards, I will have to tell them the sad news that they will have to seek employment elsewhere because their work has been unsatisfactory. This is because I will never make them partners or pay them what I am making. They will get a decent job reference from me if they don't cause any trouble before they leave. I will then get two more J-1 Visa Doctors to replace them and start all over again for a 3 or 4 year cycle. This way I get the benefit of collecting the money normally generated by 2 Doctors and only have the expense of paying for 1 because of their immigration status. I just work the system as best I can. I absolutely love healthcare in America.

I am teaching Jim these subtleties of the Anesthesia business so that he may continue in this manner after I have retired, which will be in 3 years when I am 55 years old. At that time, my other business partners and I will have paid off the loan for the professional arts office building. The additional income from that will partially replace the income I make working at the Hospital; add to that an annual income of about $600,000 from my stock, bond and mutual fund portfolios and rental properties. This will add up to a retirement income of well over $800,000 per year, with no debt.

I also have $2 million cash in my local bank for a rainy day fund. We built the professional arts office building about 9 years ago for $3million, but it is worth $10 million today. Every 2 or 3 years we can raise the rent we charge the 40 or so Doctors who occupy the building and so, keep a lively cash stream coming in from that. Yeah, I'm doing alright.

While I am drinking coffee in the Surgeon's Lounge, I get a call on my Hospital-issued cell phone: "Ready for you in OR 8," the Nurse says. I just watched them roll the patient on a stretcher past me about 4 minutes ago, heading to the Operating Room and knew they should soon be calling me. I could have just gotten up and followed them to the OR after a few minutes, but I make them call me on the cell phone. You never let them forget who the boss is; that is Deluna's Law. I get up from the computer, where I am mostly staring at the screen and not even playing the video game in front of me, and amble off to OR 8.

I pull up my paper facemask as I enter the OR and tell the CRNA "Okay," so they'll start the induction. "Turn up the temperature, it's too cold in here, and turn off that music," I say to the OR Nurse. There are CD players/radios in just about every Operating Room in America. Although I am in OR 8 for less than 3 minutes, I enforce Deluna's Law, as I do every chance I get. I walk over to the patient and tell him "I am Doctor Deluna, I am here now, and I will get you off to sleep now," as the CRNA is pushing the induction drugs into the IV. As soon as the patient's eyes close, I walk over to the Anesthesia machine to sign the Anesthesia Record and leave OR 8 because I need to get to another OR to do the same thing over again. All the patient is likely to remember, if anything, is that Doctor Deluna put me to sleep. This is what you do when you have 2 or 3 ORs starting cases simultaneously.

I can legally supervise 4 Operating Rooms at once. I don't know what government idiots decided we could be in 4 places at once and made this the law for getting reimbursed from Medicare and Medicaid, but I just go with the system I have to work in. Sometimes more than one room is starting at the exact same time. In that case I just call the CRNA and tell them to go ahead in the first room while I go to another room to quickly sign the Anesthesia Record, then leave and go to the first OR to sign the Record.

Never have I had all 4 rooms starting at the exact same time, but there have been times when 3 ORs are starting at the exact same time. In this case I will have to call 2 CRNAs to tell them to go ahead and start the induction without me while I go to one room to actually be present for the Anesthesia induction. Then, I backtrack to the other 2 ORs to sign the Anesthesia Records. The beauty of this system is that I get to collect ½ the money for each case; multiplied times 4 ORs, this means that I make double what I would make if I were actually doing the Anesthesia myself. I love America.

The Anesthesia induction takes place after the patient is connected to the EKG, blood pressure monitor, and pulse oximeter. This is where you let the patient breath oxygen right before or, as the medication to put them to sleep (Diprivan or Thiopental) is being given through the IV. For example, with gallbladder surgery, you give a drug to put the patient to sleep which lasts 5-8 minutes. After the patient is so deeply asleep that they have quit breathing (usually about 1 minute after the drug is given in the IV) you establish that you can breathe for them with a mask (which is connected by some tubing called a breathing circuit to the Anesthesia machine) held tightly on their face. Once ability to ventilate (take over breathing for the patient) the patient is established, a paralyzing agent is given via the IV. The paralyzing agent is given to facilitate passage of the Endotracheal Tube (called the ET tube) between the vocal cords, which is then connected by the breathing circuit to the Anesthesia machine. After the ET tube is placed in the patient's windpipe (trachea), a small balloon on the far end of it is inflated to help secure it in place and make a seal so that none of the oxygen and Anesthesia gas is leaked into the Operating Room.

Patients are kept asleep during surgery by a vaporized Anesthesia drug (which is called a gas), which is mixed with oxygen. Regular people refer to it mistakenly as getting the gas for surgery. We even refer to it as gas, but it is actually a vaporized drug. It is created when oxygen with or without nitrous oxide is passed over the liquid medication, which is in a vaporizer. There is a dial on top of the vaporizer with which you can simply dial the concentration of the drug up or down. Then, the ventilator is switched on to breathe for the patient, the vaporizer is turned on which will deliver a precise amount of a vaporized drug with oxygen to the patient to keep them asleep, and the skin prep and draping can begin. Putting the patient to sleep and placing the ET tube usually happens within 2-3 minutes. Once the vaporizer is turned on, amnesia is virtually guaranteed. If the vaporizer has run out of the liquid medication and has not been refilled, then you end up with "recall" which is all over the media these days.

Paralyzing medications are frequently given throughout the surgical case for 2 reasons: to use less Anesthesia gas, and to keep the patient absolutely still during the case. It actually takes very little Anesthesia gas to keep a person's mind asleep and amnesic. It takes much more to keep the patient from moving when the Surgeon's knife cuts the skin, which is why narcotics and paralytic drugs are given. These drugs keep you from having to give the patient a really heavy dose of Anesthesia gas, which would drop the blood pressure due to dilating the blood vessels and depressing the heart so it doesn't pump as vigorously as it normally does.

As soon as I leave OR 8, I get a call from OR 7 telling me they are ready for me. And, as soon as I hang up, I get a call from OR 6 with the same message. I tell the Nurse in OR 6 to tell the CRNA to go ahead, I'll soon be there, and walk into OR 7 to repeat the exact scene from OR 8. Two minutes later I walk into OR 6. The patient is already asleep and intubated, so I just sign the Anesthesia Record and leave without speaking to anyone. In about 10 minutes I have 3 operating rooms going on this floor and a C-section going on the floor above. I will never venture to the floor above; the CRNA doing the C-section will do everything, complete the paperwork and bring me the Anesthesia Record to sign after the case is finished and the patient has been delivered to the C-section Recovery Room on the 2nd floor, near the C-section room.

This Hospital has 11 operating rooms plus 2 C-section rooms (although we usually use just one 1 C-section room). An Anesthesiologist can supervise up to 4 Operating Rooms at once legally, even though 1 person cannot be in 4 places at once. This is the way the vast majority of Operating Rooms in American hospitals function. I have very few patient care problems sitting in front of the computer, playing video games, or napping in my office. Besides signing Anesthesia Records, napping and playing on the computer are my main activities to pass the time of day at work. Most patient care problem situations are routinely handled by the CRNAs who are doing the cases.

The only distractions I have are the phone calls from PACU and Same Day Surgery, which interrupt me frequently during the day. I will give the Nurse who calls me with a problem a Verbal Order for whatever the patient needs and I never even have to leave my seat. The Nurse will document the Verbal Order on the Physician's Order sheet in the patient's chart. At the end of the month a clerk with a pile of charts to sign will deliver them to my office, and then I can sign them all at once. I believe in conservation of energy, especially my own.

Occasionally, I am called to the OR because a patient is doing poorly or trying to die and I have to direct the situation or code personally. Over the years, I have subtly influenced the CRNAs to handle these situations and not call me because that would interrupt my video gaming or napping, and expose me to more risk from the 600 pound gorilla. As a result, I rarely get these calls.

There is a cookbook to manage these critical situations called ACLS (Acute Cardiac Life Support). All of the OR staff, and the CRNAs have to take an ACLS class every 2 years to maintain their certification. You just follow the protocols of ACLS, and if the patient dies, they die. You reduce your individual liability substantially if you just follow the ACLS protocols. If you deviate from the cookbook, you better have a very good reason, because if you do, you make yourself vulnerable to the 600 pound gorilla, Medico-legal Liability.

It doesn't take me very much time to walk from OR to OR and sign Anesthesia Records. Rarely do I every have to actually participate in patient care to any extent. I manage to sit in front of my computer about 4 hours during an 8 hour shift and I usually take a 1 hour nap after lunch. Kind of a boring day, but oh well, it pays the bills and I am used to it after many years.

Joe, the CRNA who has been doing the C-section, comes over to me sitting in front of the computer and presents me the Anesthesia Record to sign. "You should have seen that shelf butt (referring to the pregnant woman's large posterior), 5 feet tall and 375 pounds," he tells me. "You could have put a doily, lamp, and vase of flowers on her ass when she sat down. Her ass was at least 3 feet across," says Joe. "I'm sure all this is true, but she is far from the record holder," I say to Joe. He laughs and then says "Yeah, you're right, that girl a couple of years ago was over 500 pounds, but at least she was over 5 feet tall." "We grow 'em big down South," I say to Joe as he turns chuckling, to go file the paperwork for the C-section. We have had this exact conversation 2 or 3 times a year, for the past several years; much of Anesthesia is very repetitive and usually boring.

The U.S. has far more of its children born by Caesarian Section (C-section) than any other industrialized nation in the world. What happened to regular old-fashioned vaginal deliveries you might ask. It's the old 600 pound gorilla again. If any problem occurs with the old-fashioned vaginal delivery, or the child is perceived as developmentally delayed after birth (never mind that the highest IQ of either of his parents is only 80), the parents have 18 years to sue the OB-GYN. Just imagine having an ax hanging over your neck for 18 years; who in their right mind would agree to that? Lawyers are masters at making little Johnny look very pitiful to a court; so much so, that about 98% of these cases never go to trial. They are settled out of court and once again, most of the money ends up in the Lawyer's pocket.

These cases are settled out of court to avoid a smirch on the Hospital's reputation, and more importantly, to avoid the OB-GYN's name ending up on the national databank of practitioners who have been sued and lost the decisions. There are 2 ways to avoid getting your name on this national databank: work for a Hospital or government agency instead of private practice, or settle the case out of court. It is also financially far cheaper for Healthcare facilities and practitioners to settle these cases out of court. Cutting your losses is the name of the game.

The Lawyers on both sides of the fence are well aware of this and both groups profit from it. These games are played everyday in America and it is one of the driving forces causing Healthcare to be so expensive because these costs are passed on to the consumer—the patient. It got so bad in the 1990's that many OB-GYN Doctors had to go out of business because they couldn't earn enough money to pay for liability insurance and make a living. These were good Doctors being punished by the legal profession causing liability insurance to go through the roof for all the practitioners in the country. The other way Doctors escaped the problem was to sell their practice to a Hospital. When you are an employee of a Hospital, it basically removes your individual liability because it becomes encased in the Hospital liability insurance. Also, you don't have to pay for liability insurance when you are a Hospital or government healthcare agency employee; they provide it to you free of cost. This, of course, increases the cost of doing business for the Hospital. You've probably guessed it by now, these costs are passed on to the consumer—the patient.

Many Lawyers have made their entire career out of this type of work, and they have made out like bandits. Some of the more famous ones had a hard time finding a Doctor who would take care of their pregnant wives and deliver their children because of the fear of litigation if everything didn't turn out perfect. As a result of all of this, one of the most common diagnoses for proceeding to C-section is nonreassuring fetal heart tones. OB-GYN Doctors have a very low threshold for proceeding to C-section these days. The name of the game is be cautious and CYA (cover your ass), and we foolishly think that if we get good at this game, it will protect us, hah!

After surgery, if there is any problem with a patient whose case I am supervising, I will be called by the PACU (Post Anesthesia Care Unit) Nurse on my Hospital-issued cell phone. 99% of the time I can handle a problem by giving instructions to the PACU Nurse over the phone, this way I never have to get up from my seat in front of my computer. This is called a Verbal Order. The PACU Nurse will write the order on the Physician's Order sheet, date, time, and sign it. A month later, it will arrive in a cart delivered to my office carrying other charts to be signed by me. I believe in conservation of energy, especially my own.

On an average 8 hour day, I will supervise about 20 surgical cases which will result in about 30 to 40 hours of billable Anesthesia time, plus extra units for more complex cases or other factors such as an elderly patient. It's a funny thing, if a CRNA by himself does a complicated case on an elderly patient, Medicare and Medicaid won't reimburse him more for the additional work. If however, that same CRNA is supervised by an Anesthesiologist, the reimbursement is much higher, even though the work involved and the complexity of the case are exactly the same.

Anesthesia time is reimbursed by Medicare at a rate of about $16.00 per 15 minute increment. Private insurance pays up to 3 or 4 times more. If you are an Anesthesiologist, or an Anesthesiologist supervising CRNAs, you get extra units for an elderly patient, a patient under 1 year old, or a patient with multiple health problems. The reimbursement is much higher for Hospitals this way, so it is in their interest to have CRNAs supervised by Anesthesiologists. Generally, the ASA (American Society of Anesthesiologists) takes the position that it is a quality of care issue instead of a financial issue. They take this stand despite the fact that all research has proven that patient outcomes and safety are no different whether CRNAs or Anesthesiologists are doing the Anesthesia.

If I do a procedure myself, such as a labor epidural (Medicaid pays $500.00; private insurance, up to $1,200), it can really add up to a tidy day; added to the revenues I generate from the OR. Many procedures I do can be worked into my day while I am supervising my 4 ORs. If I get busy, I can do up to 3 procedures per hour, and I don't have to share this money with anyone like I have to share ½ the Anesthesia fees for surgery with a CRNA. Some weeks I can generate $20,000 between supervising surgical cases and doing procedures. This Hospital is a money-making machine for me.

11 A.M., time for lunch. I call Jim Turner and tell him to keep an ear open for my rooms while I am gone. I have 3 ORs running at this time and they will continue to go for quite a while. Another room is due to start soon, but if I am called while I am at lunch, I will just call and tell them to go ahead and start and I'll be there soon. I walk over to the Doctors Dining Room, which is close to the Operating Room. You have to know a number code to punch into a combination lock to get into this dining room.

"Hey," I greet the chef, whose name I can't remember. "How's it going Doctor Deluna?" He says, "We have roast beef, grilled shrimp, and fried fish. We have steamed vegetables, corn on the cob and green beans, plus garden salads and cold salads. What can I prepare for you?" "I think I'll have the shrimp over rice pilaf, steamed veggies, and a Caesar salad," I tell him. "No dessert today?" he asks. "I'm trying to cut back," I reply. "Okay Doc, you can pick up your salad right there," he gestures to his left at the cold macaroni salads, bean salads, and green salads on the refrigerated table. "I'll bring your food over to you in a couple of minutes, just have a seat," he says to me. This guy never stops smiling while he is talking to me.

I mosey down the empty lunch line to pick up my Caesar salad, eating utensils, and bottled water, and take a seat at one of the 8 tables in the room. I nod to 2 other Doctors in the dining room whom I vaguely know. We Surgical folks don't associate very much with other Medical practioners. I busy myself with my bottle of water and salad to keep myself occupied until the main course arrives.

We Doctors do not eat with the other Hospital staff and patients' family members in the regular Hospital cafeteria. The regular Hospital cafeteria food is like prison food, poor quality and almost no taste to it. Also, there are long lines of people making too much noise and moving too slowly to contend with there. It is amazing to see some people completely befuddled by the choices in a cafeteria line. How the hell do they make it to the bathroom by themselves? The food served in this dining room is cooked to order and of very high quality. I am early, it is only 11:10 A.M. now, but the Doctors' Dining Room will be nearly full by 12 Noon. I like to get here early so I don't have to deal with a large crowd and a lot of conversation with people who I could care less about for the most part. Oh, did I mention, lunch is free here for Doctors.

5 minutes later, my entrée arrives, presented by the always cheerful chef. "Enjoy, Mon Capitan," he says with a big smile, as he gently places the plate of shrimp pilaf and vegetables in front of me. "Thank you," I reply. The plate is steaming hot and attractively presented, and the smell is out of this world. This chef knows what he is doing, he doesn't just plop the food onto the plate. I finish the last bite of my salad and then slide the plate of shrimp over to take its place in front of me when I hear "Hey Jerry, how's it hanging?" The greeting takes me aback, but I recognize the voice, and start smiling at the thought of who is calling out to me.

I look up to see Doctor Jesse James, Ear Nose and Throat Surgeon extraordinaire, smiling back at me. This is a great guy and a great Surgeon. He can knock out 12 to 15 small, quick cases by lunch. His patients almost always have private insurance and for many years I have made sure I am supervising his cases. These are quick and easy cases which generate a lot of money for a minimum amount of effort on my part. We have also been fishing and drinking buddies for many years.

"Oh, I guess I'll make it," I reply, "Is your last kid out of Brown yet?" "One more semester to go and I'll be done," he says. "Yes, sending 3 kids to Brown University isn't cheap. You'll be getting a big raise later this year then," I say to Jesse. "You know that's right," he says to me. He asks "How's Nate doing?" Nathaniel is my only son from my first marriage; Shirley (wife #2) and I have had no children. I tell him "Nate is doing quite well with that Plastic Surgery practice in Dallas; he's knocking down 7 figures and it's only his second year with the practice." "Wow, that's good, I'm glad he is doing so well. You think he'd make me a loan?" Jesse says while grinning. "Shit, Jesse, you've got more money than both of us put together," I laughingly reply. We love to joke and go on about money because neither one of us is lacking for it.

"Hey, you want to go fishing this weekend?" Jesse asks. "No, the wife and I are going to the beach house," I reply. "We try to get over there one weekend a month," I tell him, "It's good to get away from everything once in a while." "Once in a while!" Jesse exclaims, "You are on vacation every other month!" "It's a tough job, but somebody's got to do it," I tell Jesse. He erupts into laughter at this comment and says "Yeah, yeah, I hear you." Jesse is a great guy with a good sense of humor and a ready laugh. We have this exact conversation 2 or 3 times a year, and we always have a good laugh over it.

We spend the next few minutes talking about vacations and mutual fund investments, and then I glance at my Rolex gold presidential watch (custom made for $50,000). It's 11:30 A.M. and I have finished my lunch while talking with Jesse. Medical people tend to eat too quickly. He's a good friend, always looking out for me. I always try to look out for him as well. He is a good guy and an excellent Surgeon, a rare combination. There is a peculiar relationship between arrogance and skill level in Surgeons that I have noticed over the years. The poorer the skill level of the Surgeon, the higher the arrogance level. "Well, I guess it's time for me to get back to the Operating Room and spell Jim for lunch," I say to Jesse, "Are you done for the day in the OR, or will I see you back there?" "I've got a laryngectomy to do, so I'll be in the OR for a couple more hours before I'm done for the day," he says. "All right, I'll see you there," I tell him.

A laryngectomy is a surgery where you take out a large portion of a patient's throat to remove cancer. Jesse James is one of the best Surgeons I have ever seen doing this procedure. He is very quick, does excellent work, loses very little blood, and his patients have very few post-op complications. He is just one of those Surgeons who has the magic touch.

I head back to the OR and briefly check on my rooms by looking through the windows in the OR doors. The people in the ORs don't notice me looking into the rooms. Everything is going as smooth as usual, so I head back to the lounge. Walking down the OR hallway, I see people and equipment coming and going continuously. The OR is a beehive of activity in the middle of the day. Going through the door to the Doctor's Lounge (we would never share one lounge with the OR Nurses) I see Jim Turner. He is at the computer, booking reservations for a Caribbean trip.

He loves to go bone fishing in the Caribbean. His wife, Janet, loves to lie out in the sun and go shopping when they go there, so it's a win-win situation for them both. How somebody could spend a whole week fishing, I'll never know. "I'll listen out for your rooms now if you want to have lunch," I say to Jim. "Thanks, I should be done here in 5 minutes, and then I'll go," he says to me. "Very good, try the shrimp pilaf, it is excellent today," I tell him. "Okay, thanks," Jim says to me before turning to finish up his reservation-making on the computer. "Are you going to a conference or is it just vacation," I ask him. "Just vacation, you know how much I love fishing in the Caribbean" he replies without looking up from the computer screen. He is very focused on what he is doing on the computer.

About 2 minutes later Jim says "All right, I'm all done. My trip is locked in, and my reservations are set. I'm going to lunch. I'll be back in a few." He gets up from his chair in front of the computer, stretches, and turns to head out of the Surgeon's Lounge. Lunch time is a good break from the activities of the Operating Room. Sometimes you just need time to pause from the constant running around from OR to OR and question-answering on the cell phone.

Chapter Three

Doctor Jim Turner, My Partner

Jim Turner came into town 5 years ago, very much the same as I did 20 years before. He was driving an old, unreliable Buick, and was strapped with $120,000 worth of college loans and credit card debt. He and Janet were newly married, after living together for 3 years during his Residency. You do get paid while you are in Anesthesia Residency, but it is a nominal amount of money. You can live off of a Resident's pay, but you can't live well. They were very much in love at that time, and still are. They are that rare couple, focused on the prize at the end of their struggles.

Immediately after arriving in town, they moved into a nice 3 bedroom apartment. They lived there for almost 2 years, so Jim could use 1 bedroom for an office in which to study for boards (national certification exams, which are taken a few months after finishing up your Residency), and have 1 bedroom available for visiting guests and family. Other than buying a new car, they spent no unnecessary money, they were not extravagant. They saved their money for a new house and the buy in on my Anesthesia Corporation. During this time, they decided on which end of town they wanted to live, and which subdivision they wanted to purchase a home in. They now live in a very nice 4,000 square foot home with 4 large bedrooms and 3 and ½ bathrooms. Also, there is a nice, large back yard to play with their son in.

Their son, James Allen Turner II is 3years old now. He was born shortly after they arrive in town. Janet is now expecting their second child. Janet is hoping for a girl this time, so she can get her tubes tied afterward. They only want to have 2 children, even though they could easily afford to have more. These people plan everything. In a couple of months, she will have an ultrasound to see if her hopes for a girl have come true. This pregnancy is not going as smoothly as the first, but Janet is doing fairly well, having no major problems. It brings back fond memories, watching this young couple going through stages of life that I have already experienced.

I want them to do well. It's nice to see such a happy couple on their way to having a very nice life. I never had things so smooth when I was at their stage of life. My first wife had a lot of emotional problems which eventually drove us apart, and drove me into my present wife, Shirley's arms. My first wife, Judy, also had a lot of problems with her pregnancy. Our son, Nathaniel, was born perfectly healthy, but the pregnancy took a toll on her. She had terrible bouts of morning sickness in the beginning and spent the last 6 weeks of her pregnancy on bed rest. It was rough on her and I think she resented me for it. A lot of hard feelings grew between us during that time.

Jim comes up and says to me, sitting in front of my computer, "I'm back from lunch, is everything going smooth?" "Smooth like butter," I say back to him. He laughs and tells me he is going to go see if Avi or Arnash want to take lunch now. Off he goes, taking care of business. Jim is all business at work, but he enjoys playing tennis and the piano after work. He also spends a lot of time with his son, which gives Janet a break so she can go to the Gym and workout. She and Jim are both in very good physical shape, unlike me. I am about 50 pounds overweight, and the only outdoor exercise I ever get is playing golf 1 or 2 times a month and going fishing 3 or 4 times a year. Shirley is my main source of indoor exercise, and that is only once or twice a week, at most. At this point in my life, this is about all the exercise I can stand or care to have.

The Indians, as I privately refer to Avi and Arnash, will either get lunch with Jim looking out for them, or they will look out for each other for lunch. That is what they usually do. I am getting sleepy and glance at my watch. It is 1:00 P.M. now, only a couple of hours to go before I start maneuvering to get out of here. I'm pondering whether or not to go to my office and take a snooze on my sofa for an hour or should I try to just stay awake until I leave here. There are no errands for me to run after work today, so I will be going straight home once I get out of here. After I get home, I'm planning on going to bed early anyway, probably around 9 P.M., so I can be well rested for call tomorrow. Decisions, decisions.

Arnash comes up to me and says, "My last room is finishing in a few minutes, so I will look out for Avi's rooms while he takes his lunch and then I'll go home after that." "Okay," I say to Arnash. He was on call this past weekend (from Friday through Sunday), and that makes him the first Anesthesiologist out on Monday. Jim is on call today, then Wednesday, Friday, Saturday, and Sunday; after which he is first out on the following Monday. The first week of the call rotation he will be on call Tuesday and Thursday. The second week he will have no call. The third week of the call rotation he will be on call Monday, Wednesday, and then Friday, Saturday, and Sunday. The fourth week he will have no call.

This is the way that call rotates when all 4 of us are here. I am on call tomorrow and Thursday of this week, and then we rotate through all of us who are here. Every third week at least we have no call. Every other month we have a week of vacation. This establishes a pecking order for who gets off work first, second, and third. This is one of the rare weeks when all 4 of us are here. We each have 6 weeks of vacation plus 1 week for continuing education per year, so for about 24 weeks out of 52, there are only 3 of us present to work at the Hospital. I manage to take another 5 days off per year (attributed to sickness or special business) so that I am only here about 10 months out of 12.

Part of my responsibility as the perpetual Chief of Anesthesia is making out the call schedule for the Anesthesiologists. I make it up 2 months at a time, so we live our lives around the call schedule, 2 months at a time. You can never take more that 2 weeks of vacation at a time. This means that you have to have your vacation, continuing education, or other leave requests on the calendar ahead of time. We usually only take 1 week of leave off at a time.

It really pisses me off that the Hospital has given the 14 CRNAs who work here the same amount of vacation (6 weeks) and continuing education (1 week) leave as we Anesthesiologists have. It never used to be that way, but they are in such short supply that they have all kinds of perks now that they did not have 10 or 15 years ago. Now, the demand for CRNAs is so great, if we shit on them too much, they can turn in their 30 day notice tomorrow and be working at another Hospital next month somewhere else. We supervise them to make our money, but at least we don't have the pay them. They do the vast majority of the Anesthesia work involved in the surgical cases while we Anesthesiologists handle the preoperative and postoperative problems. They are all hourly employees of the Hospital, so they get paid even if the patient has no insurance or money to pay for their healthcare. Most Anesthesia Departments in the U.S. operate on this model with very slight differences in who does what.

I try to get along and treat the CRNAs well, because after all, they help me make my money. Some Anesthesiologists get so caught up with the 'I'm the Doctor, I'm in charge' mind game that they look down on and abuse the CRNAs routinely to inflate their own pitiful egos. Some are such control freaks, that they keep their foot on the CRNAs neck as far as professional practice goes, and dictate every minute detail. They only want CRNAs who will follow orders, not think for themselves. They think that they can have a kind of cookbook Anesthesia process, and all the CRNA needs to do is just follow their cookbook. Anesthesia Departments with these kinds of Doctors have a lot of CRNA turnover, and they have an unhappy workforce. Having a lot of staff turnover costs a Hospital a lot of money. What used to amaze me is that, outside of the Operating Room, very few people even realize that CRNAs exist at all. This is in spite of the fact that they do 2/3 of the Anesthesia in the U.S., and there are 10 times more of them than there are of us.

It's kind of funny; almost everyone in America thinks that Anesthesiologists actually do their Anesthesia. The only Hospitals where an Anesthesiologist actually does a patient's Anesthesia are the ones where there are only Anesthesiologists, no CRNAs. There are a few of these in the country, but not many. There are also a few Hospitals in the country where there are only CRNAs and no Anesthesiologist. These are usually smaller, rural Hospitals. We actually try to minimize our participation in the actual Anesthesia because that minimizes our liability. If anything goes wrong, we can testify that we didn't do that, or we didn't order that; it's the CRNA's fault. They did something wrong, or they didn't check with us first. Another peculiar thing about this profession is that both Anesthesiologists and CRNAs are taught Anesthesia by Anesthesiologists and CRNAs. We have that MD (Medical Doctor) degree however, and even if we can't manage to pass our board exams and become certified, we can still practice Anesthesia and be in charge of CRNAs who have passed their boards. If a CRNA doesn't pass their boards, they cannot practice Anesthesia until they do. Isn't this great? I love the power structure of Medicine in America.

It is now 2:00 P.M., and I have just started my last 2 cases of the day. I guess I'll forgo the nap in my office because I'll soon be out of here. My last 2 cases are a laparoscopic cholecystectomy and a laparoscopic appendectomy. The first case is the removal of the gallbladder using endoscopic instruments and the second is the removal of the vermiform appendix using endoscopic instruments. People think these surgeries are done with a laser, which is just a focused hot beam of light. In actuality, they are almost never done with the use of a laser. Lasers were once used in these procedures, because they are good at cutting tissue. They are very poor at stopping bleeding however, for this you need the electrocautery. The Laparoscopic Surgeries are performed these days with electric cautery, scissors, and graspers which fit through the 5 and 10 millimeter ports inserted through the patient's skin to gain access to the inner organs.

Before World War II, people sometimes used to die from infected or ruptured gallbladders and appendices. During World War II, we could use the antibiotic Penicillin to fight infections and the surgery to remove these infected or ruptured organs was refined to a high degree. The old fashioned gallbladder scar was about 6 to 8 inches long and the patient felt awful for about 4 to 7 days afterward. The old fashioned appendectomy scar was about 2 to 3 inches long and the patient felt awful for about 1 to 3 days afterward. Full recovery to be able to work vigorously was usually 2 months. With the new laparoscopic techniques, you have a ½ inch incision over you navel and 2 to 4 other ½ inch incisions in your abdomen. These incisions are usually covered with band aids instead of large, bulky dressings. Now, you feel better the next day after surgery, but full recovery takes 6 to 8 weeks. Also, now you are usually sent home the day after surgery with prescriptions for antibiotics and pain pills so you won't hurt or get a post-op infection.

Both of these cases should be done by 3 or 3:30 P.M., then, I will take care of some paperwork in my office and be out of the hospital by 4 P.M. No, I think to myself, I think I'll just slide out of the Hospital right before the patients leave the Operating Room and go to the PACU. I can take care of the paperwork tomorrow, when I am on call. The Nurses in PACU know to call me on the cell phone if they have any problems. Not only that, but the CRNA on call and Jim (the Anesthesiologist on call) can take care of any patient care problems in the PACU if more immediate attention is required.

3:00 P.M. and I decide to get up from the chair in front of my computer to walk over to Operating Rooms 6 and 7, where my 2 cases are going. I stick my head just inside the door of Operating Room 6 and see Jake Barns, the General Surgeon removing his gown and gloves (this means he is finished with the surgery he has been doing). He will now leave the OR and go to the dictation phone to dictate the surgical procedure he has just finished. This dictation will be listened to and typed up by a

Medical Transcriptionist. This typed surgical report will come back in a couple of days and the Surgeon will read and sign it, after which it will go into the patient's chart to be part of the permanent record. The OR team (Scrub Tech and OR Nurse) will soon be taking down the surgical drapes and the OR Nurse will be putting on the dressing. After that, the CRNA will wake up the patient, the OR staff will move the patient over to a stretcher, and it's off to the PACU they go. I look over at Elizabeth, the CRNA doing the case, and say "Any problems?" She says "No, no problems at all." "See you tomorrow," I tell her. "See you," she says back as I turn from the door to OR 6. Then, I walk over to OR 7, where Bob (the CRNA) is doing the appendectomy. Opening the door about a foot, I can see the General Surgeon, Stuart, is closing (sewing up) the incision. He has his head down, focused on his work and doesn't notice I am looking through the door as he sews up the patient. This case is done, I think to myself. I look over at Bob, and ask "Any problems?" "Nothing but smooth sailing all the way," he replies. "I'll see you tomorrow Bob," I say to him, "Say Bob, are you on call with me tomorrow?" "Yep, I'm on with you tomorrow," he says back to me. I reply "All right, I'll see you tomorrow Bob."

I like to be on call with Bob, He has 20 years of experience in Anesthesia, and he makes my job very easy. Bob can handle any problem or situation that arises at this Hospital. The first 5 years of his Anesthesia career he spent at a Level 1 Medical Center. A Level 1 is the highest level of Medical Center, where lesser Hospitals such as this one (we are a Level 3) send the sickest patients, which we are ill-equipped to handle. Smaller Hospitals just don't have all the Medical specialists you need to take care of every type of healthcare problem. You have to have Neurosurgeons (brain) and Cardiothoracic (heart) Surgeons available to be a Level 1 Medical Center. After that, Bob did free lance Anesthesia, and worked all over the place for 5 years, at all types of Hospitals; from large Trauma Centers (Level 1) to 50 bed Hospitals where he was the only Anesthesia provider there. He has seen and done just about everything in Anesthesia. Not only that, but he possesses a keen mind, enabling him to adapt to new situations readily; and to top it off, he has a great sense of humor. Yes, I don't have to worry about a thing when I am on call with Bob. I can rest easy tonight knowing I am on call with him tomorrow.

I head off to the Physician's Dressing Room to shed my scrub suit and slip back into my street clothes. Having my own locker in my own dressing room is great; we don't allow any Nurses in the Physician's

Dressing Room. This is one place where we can talk amongst ourselves about the patients, the Nurses, and anything else, and we don't have to look around to see who might be listening. This is a blessing, because we love to tell dirty jokes and gossip, and we wouldn't want to offend anyone's delicate sensibilities. Even more important, we wouldn't want to be reported to Administration by the Hospital staff for telling offensive jokes, not that it would really have any impact on us Doctors.

As I am getting out of my scrub suit, Jake Barns, the general Surgeon, walks in and says "High Jerry, how are you doing?" "I am doing great, Jake, I'm getting out of this place," I say. "Yeah, I know the feeling, sometimes it feels like a prison," he says back to me. "Say Jerry, did you see that new X-Ray tech who came in to do my cholangiogram?" A cholangiogram is an X-ray taken after dye is injected which shows the ductwork around the gallbladder. It is done during gallbladder surgery to see if there is a gallstone or other blockage of a duct. "No, I didn't see her," I reply back to Jake. "Well you sure missed something special there, that girl is built like a brick shit house," Jake continues, "She must be a new employee. I think I will get cholangiograms on all my gallbladders from now on, just so I can see her swivel her ass." I tell Jake "Watch out, you old dog, that girl will hurt yooou." He laughs loudly, and then Jake says to me "There's nothing wrong with looking at a little eye candy from time to time." "That's true Jake, but you are on wife number 3 and you can't work until you are 100 to pay for all of the women you lust after," I tell him. "Oh, you're just a killjoy," he says back to me, laughing like a fool. "Jake, you know the difference between sex for free and sex for money?" "I'm not sure Jerry," Jake says. "Sex for free is more expensive Jake. You know I'm right," I say to Jake and we both laugh like crazy as I finish getting dressed.

Chuckling to myself at the conversation I just had with Jake, I walk out of the Physician's Dressing Room into the main hallway of the Hospital. Jake is a good guy, he just can't keep it in his pants. I hang a right in the hallway and head to the end, toward where I'm parked in the parking deck adjacent to the Hospital. They finally got rid of that skuzzy assed carpet I notice as I'm walking down the hallway. They actually picked out a nice linoleum to cover the floor; it looks like parquet flooring. It is a long hallway, but I finally arrive at the end and hang a left to check my mailbox in the Doctor's Mailroom next to the regular Physician's Lounge.

Only Doctors who are Surgeons or Anesthesiologists ever come around the Operating Room, the other Doctors avoid it like it has the plague. That is just fine with us because we feel we are superior to them. We are real Doctors, the last cowboys of Medicine. We yawn while dealing with life and death situations. We deal with life and death situations so much that it really becomes just another routine to us. Surgeons and Anesthesiologists deal with acute, critical situations. Other Doctors deal with chronic conditions which take years to develop and have to be dealt with for years. The other, lesser Doctors decompensate and fall apart in critical situations which we can handle with no drama at all. We are the true miracle workers.

Looking into my mailbox, I pull a huge wad of papers out of it. 99% of it goes right into the trash. Don't these people have any mercy on our pine forests, wasting all this paper on this garbage I think as I go through it. The stack of mail is about 4 inches thick, and all I end up keeping is my professional journal and 2 letters about Anesthesia conferences from continuing education (CE) companies. I open the first of the letters on Anesthesia conferences; it is for an Anesthesia cruise conference in the Mediterranean Sea. Straight into the trash can it goes, I am not going anywhere near the Middle East these days. The second letter is for an Anesthesia cruise conference in the Caribbean. I tuck this one in my professional journal. This one might be nice to go to this winter, to get away from the cold weather here. They will offer special rates for the cruise ship, and all the food and drinks are usually included. This might be a good way to relax and get my mandatory continuing education hours in at the same time.

I always try to find 1 or 2 conferences a year to go to which are in really nice locations. I have never been on an Anesthesia cruise conference. If I exceed my allotted days for continuing education, no one will say anything because I am Doctor Jerry Deluna, the Chief of Anesthesia. You get really reduced Hotel room rates with Anesthesia conferences, plus, it is a tax write off. As a result, I have been to Las Vegas, New Orleans, New York and San Francisco about 5 times each. Now, the most important feature I look for in an Anesthesia conference is one that lets out at noon or 1 P.M., at the latest. That way I can go back to my Hotel room after a nice lunch and take a nap. This allows me to be well rested so I can have a busy afternoon and evening and not be too tired or hung over in the morning, when the conference starts again.

If I am too hung over or tired in the morning, I just stay for an hour so I can sign up, get some of the free breakfast, and knock down some orange juice. I may or may not actually sit down in the conference and listen to the lecture, but if I sign the sign up sheet, I will get credit for it and get my CE hours. Surgeons, CRNAs, and Anesthesiologists must get 40 Continuing Education hours every 2 years to maintain our licenses. Thank goodness the expense of doing this is an income tax write off. That means that if you make $500,000 a year in taxable income and you spend $10,000 a year on medical conferences, you only pay taxes on $490,000. Doing several little things like this over and over add up to help preserve a Doctor's income; by reducing your taxable income while paying for the things you have to have anyway. By doing several of these types of things every year, you can easily keep from paying an additional $10,000 a year in taxes. I didn't write the rules, I just try to play by the rules they give me.

Chapter Four

Sex and Shopping

As I turn to head for the exit door, I walk past the Physician's Lounge, and the door opens. Out comes Junius Britt, who is a Vascular Surgeon, holding a cup of coffee. "How's it going Jerry?" he says to me. "It's going great because I'm going home," I say back to him. Junius laughs and says "Yeah that is good, especially when you're going home to that hot little number you're married to. You lucky dog."

Junius got divorced last year from his wife of 20 years and then married his office Nurse, Kelly. They got married 3 months ago and went to Hawaii for a 2 week honeymoon. When they got back Kelly was wearing a $50,000 black pearl necklace. She is 28 and very pretty; he is 47 years old and very average looking. Kelly is a tall (2 inches taller than Junius), willowy blond who started working in his office 3 years ago.

They started having an affair about 4 years ago, soon after they met in the OR. They kept it pretty quite until about 1 ½ years ago. That was when Junius' first wife confronted them coming out of a motel on the edge of town. Jennie, Junius' first wife, was in the parking lot, standing by her Mercedes, yelling at Junius. Kelly walked right up to her and got in her face. She then said "I'm in love with Junius and I'm going to marry him." Jennie said "You whore, you can have him!" She got back in her Mercedes and took off, burning rubber as she left the motel parking lot. The people in the Operating Room are still abuzz over it, talking about it over a year later. Small towns in the South are pretty boring places and the people don't have much excitement, so they really get to talking when something like this happens. It'll keep them talking for years.

"You are the luckiest man in the world Junius," I tell him, "Kelly could pose for Playboy." "Yeah, but she cost me a $2 million cash payout to Jennie, even though Jennie is worth more money than me," Junius says to me. Junius' first wife came from a wealthy family in Boston. They met when Junius was in his final year of Vascular Surgery Residency at Massachusetts General Hospital. "Well, is Kelly worth it?" I ask Junius. "She sure is," Junius replies. "There is nothing like firm, young flesh in bed," he says. "You know what I'm talking about, Jerry, that Shirley is a real hot looking woman," Junius says. "Yeah, she is, she should be, she works out at the health club 10 hours a week," I reply, "I am a lucky man Junius, you are right."

"Did you buy Kelly a red Corvette convertible recently?" I ask Junius. "Yes I did," Junius says, "We were riding by the Chevrolet dealership when she saw it and said to me, God, that's a pretty car." "So, we pulled into the dealership, and one hour later she was driving it home." Junius adds "Man, she fucked my brains out that night, let me tell you." "I'll bet she did," I reply to Junius, "I thought I saw her in that beautiful car last weekend." "She loves that car and she has loved me every night since she got it," Junius says. He continues, "As long as I get her a nice present every 2 or 3 months, she absolutely wears me out in the bedroom." "It'll probably kill me one day, but at least I'm gonna die with a big smile on my face." "Haa ha ha," Junius laughs like a hyena.

"Hey, did you hear what happened to Stuart (General Surgeon) last week?" Junius asks me. "No, I didn't," I reply. Junius says "You know that real cute brunette Nurse, Laura, who works up on the fourth floor?" "I think so," I say back. I really don't have any idea who she is. Junius continues, eager to relate this tale, "Last week, about 10 P.M., Stuart was up on the fourth floor making rounds on his patients. Laura told Stuart that she needed to talk to him, and to please follow her down the hall." "She took him around the corner to an empty office, went inside with him, locked the door, turned around and gave him a blowjob." "She blew him off in the Hospital, can you believe it?" "Stuart told me this himself," Junius says. He continues, "The crazy part is that after she had sucked him off, she went back to the Nurses' station with some of his cum on her lips for everyone to see. Not only that, but she told the other Nurses what she had just done. Can you believe it?" "Wow, that's really crazy," I say.

Actually, some Nurse gets caught having sex in the Hospital every 2 or 3 years and probably many more engage in this activity and don't get caught. Junius says, "Man, that Stuart is one lucky bastard, he's not married and his girlfriend will never find out about it because she doesn't work at the Hospital." "You're right, that is lucky for Stuart, but he's still crazy for letting that Nurse do that to him in the Hospital," I say to Junius. "Yes, that is crazy, I sure wouldn't do something like that in the Hospital," Junius replies. "Neither would I," I retort. "Thank God we both have hot wives waiting for us at home," Junius says to me. I reply, "Amen, brother." "See you later Junius," I say as I turn to go out the door and out of the Hospital. "Take care Jerry," he says back to me as I walk toward the exit door.

When you have men and women working closely together in intense situations, like the Hospital setting, these types of sexual adventures happen from time to time. Sometimes Nurses and Doctors spend more time together than they do with their spouses. But all this is nothing new. Nurses and Doctors having sex (extramarital or otherwise) in the Hospital is an old story and a time-honored tradition in America. In fact, one of the benefits of being a Doctor is that you have an unusually large pool of women (Nurses, X-ray technicians, Respiratory Therapists, and other assorted clip board carriers and mid level managers) from which to pick for your next tryst. Some young, egomaniac, over-sexed young Doctors almost view the Nursing staff as their personal harem and try to screw their way through the lot of them. As a result of this, the vast majority of Doctors' wives are former Nurses. Also, the divorce rate for Doctors and Nurses is much higher that the national average.

It is raining pretty hard outside, but this is no problem for me because my Mercedes is protected by the roof of the parking deck. Only the Doctors, Administrative Staff, and Department Heads get to park in this deck. The Nurses, middle and lower level managers, and other support staff all have to park in a large black topped lot in the back of the Hospital. This means that 90% of all the people who work in the Hospital have to park out in the open, exposed to the elements, and hike up to the building in all kinds of weather.

I open the door and slide into the glove-soft padded leather seats of my SUV. Closing the door with a heavy thunk, I muse about the conversation I just had with Junius. What a crazy story, but this type of thing happens from time to time. Nurse Laura, the instigator, stands a good chance of getting fired for having sex in the Hospital while on duty. Some fellow Nurse, probably a religious person or another jealous Nurse, will rat her out sooner or later to the Nurse Manager on their unit. Doctor Stuart will probably never hear a word about the episode, and he will certainly never have any consequences to pay. I love the power structure of modern Medicine.

I fire up the Mercedes' big V-8 engine. This engine has over 400 horsepower and emits a gratifying growl when you press on the gas peddle. It really is amazing; this big, heavy SUV is nearly as fast as a Corvette sports car. Yet it is so large and comfortable; it is like a small living room on wheels. This baby requires premium gas and only gets 14 miles per gallon on the highway, but because I only drive a few miles to and from work, I only have to cough up $60 to fill her up every two weeks. It is expensive to take a road trip in, but what the hell, it's only money.

As I back out of my parking space, I look at the sign bolted to the wall in front of my SUV. It reads: Dr. Jerry Deluna, Chief of Anesthesia. Yeah, that's me, I am the man. A warm glow comes over me as I put the SUV in drive, punch the gas peddle and let out a little tire squeal as I head down the parking deck ramp. I love driving fast. As I round the last turn in the parking deck to approach the exit, I have to slow way down to give the crossbar a chance to rise. Other people know to look out for me in this parking deck. I gun the V-8 and head out into the rain. I check my gas gauge, there is plenty of gas in my tank, and so it is a quick ride home.

I call home to see if Shirley will be there when I arrive. She answers "Hello." "High honey, I've just left the Hospital and I'll be home shortly," I say to her. "Okay, I'll be here when you get here," she says back to me. "Love you," I say. "Love you," she says to me, and then hangs up. A few minutes later, I am pulling into my driveway. I hit the button on the garage door opener and slowly pull up out of the rain next to Shirley's Jaguar. Once I am in the garage, I hit the button to lower the garage door and turn off the Mercedes' engine. After getting out of the big SUV, I head across the garage to the door which leads into the house through the kitchen.

"Hey baby, how was work?" Shirley says right before she gives me a big hug and a kiss on the lips. "Same as usual, not much excitement today," I tell her. "Well, you've got me for excitement," she says as she hands me a gin and tonic with a wedge of lime perched on the lip of the glass. "Thank you baby," I say emphatically back to her as I take the drink from her. I love a good gin and tonic, with a lime wedge. "How was your day," I inquire as we walk to the living room and have a seat on the big sofa. "Not bad, I had a good workout at the health club, where I met up with my compadres, Suzie and Cindy." Shirley says to me. She has known Cindy for about 6 years, and Suzie for more than 15 years. They are both married to Doctors whom I have known for a long time. Suzie has been married to Jesse James (ENT Surgeon) for more than 20 years, a rare occurrence in the medical world. Cindy is the second wife of Brett Smith, a general Surgeon whom I have known since he came to town, 15 years ago.

"What trouble did the three of you get into today?" I ask Shirley. "Not much, we had salads for lunch at 'La Bistro'. We love that place for lunch," she says to me. "Do they still have the guy teaching Italian lessons over the speakers in the bathroom?" I ask her. "No, they have switched to French lessons. I guess someone finally told them it was improper to have Italian lessons taught in a restaurant with a French name," she says. "Ha ha ha," I laugh at this. "That's true babe, but what can you expect in the South. That sure is funny though," I say to her. "I want to show you something I found today, let me go and get it," Shirley says. "Oh no, you've been shopping," I tease her. She laughs as she gets up from the sofa, saying to me "It'll be alright dear."

I finish off my gin and tonic and go over to the wet bar to make another one. As I am putting ice cubes into the glass I am thinking, I hope this shopping spree of Shirley's wasn't too expensive. I pour the glass 1/3 full of Bombay Sapphire gin, 1/3 tonic water, then squeeze a wedge of lime into the glass and drop it into the glass. After I stir the mixture with my index finger, I take a big drink. Man, that's a good drink, I am thinking as Shirley returns to the living room with a shopping bag.

"Sit down over here," she says as she motions toward the sofa with her hand. After I am seated and giving her my full attention, she pulls a shoe box out of the bag. She has the biggest smile on her face when she is doing this; you'd swear she'd be getting ready to give me a brick of gold or something. Why is it that every American woman wants to emulate Imelda Marcos I think as I watch her proudly preparing to show me her latest 'find'. Shirley already has at least 100 pairs of shoes. "Check these out," she says as she opens the box and proudly presents to me her latest purchase so that I too can be amazed. In her hands are 2 skinny, almost invisible shoes that remind me of the sandals you find for sale at the Mexican border for $2.00 a pair.

"What are they?" I ask. "They're Jim Chow shoes, silly," she says, smiling ear to ear. "Oh, what are those?" I ask. "Why they're the absolute hottest thing in women's shoe fashion from California," she replies. I just can't help myself; I have to ask "What does the latest in women's shoe fashion from California cost?" "$1,200," she returns, still smiling. "Wow!" I exclaim. "Don't you think they're gorgeous? I want to wear them out to dinner tonight," she says to me. I'm not stupid, I tell her "They are pretty, and they'll go well with some of the outfits you have." She gives me a big hug and says "I knew you'd like them honey. I fell in love with them the moment I laid eyes on them. I just can't believe how cute they are." I just can't believe anyone would pay over $10 for them, but I certainly don't share these thoughts with Shirley, oh well.

Chapter Five

Dinner With the Deluna's

"Let's call Suzie and Jesse and go out to dinner at 'La Fleur" tonight. What do you think dear?" She says. "I love 'La Fleur', let's do it," I say. We go out to eat about 3 or 4 times a week. I have to eat supper at the Hospital 2 or 3 times a week because of call duty and committee meeting obligations. We Doctors have committee meetings at the Hospital every week, where we waste time making policies that no one pays attention to because every Doctor pretty much does as he pleases with no repercussions. The Hospital provides a nice, free meal at these meetings, so at least they aren't a total waste. As a result, we only eat supper at home once or maybe twice a week. I enjoy our cozy dinners together.

Actually, I do love the restaurant 'La Fleur'. It is an excellent restaurant, but it is not cheap. They have fabulous appetizers, great steaks, great seafood, and a chocolate soufflé to die for. The wine list is extensive, the drinks are strong, and when you order a Stolichnaya Vodka and orange juice, they squeeze the juice from a real orange right then and there to make your drink. I don't mind spending $100 or more per person to eat a meal at a restaurant of this caliber.

I also love the company of Jessie and Suzie James. We have known them for a long time. They are a great couple of friends. Jesse has a great wit and really tells good stories about his travels. He goes on a Medical Mission trip every year. His wife, Suzie is a real pistol as well, with a great sense of humor. She just exudes joy and a zest for life that is rare. They are as nice a couple of people as I have ever met in my entire life.

I tell Shirley that I'll give them a call. "Don't bother," she says, "I've already made the arrangements; our reservation is for 7 P.M." "Suzie and

I went shopping today, after meeting at the health club and then having lunch. She bought a pair of Jim Chow shoes also, but of course hers look different than mine. We made our plans then and she called Jesse, so, it's all set," Shirley says all this to me without taking a breath. "Wow, you sure work fast," I reply. I am amazed at how quickly she can put such a plan together. She is an absolute whiz at organizing any kind of social activity.

It's 5:30 P.M., and I walk over to the wet bar to fix my third drink. Shirley is busy trying on her new shoes and admiring them on her feet. She is walking around the living room, parading and showing me how good her new shoes look while I am mixing my drink. After I stir the gin, tonic, and lime mixture with my finger, I take a healthy swallow. Man, what a good drink. I am really beginning to unwind from my day at the Hospital and feel at ease in my sanctuary, my home. Here, I am surrounded by comfort and beauty, and not one of my nerves is on edge.

"I guess I'll go take a shower and get ready to go out," I tell Shirley. "You go right ahead. I just need to freshen up my makeup and get dressed, I showered after my workout" she says to me. "Gee babe, you already look gorgeous to me," I tell her as I lean toward her to give her a passionate kiss. "Oh, you," she says and giggles right before she gives me a close hug and passionate kiss in return. I can feel Shirley's large breasts pressing into my chest and I cup her left butt cheek with my right hand as we hug and kiss for a few seconds. I am starting to get hard as she wriggles free, smiling that big, beautiful smile at me. "We don't have time to fool around now. We both have things to do to get ready for dinner, maybe when we get back home," she says to me, smiling while backing up a little. "Oh, okay," I reply and then turn to head for the bathroom. Man, I love those big tits pressing on me, I think as I pause on the way out of the living room to pick up my ½ drink from the coffee table and polish it off in one last, big swallow. As I rinse out my glass at the wet bar, I admire Shirley's long legs and rump while she bends over to gather her shoe box and shopping bag. The contour of her ass and thong are plainly visible through her tight dress as she is bent over. Man, what a fine piece of ass, I am a lucky man I think to myself as I turn to head to the bedroom. Yeah, I'm doing alright.

Going through the bedroom door, I take an immediate right turn to go into my walk-in closet. I have to walk through my walk-in closet to get to my bathroom. Flipping on the light, I walk into the closet and begin to get undressed, tossing my old clothes into the dirty clothes hamper. I have only worn them to work and back, but they are wrinkled, so I don't want to wear them again.

Our maid will either wash my clothes and fold and put them in the appropriate dresser, or take out the finer articles to be dry cleaned or pressed at the cleaners. Once a week the cleaners deliver our nicest clothes back to our house. The maid works at our house Monday through Friday, 8:00 A.M. until 2:00 P.M., and keeps the house spotless. She generally arrives after Shirley is awake, and is gone before we return in the afternoon. We don't have to concern ourselves with things like vacuuming, dusting, mopping floors, washing dishes, or washing dirty clothes. Our maid has worked for us for the past 8 years. She is very trustworthy.

The more money you make, the more people you hire to do the chores of everyday life for you. We have a landscaping service that takes care of our yard and the flowers, a pool guy who takes care of our swimming pool, the maid, and a housekeeping guy from the Hospital that comes over every 2 weeks to wash, wax, and keep our cars looking new. Shirley drives a metallic sea foam green Jaguar convertible with a white leather interior. Our lives are filled with other activities and concerns besides the maintenance duties of everyday life. Yeah, I'm doing alright now.

After getting naked, I walk through my walk-in closet and into my bathroom. I look at myself in the mirror. 50 pounds overweight and a bit more than slightly grayed, I still look decent for my age, I think to myself. In fact, I look like a successful man, especially when I dress in my tailor-made clothes. All of my shirts, pants, suits, and tuxedoes are tailor-made; there are no double buttons on my shirt sleeve cuffs. Putting toothpaste on the electric toothbrush, I am trying to decide what pair of shoes to wear tonight; I only have about 40 choices. I think I'll go with black dress shoes; black always looks classy and goes with anything.

I shaved this morning, so I jump into the shower after brushing my teeth. Man, I love this shower. It has 6 shower heads and 20 different programmed settings to shower with. I especially love the pulsating massage that beats on my back, it is so relaxing. Fifteen minutes later, I jump out of the shower, squeaky clean and feeling great. I look over at the clock on the wall; its red LED numbers read 6:15. Not to worry, it doesn't take me long to get dressed because my closet is very well organized. We'll be out of the house in 20 to 30 minutes and on our way to a great restaurant for good times with good friends.

Getting dressed in my large closet, I put on a yellow cotton shirt and khaki pants. Checking myself out in the full length mirror, I admire the way the clothes look, yeah, I look sharp. After going back into the bathroom to comb my hair and eyebrows, I walk out into the bedroom, where I am stopped in my tracks. Shirley is dressed in a short black dress and looks stunning. "Wow babe, you look like a fashion model," I say to her. Shirley thrives on these comments. She smiles back at me, snow white teeth showing between blood red lips. "Why thank you darling. You really think I look good for my age?" She asks. She is only 38, has never had any babies to stretch her body out of shape, and works out 5 days a week. Hell yes she looks good for her age. "Baby, you look good for any age. And your new shoes look great too," I tell her. She beams with pleasure at this comment. I am buttering my bread so I will get some booty later tonight.

We set the house alarm and head out of the house and into the garage. I press the button on the Mercedes' fob to unlock the doors. I walk behind Shirley toward the SUV, mostly so I can admire her ass swivel as she walks. Walking around the SUV with Shirley, I open her door for her. She likes me to do that and I like to do it so I can admire her tan, shapely legs as she sits down and swivels around into her seat.

Heading to 'La Fleur', we are both excited about seeing Jessie and Suzie. It's been almost 2 months since we have been out to dinner with them. They are a fun couple, and Jesse loves to tell dirty jokes and travel stories, both of which my Shirley loves to hear. "Now don't you forget to notice Suzie's new shoes tonight," Shirley admonishes me. "I won't dear, I'll be sure to compliment them. I hope they are as nice looking as yours," I say back to Shirley. Yes, I am buttering my bread. Shirley loves to be complimented. "Do you really think they are sexy?" She asks me. "Hell yes, they are hot looking and you are hot looking in them," I reply. "Oh honey, you are so sweet," she says as she leans over to give me a kiss on the cheek. I love the idea of entering a really nice restaurant with her lipstick on my cheek. Warm and fuzzy feelings are all I am having as we back out of the garage and head to the restaurant.

Ten minutes later, we pull up to the front door of 'La Fleur'. After we stop, with the engine still running, a red coated young valet opens Shirley's door for her, and another opens mine. As I get out of the SUV and stand up, I reach into my pocket for a $5 bill to hand the valet. "How are you and the wife doing tonight Dr. Deluna?" He asks me as he takes the $5 from my hand. "We're doing very well, thank you," I reply to him as I turn to walk around the SUV. I recognize his face, but I can't remember his name for anything even though I have seen him many times.

I walk around the large SUV quickly to catch up with Shirley, who is standing on the sidewalk in front of the entrance to the restaurant, fussing with her dress. She is bent over, her dress pulled tight over her ass, dusting an imaginary piece of lint off of the hem. The other 3 valets, all young men, are definitely checking out the situation. I think Shirley just naturally preens and poses in front of men. She just can't turn it off. It comes so naturally to her. It's how she got my attention, years ago. And she is just so damn hot looking; many men turn their heads and look at us as we walk up the steps and through the front door, which is held open for us by a smiling man in a black coat. "Good evening," he says as we walk past him. We do not reciprocate as we enter the restaurant.

Once inside, we walk up to the Maitre De's desk where our old acquaintance, Jackson greets us. "Ah, Dr. Deluna and Shirley, my, but you look lovely tonight Mrs. Deluna. What a handsome couple you make, will you be joining anyone for dinner?" He asks. This guy really knows how to treat his patrons. "Yes, Jackson, we are joining Dr. James and his wife for dinner tonight," I reply. "Oh yes, they have only just arrived, and are seated by the window overlooking the river. Would you like me to walk you over to them?" Jackson asks. "No, thank you Jackson, I think I know exactly where they're seated," I say. This is not a very large restaurant. Jackson smiles and says "Very well sir, I hope you have a lovely evening with us. If there is anything at all I can do to make your stay with us more pleasant, please don't hesitate to tell me." "Thank you Jackson, I'm sure we'll have another great meal here," I tell him as we turn to walk into the restaurant's dining room. "Yes sir," he says after us as we walk away from him.

I am getting more and more excited in anticipation of having dinner with Jessie and Suzie as we walk through the restaurant. It has been more than 2 months since we have gotten together with them. We just get so damn busy. Jessie has been on a Medical Mission trip since we last saw them, and I can't wait to hear about the trip.

I already know almost exactly where Jesse and Suzie will be found in the restaurant. They love to sit by the windows on the far side of the restaurant, overlooking the river. We have met for dinner here many times over the years. "Oh, look, there they are," Shirley says as soon as she spots them. Jessie and Suzie are huddled over the table in a close conversation, and don't notice us as we approach. "What are you kids doing?" I say loudly as we get within a few steps of them. They both look up at us, smiling from ear to ear.

Immediately, they both stand up and Jessie proceeds to give me a firm handshake and tell me how nice it is to see Shirley and I. "You are always the fashion model," he says to Shirley as he leans over to give her a kiss on the cheek. He steps back and looks down at her feet and says, "Are those your new shoes? They look great, especially at the end of your legs." Shirley giggles like a school girl at this. Not to be outdone, I tell Suzie "Show me yours, Shirley told me you got a pair also." Suzie steps forward so I can admire her new shoes. They have a little more material to them and look a little more substantial than the pair Shirley is wearing, and they do go with her dress quite well. "Those are some great looking shoes. I think you and Shirley made some good choices," I tell her. Suzie smiles and is obviously pleased with all this.

After our greeting and shoe fussing, we sit down at the table overlooking the river outside. The large windows give us a panoramic view of the river and the far bank. It is a beautiful scene. Within 10 seconds, a waiter is at our table, filling our water glasses and asking if we would like anything to drink. Before the last words of the question finish crossing the first waiter's lips, another waiter approaches our table with a bottle of wine in his hands. Jessie has been busy ordering wine for us. I don't mind because he has excellent taste in wine.

Jessie says "Suzie wants fish and I wanted to eat steak, so I ordered a nice Merlot from Peru that I know will go well with both choices." I look at Shirley and she nods, indicating that this wine selection will suit her as well. "We'll go with the Merlot from Peru as well," I say to the waiter. "Very good sir," he says to me before pouring a tablespoon of the Merlot into Jesse's glass so that he may observe its color and sniff its bouquet. After this, Jesse takes the wine into his mouth, swirls it around, and swallows it. About 2 seconds after swallowing the wine, Jesse breathes out through his mouth, sighs, and pronounces the wine fit for consumption. Our waiter then proceeds to pour wine into all 4 of our glasses.

I ask Jesse how his mission trip went while the waiter pours the wine into our glasses. "Great, it was an unbelievable experience Jerry," Jesse says. Suzie raises her wine glass and says "I want to make a toast to Jesse and the mission trip." We all raise our glasses as she says "To doing good work in the world and making a safe trip home." "Hear hear," we all chime and take a swallow of the wine. This stuff is really good.

Jesse takes a Medical Mission trip to the Dominican Republic every year. Some of his church members and a few other Doctors and Nurses go with him, about 12 people all together. They save up drugs, equipment and supplies all year long to bring down there with them. Although they are only there 1 week, they perform surgeries, provide all kinds of health services, give out donated eyeglasses, and help build and repair houses. They try to do their best to do whatever the people need doing while they are there. All in all, they probably help out more than 1,000 people in that 1 week, and the people really appreciate their efforts. Jessie's church provides for the meals down there and sends donated supplies with them. They have to pay for the travel expenses out of their own pockets. The church Jesse and Suzie go to has organized 2 teams for 2 Medical Mission trips a year; and they have been doing it for 10 years.

Initially, we just talk about how nice it is to see each other again and catch up on what's been going on in our lives, but Suzie has other plans for conversation. "Tell Jerry the story about the old woman and the glasses," Suzie says excitedly. She looks like she can barely contain herself. "I will after we order appetizers," he says. Our waiter comes up and we order crab cakes and calamari for appetizers. We also order another bottle of the Peruvian Merlot because it will not take the 4 of us very long to polish off this one. Man, this stuff is smooth and delicious. Suzie says "Tell them about the old woman!" Jesse laughs and takes a good drink of the Merlot and starts his tale about the old woman.

I performed 30 to 40 surgeries per day for the 5 days we were working there. Not just ear and nose surgeries, but all kinds of surgeries. One day, I was taking a break from doing surgery and eating a sandwich, when Jack Branch, the team leader came up to me. He asked if I could give Gene Smith a break for just a few minutes so he could grab a sandwich and go to the bathroom. Gene had been working for 6 hours in a shack to our left without a break for food, water, or a bathroom visit.

Gene's job that day was giving people a simple eye test, then giving them a free pair of eyeglasses to correct their vision as best as he could. The eyeglasses were donated by members of the church, and their friends and families. Gene owns a hardware store back home. He is not an Optometrist. Other than wearing glasses himself, he knows very little about them. He was given instructions on how to conduct a simple vision test, and provide the glasses to help with the vision problems. I told Jack "Sure," and finished the last bite of my sandwich.

As I walked toward the shack where Gene was working, I noticed a line of about 20 people waiting outside to be seen by Gene. When I walked through the burlap covering of the shack door, Gene looked at me and said "Thank you buddy!" He handed me a box with about 50 pairs of eyeglasses in it and said that they were for reading and the box on the table were for far vision. The table was a crate, turned on its side. There was a simple eye chart tacked up on the wall. About 10 feet away there was a line drawn in the dirt where the 'patient' was supposed to stand. There was no chair in the shack. At least there was some burlap covering the windows and doorway.

The helper/translator yelled out for the next 'patient' to come in. An old, short, fat woman came in. She stated that she was 80 years old and couldn't see to read any more. I told the translator to tell her that I would give her some glasses so she could read again and that I would have to give her a simple eye test first. The old woman smiled at me for all she was worth. She had 1 tooth in her mouth. This was amazing to me for 2 reasons. There are very few fat people in the jungles of 3rd world countries; there is not that much food and they have to work too hard to survive. Second, it is exceedingly rare for a person to live to the age of 80 years in a 3rd world country.

After I gave her the eye test, it came down to 2 pair of glasses; they were different styles, but corrected her vision about the same. I told the translator to ask her which pair she wanted. The old woman reached out for the pair she liked the best. She put them on and looked at her hands. At this point she struggled down to one knee while holding the translator's hand for assistance, and started what sounded like singing to me. I asked the translator what the old woman was doing. The translator then told me that the old woman was singing her prayer of thanks to God for sending his angel (me) to her with these glasses so that she might see to read her Bible again.

This really touched my heart. When Gene came back to work and I left that shack, I felt like I was walking 3 feet off the ground. There is no better feeling on this earth than that. You can't buy anything close to that feeling. Jessie stopped talking and took a drink from his wine glass, indicating that his story was done. We were all stunned for a moment by what he had just told us.

"Wow!" I exclaim, "That was an amazing story." I look up at Shirley and see that she is crying. "Are you okay honey?" I ask her. "That story was so touching, I just couldn't help myself," she says, "Suzie, will you come with me to the bathroom?" Suzie says "I sure will, I cried like a baby when Jesse first told it to me too and it still brings tears to my eyes every time I hear it."

The girls both get up from our table, dabbing their eyes, and go off to the bathroom to dry their eyes and freshen up their makeup. "Jesse, you are an amazing guy, going on those Medical Mission trips every year," I say to him, "How do you manage to do it with such a busy practice?" He says to me "Jerry, I feel very blessed in life and I feel it is my duty to give back to others." He continues "Besides, in a 3rd world country you can work as fast as you are able to help as many people as you can and you don't have to worry about the 600 pound gorilla like you do in this country." "Yes, that's true," I reply.

"Those people view us as saviors and they appreciate every thing you try to do for them. They would never think of trying to sue you if everything doesn't turn out perfect like people do in this country," Jesse says, "They know we are there to do our best to try to relieve their misery, and they appreciate us for it." He continues "It's too bad we have the legal system we do in this country; it probably adds a 3rd more to the cost of providing health care, and prevents a lot of people from even getting health care, but everyone's afraid to talk about it or confront the issue." Jesse says "Lets face it, the damn Lawyers make up all the rules and hold all the cards; we don't stand a chance going up against them in their system." "That's the damn truth," I reply.

The girls return from the bathroom a few minutes later, all dry eyed and makeup freshened. "Jesse, thank you for sharing that story with us, it really touched my heart," Shirley says as she takes her seat next to me. She is a good-hearted woman and I love her for this. That is another reason why I married her. Shirley sits down next to me and gives me a big smile as I assist her with her chair. I feel happy.

While Jesse recounted his tale, the appetizers arrived steaming hot but we did not take a bite because we were so enthralled. Now, however, they have cooled off enough to eat and we pounce on the crab cakes and calamari like we are starving. The Peruvian Merlot is excellent, and it stimulates the appetite. Plus, we are nearly finished with the second bottle of wine. In a few minutes, our waiter approaches the table and asks if we are ready to order dinner. Jesse says "Yes, I'll have the filet mignon, cooked medium well and she will have the flounder." I say to the waiter "I'll have the filet au poivre and she'll have the stuffed red snapper." "How would you like you filet cooked sir?" the waiter inquires. "Medium well,"

I reply, "Also, we want another bottle of this wine, it is wonderful." After a few glasses of wine, I am feeling good and relaxed. Good food, good wine, and good company, all is well with me right now.

While we enjoy our appetizers and wine, Jesse and I talk about our next plans for vacation. The girls talk about shopping for clothes and gossip about other women. The 4 of us carry on 2 separate conversations, only breaking into each others conversations occasionally. Men and women are seldom interested in the same things for the most part, and I, for one, am thankful for the differences between men and women. So we carry on our guy conversations while the girls carry on their girl conversations and everybody is happy. It's crazy, but it works.

This only goes on for about 10 minutes before the waiter comes up to our table carrying a platter with our salads. He cleans up our leftover appetizer dishes and the plates on which we ate the appetizers. Then he places each of our salads in front of us and asks if we would like some freshly ground pepper on them. We have been here almost an hour now and have worked up quite an appetite, so we dig into our salads.

There are so many good food smells in this restaurant that it really stimulates the taste buds and appetite. We are about halfway into our salads when another waiter comes to our table carrying our 3rd bottle of Peruvian Merlot, with which he tops off our wine glasses. The girls are beginning to get a little giddy from the wine. I can tell this from experience and the fact that they are giggling more now than they were earlier. Jesse and I are feeling good and relaxed from the wine as well.

As we are nearing the end of our salads, a waiter comes up to our table with a huge platter, holding our entrées. The smell of the steaks and seafood is fabulous. The food is still sizzling on the plates. This waiter is graceful as he picks up our salad plates and sets our main courses in front of us. The dishes of food in front of us look good and smell good. The waiter finishes his duties at our table by topping off our wine glasses. This guy is going to get a good tip. The first bite of my steak with the creamy mustard and pepper sauce is shamefully good. The taste of the pepper with the tangy mustard on the grilled steak is absolutely wonderful. We carry on drinking wine, eating, and talking. All of us are having a good time tonight!

"I plan on retiring in 3 years Jesse, how much longer do you think you'll work?" I ask. "I haven't really thought much about it. I'm 55 now, and I'm sure I'll work at least another 10 years," he says. Jesse continues, "I like what I do, I think I'm pretty good at what I do, and I just like the groove I have going in life now." "You are an excellent surgeon," I tell him. "I'm pretty well set financially, maybe when I have a bunch of grandkids to fool around with in a few years, I'll think about slowing down," he says. "That's not a bad plan," I tell him. "I plan to retire in 3 years so I can devote more time to Shirley, traveling, and just having fun," I say to Jesse. Shirley hears this and comments "Oh really, you plan to start going to the gym and going shopping with me?" "Well, I'm not exactly sure about all that," I say to her. We all have a good laugh at this and go back to our eating, drinking, and our separate guy and girl conversations.

My filet with the pepper and mustard sauce is so good that I am almost sad when I come to the end of it. I wash down the last bite with a swallow of wine, savoring all the wonderful tastes on my palate. I am really feeling good and relaxed after such good food and many glasses of wine. A waiter comes up and asks if he may remove my dishes, to which I reply "Yes." One minute after he has cleared my plates, another waiter comes and asks if I would like a cup of coffee, and again I say "Yes." Looking around our table I notice that Jesse is just about finished with his steak, while our wives are only about halfway done with their meals. I guess it's because they talk a lot more than Jesse and I do. Either that or we talk more with food in our mouths than our wives do.

A short time later, a waiter arrives at our table with my coffee, cream and sugar. I enjoy a cup of coffee after a good meal. As I sip my hot coffee, Jesse finishes his steak, exhales and exclaims "Wow, what a great meal that was." Our wives have stopped eating and pronounce themselves full.

It is now about 9:30 P.M., and we have been drinking, eating, and talking for about 2 ½ hours. Soon, it will be time to pay the bill and wrap up the evening. Very few medical people stay out very late during the week. This is because you have to wake up around 5 o'clock in the morning to make it to work by 6:30 or 7 A.M., and many people like to get to work a little early to drink some coffee and organize themselves before their day starts.

I flag down a waiter who happens to be near. He comes over to our table right away. "Could you bring me our bill?" I ask him. He is not our waiter, but he will pass our request on to our waiter. "Jesse, this has been such a wonderful evening. We always have such a good time when we are out with you and Suzie," I say. Shirley chimes in with "How about joining us at the beach house next weekend, it would be great to have you there?" "No can do," Jesse says "We have too much work to catch up on for a few weeks, maybe next month we could make it." Shirley says "I'll work with

Suzie to plan a weekend at the beach house. We'll organize this." I laugh at this and say "I'll bet you will."

Just then, our waiter comes to the table with our check. I immediately take it from him and say "I'll take care of this, feeding Jesse will be my contribution to the mission effort." Jesse and Suzie laugh at this, and he says "Well alright, I guess I'll let you support the mission effort in your small way since I can't seem to drag you along for some real heavy lifting." We all have a good chuckle at this as I look at the check; $295, not a bad deal for all that we had. I slide the credit card into the check folder and a few minutes later the waiter comes by and picks it up. I cherish the times we spend with Jesse and Suzie. This has been such a fun evening, I almost hate that it is coming to an end. This makes me a little sad.

After taking care of the bill, we gather ourselves and slowly head toward the front door. We walk out of the restaurant together, talking and laughing. "Well Jesse, I guess I'll see you at work tomorrow," I say. "Yes, I've got a busy day tomorrow," he says. We wrap up our goodbyes, then Shirley and I head to our SUV, which the valet has brought around to us. "Gosh, that was so much fun. I just love Jesse and Suzie." Shirley says to me. "Yes, they are a great couple of people," I say back to her. "They sure are fun to be around, we've got to get them over to the beach house for a weekend next month," Shirley says; following with "Suzie and I will organize this, you men are just too busy." I laugh at this and admit that she is probably right.

During the ride home, Shirley leans over next to me while I am driving and snuggles up to me. "What a great evening, I am so tired, I'm going to sleep like a baby tonight," Shirley says. I am enjoying the feelings that great food and a lot of wine impart. Also, I really enjoy it when Shirley snuggles up to me; I am feeling all warm and fuzzy. We don't speak for rest of the ride home, which only takes a few minutes. After we pull into our garage and turn the engine off, I have to wake Shirley. She has fallen sound asleep.

"Hey Shirley, we're home!" I have to repeat 3 times, in progressively louder volumes before she half opens her eyes and sleepily says "I must have fallen asleep." I end up having to partly lift her out of the SUV and help her to her feet before she is awake enough to help me walk her to the door which enters the house from the garage.

We stumble through the house to the bedroom door. Shirley is not helping us move in a straight line very much. I walk with her to the bed, where she falls over into it in a heap. I take off her new shoes for her and pull some covers over her as she pulls the pillow close to her face. Well, I guess there will be no booty call for me tonight. I turn from the bed and head toward my closet to get undressed. So nice to have a maid, I think as I peel off my clothes and leave them in a pile on the floor of the closet. After putting on some silk pajamas, I head for the bathroom to take a dump. It takes me a long time to pee while I am sitting on the throne. That damn prostate, it's starting to give me trouble I think as I am waiting to pee. After a few minutes I am finally done with my business, and I stand up to pull up my pajama pants. The bathroom takes a few spins all of a sudden and I have to put a hand on the wall to steady myself. Whoo, I guess I stood up too quickly after sitting on the toilet for a while. Now, do I want to brush my teeth, or just wait until morning to do it? Aww, to hell with it, I'll just brush them in the morning.

I mosey back through my closet to the bedroom where not much has changed since I left. Shirley is still lying exactly where I left her. That wine must have hit her hard, I think as I walk around to my side of the bed. Sitting on the edge of the bed, I look at the alarm clock. Wow, it's already 11:30 P.M., and I haven't really done a whole hell of a lot since I got home. We must have spent too much time talking with Jessie and Suzie at the restaurant and in the parking lot afterwards.

Damn, I sure wish Shirley was awake so we could fool around a little. I reach over and pull the covers up over her fully clothed body as she sleeps. We are both so busy and always going in different directions these days, it makes it difficult to get together for sex. It's down to once a week or less these days. How sad this has become, I think as I lay my head down on the pillow. What a waste of a beautiful piece of ass. Still, I have a real good buzz from the wine and my stomach is full of real good food. Lying down on my back, I have the sensation that the room is spinning slowly around me, but I could still go for some sex. Poor me, I am thinking sad thoughts like this as I fall off to sleep. I am dead asleep in 5 minutes.

Chapter Six

Tuesday Morning, 4 A.M.
Call Day

I wake up choking on my own vomit. The taste of bile and vomitus fills my mouth, trying to suffocate me as I lurch up in the bed. Leaning over the side of the bed, I vomit onto the floor and begin choking and coughing. The acid and bile regurgitation threatens to enter my lungs as I hang my head over the side of the bed. My esophagus is burning from the irritation caused by the stomach acid. I am dying to take in a deep breath of air, but I dare not for a few seconds.

With my head hanging down, I just have to let the vomit drain out of my mouth so I don't inhale it when I can finally take a breath. This hiatal hernia is going to kill me one of these days, I think to myself after I finally manage to clear my mouth and take in a couple of desperate breaths of air. Gasping for air and sweating from the exertion, I look over at Shirley who is still asleep and hasn't heard any of this struggle. I could have died from aspirating vomit (getting vomit into your lungs) just now and she wouldn't know it until she woke up around 8 or 9 in the morning, I think to myself as I get out of bed and stumble to the bathroom.

Flipping on the bathroom light, I look into the mirror and get a good look at myself. Pale and sweating from the vomiting, I am not an attractive site right now. Vomit is dripping off my chin, and I am still gasping for air. My throat is raw from the contact with stomach acid. I wet a washcloth and wipe down my face, then gargle with mouthwash a few times to rinse out my mouth and erase the vomit taste from my mouth. That's a little better, whew, what a night! Still sweating profusely, I wipe my face on my pajama sleeve. I grab a towel off the rack and walk back to the bed where Shirley still hasn't moved. She sleeps like the dead, I think as I toss the towel over the vomit on the floor to cover it up, and then grab a couple of antacid tablets out of the nightstand to chew up and neutralize the stomach acid still burning my throat. I put 2 more pillows on top of the one I was laying on when this all started and then ease back on them with my head elevated so I can close my eyes and get some rest before my alarm clock goes off. I am still breathing heavily, and I can hear myself wheezing as I breathe. In no time at all, I am back asleep, exhausted from the recent exertion.

Beep! Beep! Beep! Beep! Goddamit, I mutter to myself as I lean over to turn off the alarm clock. 6 o'clock already and I am thinking that I had just about gotten back to sleep good. Sitting up on the side of the bed, I have to brace myself with both hands on the bed because my head is swimming so badly that I almost feel like I am going to pass out. After a couple of minutes this feeling subsides and I pull myself vertical so that I can slide my feet into my slippers and stumble off to the kitchen. Going through the swinging door of the kitchen, the smell of coffee hits my nose. Boy, am I craving some coffee and brandy this morning! That will ease up the train going through my brain. My headache this morning is a real ass-kicker. Just as I have done for so many years now, I pour some coffee into a mug, add some brandy and an ice cube, and begin my day. The first sip is a major shock to my mouth, as always.

Putting the coffee mug on the table after my 2nd sip, I turn on the small television on the kitchen counter so I can watch some news. I sit down at the table to drink my coffee and brandy and stare at the news program. Whew, what a day already, and I haven't even gotten to work yet. After rapidly consuming 2 cups of the coffee and brandy I feel like I am as good as I'm going to get at this point. At least I've finally rinsed the vomit taste out of my mouth. Off to the bathroom I go to perform my morning ritual. As I walk through the bedroom, I glance over at Shirley. She is still sound asleep, in her clothes from last night. Wow, what a deep sleeper!

After cleaning up and getting dressed, I walk into the bedroom and glance at the alarm clock. Only 6:45 A.M., wow, I must be on speed this morning. The faint smell of vomit lingers in the air of the bedroom; I detected it as soon as I came out of my closet. I walk over to give Shirley her morning kiss on the cheek. After kissing her cheek and whispering

"I love you," she actually sits up, eyes only half open, and says to me "Are we home?" I chuckle and reply "Yes dear." "I must have drunk too much wine last night," she says. Then she scrunches up her nose and says "What's that awful smell?" "I threw up on my side of the bed last night dear, go back to sleep, I put a towel over it, the maid will clean it up when she comes in," I tell her. This seems to satisfy her and she replies "Oh, okay," and falls back onto her pillow.

I walk briskly through the house and get into my SUV to head to work. It's almost like I'm in a hurry to get to the Hospital for some reason. A good jazz CD is playing and I am chewing breath mints in time to the music as I drive to work. I don't know if I was speeding or what, but as I walk into the hospital and glance at my watch I see that it is 7 A.M. Wow, right on time for a change. Passing through the Physician's Dressing Room, I walk right out into the Operating Room corridor with my street clothes on so that I may look at the schedule board and make assignments. No one else in the OR hallway would dare be caught standing around in street clothes. Any Hospital employee caught doing this could be fired. Making the Anesthesia personnel assignments for the day's work takes me less than 2 minutes. After this, I walk back into the Physician's Dressing Room so that I can get out of my street clothes and put on a scrub suit.

As I am changing clothes, I notice that I am wearing one blue sock and one black sock. My vision must have been impaired this morning I think to myself as I pull on my scrub suit and tie up the drawstring at the pants waist. Oh well, nobody will notice I think to myself, and I don't much give a shit if they do anyway. After putting on my scrub suit, shoe covers, paper hat (to cover my hair) and mask, I walk back into the Physician's Lounge to pour myself a cup of coffee. This is just another habitual routine. This coffee is not nearly as good a quality of coffee as the one I make at home, plus it doesn't have the added flavor of brandy. It's just a routine to walk around with a cup of coffee.

My business partner, Jim Turner, is in the lounge when I walk in and has just poured himself a cup of coffee to which he is adding cream and sugar. "How was your night?" I ask him. "Awful," he replies. He continues "We had 2 rooms going until 10 and worked like dogs until after 2 A.M." "I did manage to get a 2 hour nap on the sofa in here. This coffee will bring me back to life." I ask "What kept you so busy?" "Gallbladders and C-sections mostly," he replies. "The last case finished up about two thirty and that was the one that really got my goat," Jim says to me, "You know

Michael Hanes (Urologist) is a real piece of shit." "Why do you say that?" I ask. "Well he was on Service Call last night and wouldn't come in to see one of his own private patients!" Jim says.

Let me digress. All Surgeons take call for their own practice on a rotating basis among all the Surgeons in that particular group. They get no call pay for doing this service for their patients, but they take care of their private patients who have had surgery this way. In addition to this Call, all the Surgeons of a particular specialty rotate Service Call amongst themselves. This is to take care of patients who are in critical need of their particular skills; patients, for example, who have never been to a General Surgeon but have an acute gallbladder attack and need to have surgery quickly, will be taken care of by the General Surgeon on Call. For Service Call, this Hospital pays these Doctors $1,000 per night, whether they come in and do anything or not. And the game is to avoid coming in by ordering enough lab tests, X-rays, or whatever, to keep the patient busy until morning.

The Hospital does this because it is a conduit for money to come in to the Hospital by way of surgical fees and hospitalization charges. If a Surgeon does come in to take care of a patient, they get the $1,000 plus they are allowed to bill the patient for the services they perform. This makes Service Call a pretty good income booster for Surgeons. It can easily add $100,000 a year to a Surgeon's bottom line. Not a bad bonus, but you just have to work at undesirable hours sometimes.

"What did that have to do with you?" I ask Jim. He explains "Well, one of his private patients is in the Hospital and not doing well. He was in DTs (Delirium Tremens) from alcohol withdrawal. (This can cause hallucinations and considerable patient agitation. Also, it can be fatal). The guy was so out of it that he pulled out his suprapubic catheter, in spite of having both wrists restrained. (A suprapubic catheter is a urinary catheter which is inserted through the skin of the lower abdomen, between the belly button and the pubis bone, into the bladder) Despite being on Service Call, Michael didn't answer his beeper, cell phone, or home phone. Since we couldn't get in touch with the son of a bitch, Brett Smith, the General Surgeon on Service Call had to take care of the patient and reinsert it. Remind me to never go to Michael Hanes if I ever have any Urological problems." "I wonder where in the hell he was, or what in the hell he was doing that he wouldn't answer his beeper or phones last night?" I ask. "I don't know, but that sure is unethical Medical practice to me," Jim says. "I'll look into it," I say to Jim.

Doctor Jim Turner and I can talk frankly like this in the Surgeon's Lounge right now because we are the only ones in the lounge. Normally, we only talk about other Doctors in my office. We could never talk like this if there were Surgeons in this lounge because some of them might be friends of Doctor Michael Haynes and report this conversation back to him. This would make for hard feelings. The politics of medicine is like playing chess sometimes. In a few minutes, the Surgeons will start coming in to start their day. After they start coming in, we have to be polite to them and be social, because Anesthesia relies on Surgeons for their work.

After sipping on my cup of coffee and listening to Jim ventilate his frustration, I pop another breath mint into my mouth and walk out of the lounge and into the OR hallway. I want to see what is going on and how things are going on. In this business things can get out of hand in a hurry. Plus, it's just good to be seen by the worker bees, put in a little face time, so to speak, say a few 'good mornings'. You need to stay in charge to be in charge.

It is 7:20 A.M. and I get the first cell phone call of the day; "Ready for you in OR 4." The case is for Doctor Jesse James, my old friend. It is insertion of ear tubes in a 1 year old child. These procedures are scheduled for first thing in the morning so that the children don't have to starve all day. You need to be NPO (Nothing Per Orum = Nothing By Mouth = empty stomach) to have surgery and be put to sleep safely. This procedure takes Doctor James about 10 minutes, start to finish. He has posted 16 of these procedures this morning and has been given 2 ORs to facilitate the process of getting them all done in as quick a manner as possible. The rate limiting factor in completing all these procedures in as little time as possible is how fast the paperwork can be completed. While the OR Nurse and CRNA are in the PACU turning the patient over to the PACU Nurse and completing the mountain of paperwork, the rest of the OR team is busy with OR turnover; cleaning the room after each case, and then setting up the equipment for the next case. The paper work for these cases takes far longer than the actual surgery itself. Only the speediest and most organized Nurses can possibly complete it all in a reasonable time. They try to do as much of it as possible while the surgery is going on, then they get caught up on the paperwork in PACU, before the next case starts.

As the government, increasing numbers of regulating agencies, and litigious Lawyers get their claws deeper and deeper into Healthcare, the amount of paper work increases astronomically. If the Nurses fail to fill in any blank on any form, they are severely punished by their immediate supervisor. But of course, no one considers that while the Nurses are focused on filling out reams and reams of paperwork, no one is actually taking care of the patient. In fact, no one is paying the patient any attention at all. But the bureaucrats, managers, and lawyers are delighted that 'everything is being documented'. The legal profession's position on this is 'if it isn't documented, it wasn't done'. It apparently doesn't matter to them that if it's being documented, no one is taking care of the poor patient during that time. Another point of possible slowdown is how fast the CRNA can put to sleep and wake up the patient.

Doctor James will complete all 16 ear tube cases in about 3 hours, then he will move on to slower, more time consuming procedures such as nasal and sinus cases. And so, the first few hours of my day will be bouncing from ENT (Ear, Nose, and Throat) room 4 to ENT room 5. These first 16 cases don't pay much per case, but the sheer volume of cases adds up the dollars. Later, the longer cases pay more for each one, but consume more time. This way I can stay busy in the morning and slow down by lunch. Frequently, after lunch, the pace of the cases slows down to a crawl. This allows me to take a nap quite often. It sure is nice having my own office with a comfy sofa.

In the middle of all this, I am called to start cases in OR 6, which is Orthopedics, and OR 7, which is Gynecology. I wander over to OR 6, where a total hip replacement procedure is starting. As I walk through the door, I say "Turn that temperature up, it's cold in here." The Circulator Nurse (that OR Nurse which fills out the reams of paperwork required for each surgery, and gets things for the surgeon such as extra suture or instruments) practically leaps to adjust the thermostat on the wall to a higher setting.

The patient is already hooked up to the blood pressure cuff, the EKG, and the pulse oximeter. I nod to Bob, the CRNA, who has been holding the oxygen mask over the patient's face so he can breathe in the oxygen, to begin giving the induction drugs. I then walk over to the OR table where the patient lies. "Hello John, how are you doing?" I say to the patient. John is the ex-Mayor of Ashburg, and I have known him for 20 years. He is retired now. "Better, now that I see you Jerry," he says to me. "Everything is all right, and I'm going to get you off to sleep now," I say. He is already unconscious and his eyes are closed now. I walk over to sign the Anesthesia Record and glance over to see that Bob has already placed the ET tube in the trachea and has John on the ventilator with the Anesthesia gas going. Bob will then tape the ET tube to John's face (to keep it from getting dislodged) and the Circulator Nurse will prep his hip with betadine to sterilize it. After that, the sterile drapes will be placed around the hip and the Surgeon will begin his part—removing the old hip joint and putting a new metal one in its place.

Everything is right on track here, so I then walk over to OR 7, where a TAH (Total Abdominal Hysterectomy—removing the uterus) is already underway. The OB-GYN Surgeon is just now making the skin incision as I walk into the room. I walk over to sign the Anesthesia Record (even though I was not present for the start of the case) and ask Elizabeth, the CRNA, "Is everything okay?" "Everything's great right now," she replies. She then tells me "This patient is pretty anemic from excessive uterine bleeding. (Which is why this woman is having this surgery) If the Surgeon loses much blood, I'll probably have to give her a unit or two (of blood bank blood)." "You gotta do what you gotta do," I tell her. "How old is she?" I ask. "Only 26," She replies. "What is her crit (hematocrit = the percent of red blood cells in her blood)?" I ask. "Only 26," She replies. (A normal hematocrit is about double this) "Check her crit every hour, and if she drops to 22, or the surgeon loses 500 ml (milliliters) of blood, give her a unit." I instruct Elizabeth. "That sounds like a good plan to me," She says.

Elizabeth is a solid CRNA, very conservative and patient safety conscious. She will watch this patient's blood loss and hematocrit like a hawk. If she has any problems keeping the patient's blood pressure up or keeping up with the surgical blood loss, I can count on her to notify me immediately. I then leave OR 7 and head back to my ENT rooms to sign charts (Anesthesia records). I have been gone from those rooms for about 10 minutes now and it is time to sign the Anesthesia records again for the next round of patients. Within 2 minutes I am done with signing charts in the ENT rooms, now I have 10 to 15 minutes to sit down in the Surgeon's Lounge before I have to return to those rooms and sign the charts for the next round of patients.

My rooms are not chosen randomly, but according to which ones have the most private insurance (which pays far more than Medicare and Medicaid). Also, I cluster my Operating Rooms together, if at all possible, so that I am not running all over the place to different Operating

Rooms in different parts of the surgical area. I try to organize the OR room assignment for Jim Turner, my partner, this way as well. The other 2 MDAs (Medical Doctor Anesthesiologists), Avi and Arnash, I just put where ever. They pick up the leftovers and run all over the place to monitor their OR rooms. I cluster my OR rooms to conserve my time and energy. I believe in conservation of energy, especially my own.

Chapter Seven

Getting My Niece a Job

It is now 10 A.M. and all of my quick ENT rooms are finished. Much slower surgical cases are going in the ORs that I'm supervising now, so I give Jack Gaither, the Hospital CEO (Chief Executive Officer), a call on my cell phone. "High Jack, how's it hanging?" I say. "Not bad Jerry, not bad," he says back to me. "Have you got a few minutes to talk?" I ask. "I always have a few minutes for you Jerry," he says. He understands how this good old boy network works, and he figured it out quickly when he arrived here 10 years ago. "I'll be right over to your office," I say to him. "Great Jerry, see you soon," he says back to me. He is one of the very few people in this Hospital that calls me by my first name.

Most Hospital Administrators only last about 3 years before they tick off some Doctors or someone on the Board of Directors. Then they are gone and a new whipping boy is put in place. Somehow Jack Gaither has remained in charge here 10 years and not run afoul of anyone in a major way. Mostly, he has done it by sucking up to every one he possibly can, as much as he can. Plus, he aligned himself with a few politically powerful Doctors, who are also on the Board of Directors. This has been a great help to him. I call Jim Turner and tell him to keep an ear out for my rooms because I will be out of the department, over in Administration, talking to Jack for 15 minutes. He responds with the usual "Okay." It just takes a minute to walk over to Administration, which is close to the Operating Room.

Arriving in Administration, I tell the Secretary "Tell Jack I'm here." She says "He is expecting you, Dr. Deluna, just walk right in Sir." "Thank you," I say to her. As I walk into Jack's office, he looks up at me and smiles, saying "To what do I owe the honor of this visit Jerry?" He is probably dreading my visit, but most Hospital Administrators are masters at groveling to Doctors. They have 2 masters, the Hospital Board of Directors and the Medical Staff.

I walk over and sit in one of the two plush chairs in front of his desk before I get to the point of my visit. "Good to see you Jack," I say before adjusting my butt in the chair and proceeding to the real reason for my visit. I like to build a little suspense. "Say Jack, my niece, Francine, needs a short term job. She has finished college and has been applying to Medical Schools without much success. She needs a job for 3 to 6 months while she continues to apply to Medical School and decides whether or not to apply to Graduate School, depending on her results," I say to Jack.

He leans back in his chair, trying to look like he is pondering a deep problem, and then replies "Well Jerry, there is a hiring freeze on here at the Hospital, but I'm sure we could work her into a temporary position over in credentialing or recruiting." "Would a salary of $3,000 a month help her out until she decides what to do?" he asks me. "Thanks Jack, I'm sure that will fix her up until she chooses which direction to take with her education," I say. Jack says "I'll make a couple of phone calls to find the best place for her. Just have her come by tomorrow afternoon about 2 P.M. and we'll process her through Human Resources and introduce her to her supervisor." "Is she available to do that, and will she be okay to start full time next Monday?" Jack asks me. "That will be perfect Jack, she's not doing anything at the moment, again thanks," I say to him.

Mission accomplished, I get up to leave Jack's office and say "See you later Jack." "Glad I could help Jerry," he says to me as I turn to leave. Before I get 2 steps toward the door, he says "Say Jerry." This stops me in my tracks. "Yes Jack," I say as I turn back toward him. "We have a small problem. At the Medical Practice Committee meeting last night they voted in a resolution. It requires that an Anesthesiologist go in person and evaluate all ASA 3 and above patients that the CRNAs have seen before they go to surgery," he says to me. "No problem," I say to Jack, "I'll pass this info on to the other Anesthesiologists and take care of it." "Thanks Jerry, I knew that I could count on you," he says back to me. "Anytime, Jack, see you later," I return; then I turn and exit his office and head back to the Operating Room.

Let me explain. The ASA (American Society of Anesthesiologists) developed a patient classification system years ago. It stratifies patients according to increasing health problems. The system is numbered from 1 to 5. The higher the score, the more health problems and the more severe the health problems a patient has. An ASA 1 patient has no health problems; whereas an ASA 5 patient is moribund. There is also an E (emergency) qualifier that can be added to any patient's score. The number one effect of this system, as far as I am concerned, is that the higher the score, the more I can charge and get paid. Only Anesthesiologists can charge more and get paid more for higher ASA score patients, not CRNAs. In a CRNA only Anesthesia practice or, in a small Hospital that only has a single CRNA providing care, they do not get more money for taking care of sicker patients, or Emergency patients in immediate need of care, only Anesthesiologists do. I love healthcare in America!

I am smiling as I leave Administration. My sister will be pleased that I was able to pull a few strings and get Francine a good paying job at the Hospital, temporary though it may be. The fact that it is a temporary job will be more of an incentive for her to get busy applying to Medical Schools, or if she doesn't get into Medical School, then deciding which Graduate School program to apply to. I'll call my sister, Ann, this evening and tell her the good news about the job for Francine, and tell her to make sure that Francine reports for duty tomorrow afternoon at 2 P.M. Francine, that lazy little shit, if she had spent more time studying instead of partying, she would have made better grades in college. Then she would have been able to get into Medical School, and we wouldn't have this situation.

That new Medical Practice Committee resolution won't be any problem for me either. I was elected the head of the Medical Practice Committee last year. Just because I went out to dinner last night instead of attending the committee meeting, they snuck this resolution in without my knowledge. I only attend about ½ of these committee meetings anyway, because they are so boring. The bickering and infighting amongst Doctors is relentless. I'll find out who was responsible for this, and make them sorry that they did this to me. How dare someone try to control Anesthesia without talking to me first? No body messes with my baby here at this Hospital.

Medical politics can be brutal. If I just ignore the new resolution completely, there will be absolutely no consequences for me at all. Someone will get pissed at me if I just ignore their silly-assed resolution, but they can't really do a damn thing to me. I am too politically powerful and too well connected. Just to keep the peace and make them happy, I'll follow the new rule, when it's not too inconvenient. There used to be a country and western song about it being good having friends in low places, but it really helps to have friends in high places, I think as I head back to the Operating Room. It's really great being a big fish in a small pond.

When I return to the Surgeon's Lounge, I see Jim drinking a soda. "Any problems while I was gone?" I ask him. "No problems at all," he says to me. "Great, anything I can help you with?" I ask, to be cordial. "No, everything's going pretty good. My rooms will soon be finished and I'll be on my way home for a nap," Jim says. He was on call yesterday, so he is the first Anesthesiologist out today. He abruptly stops talking to me to answer 2 back to back calls on his cell phone. They are phone calls from the 2 CRNAs whose cases he is supervising. They are reporting the progress of the cases to Jim because they know that he is up to leave as soon as the cases are finished.

It is now 11:00 A.M. and I am kind of tired and hungry. I have already signed in on 22 cases and have generated a bundle of money. Things should be winding down from the fast pace of the morning activities, and I'm thinking that lunch would be nice about now. The afternoon schedule of surgical cases will involve longer procedures, allowing more planning for afternoon activities and a more relaxed pace. Jim has finished talking on the cell phone and says to me, "The 2 C-sections are finished, so I only have one room going which will be done in 15 to 20 minutes. Why don't you have lunch now, I'll listen out for your rooms and then I'll go home since I was on Call." "Okay Jim," I say. I then walk out of the Surgeon's Lounge and call Arnash on my Hospital cell phone and tell him "Hey, I am going to go have lunch now, keep an ear out for my rooms if Jim leaves before I return." He replies "Okay Chief." He knows better than to reply anything else. It's great being Lord and Master of your domain.

If one of my rooms starts a case while I'm at lunch, either Jim or Arnash will show up for the induction, and then I'll just sign the Anesthesia Record when I return, so that I can bill and collect for the case. Except for Jim, the other Anesthesiologists are already supervising 4 Operating Rooms (the maximum allowed) each, so they can't sign in on my rooms when they are present for the induction. If the Circulator Nurse calls me to start a case, I'll just tell them to call Jim or Arnash. Now that that's double covered, I'll just mosey down to the Doctor's Dining Room to have lunch.

As soon as I enter the Doctor's Dining Room, the chef (whose name I can never remember) greets me with a hearty "Good morning Doctor Deluna." He is so damn enthusiastic. "Good morning," I say back to him. "What have you got for us today?" I ask. "Well, we have tuna steaks, beef stroganoff, or chicken and sausage gumbo," he replies. "Is the tuna steak encrusted in sesame seeds or herbs?" I inquire. "It is cooked in herbs, parmesan, and butter. It comes with steamed green beans, broccoli, or Greek potatoes also," he says. "I think I'll have the tuna steak with the steamed broccoli," I say to the chef. "Very well sir, if you want a salad, you can choose one just down the counter there and start with that. I'll have your entrée to you in about 5 minutes," he says to me. I move down the counter and pick out a bottle of water and a small macaroni salad with peas and ham to nibble on until the real food arrives.

A few minutes after I sit down and start eating my macaroni salad, Doctor Michael Hanes (Urologist) comes into the dining room. I wave 'high' to him and motion for him to come over to my table, which he does after placing his lunch order with the chef and grabbing a salad. "High Jerry, how's it going?" he asks. "It's going pretty well Mike, not an unusually busy day, just the normal amount of excitement. I heard you missed out on some excitement last night," I say to him. He says "Yeah, the wife and I were at the beach house having a party. We had about 2 dozen people over for drinks and grilled seafood. Thank God the General Surgeon on call was available to replace that suprapubic catheter for me. That Brett Smith is a good guy." "Yeah, he sure is," I reply. This kind of thing happens from time to time, and the patient is usually taken care of by a Doctor who happens to be in the Hospital. Rarely does a patient die from this kind of neglect, but it does happen on occasion. Doctors who are in the Hospital will usually cover absences from other Doctors in an emergency situation; it is just ingrained in us to look out for each other.

Doctor Michael Hanes' beach house is a 2 hour drive from Ashburg. I don't even bother to discuss with him that it is unethical for him to be on Call at the Hospital and physically be more than 100 miles away from the Hospital, not to mention having a party and drinking alcohol on top of that. In effect, the Hospital paid him $1,000 last night to have a party. I just say to him "It must be nice to be so in control." The pompous ass replies "Yeah, it is," and grins.

We actually have a General Surgeon who is a pilot and has his own plane. He will take Call and fly to his beach house on weekends. If he gets a call about a patient, he will order enough lab tests, X-rays, or whatever, to keep the patient occupied for an hour. In that hour, he can hop into his airplane and be back in town. Then, he will make phone calls to find out the results of all the tests he ordered and if necessary, he will say "Take the patient to the OR." By this time, he is pulling up in the Hospital parking lot and within 5 to 10 minutes, he will be in the OR ready to perform the indicated surgery. The Hospital staff actually have to hurry to get all the things done that he has ordered and be ready for him to operate when he arrives in the Operating Room, ready to go. He is a true master of time management.

As long as he never gets in a plane crash, no one outside of the Hospital will ever know that this crazy shit goes on. Within 15 minutes of him finishing a surgery, he is back in his plane, and 30 minutes after that, he is landing on the airstrip by his beach house. He can actually get a phone call about a patient with acute appendicitis, fly in and perform the surgery, fly back and be back sitting in his beach house, all in less than 2 hours. What a man. A Surgeon can get away with things like this at a smaller Hospital. Because in these Hospitals, they are gods.

Just then, the chef brings us our main courses, the tuna steak with steamed broccoli for me and the beef stroganoff with Greek potatoes for Mike. This food smells so good and looks so appetizing, that we busy ourselves with our meals, not really talking much after that. I have known Doctor Michael Hanes for close to 20 years, and I don't really like him. He is so pompous and self-centered, that he basically views his patients as existing only to make him money and meet his needs. We are both greedy, but I view him as stooping lower than I do, operating on a lower rung of the ethical ladder, to make his money. So, I don't care to have much in the way of conversation with him. We are not really friends, and he is not a member of the Sunday Night Supper Club. When I am done with my meal, I tell Mike it was nice to talk with him and excuse myself from the table quickly. "See you later Jerry," he says as I am leaving.

I walk back into the Surgeon's Lounge and see Jim looking at the news on the television. "Any problems while I was gone?" I ask. "No, no problems, but I started a tubal ligation for you about 5 minutes ago," Jim says. "That's fine, thanks. Why don't you head on home?" I say to him. He replies "I think I'll do just that, see you tomorrow Jerry." "See you," I say to him as he heads to the dressing room to change out of his scrubs and back into street clothes. In about 20 minutes, he will be at home getting ready to take a 2 or 3 hour nap so that he can get some rest and feel like a human being for his family later on today.

We cannot live more than a 30 minute drive from the Hospital. This is because sometimes we are done in the OR and go home in the afternoon, even though we are on Call. If another surgical case comes up, we will be called at home, and just drive back in for it. The CRNAs have to stay in house (in the Hospital) when they are on call. They get paid while they are just sleeping at the Hospital, but they are the first, immediate line of defense if a sudden emergency arises. Jim will be on Call again Wednesday, then Friday, Saturday, and Sunday. The following week, he will not be on Call at all.

Heading out of the Surgeon's Lounge, I walk out into the Operating Room hallway. It is 11:45 A.M., and the OR is a beehive of activity. Getting the OR staff time to have lunch in the middle of the day has historically been a big problem, even though they only get ½ hour for lunch. Surgeon's typically want to work in the morning and middle of the day so that they can have an afternoon office session. They can grab a snack or quick meal in between their cases, while the OR team is setting up their next case. A Surgeon makes his money doing surgery, not on the follow up office visits or lunch breaks. Lunch breaks are a luxury. The follow up office visits are a necessary evil, but just part of the business of doing surgery.

Some Surgeon's will schedule one day every 2 weeks to perform small surgeries in their office; excision of little lumps and bumps. They make out quite well on these minisurgeries because the insurance companies pay them a bonus for doing office procedures, which would otherwise be done in the Hospital Operating Room at a much greater expense. Office surgery is not as controlled an environment as surgery performed in an Operating Room, however. There are some patient safety issues involved with this as well. The Surgeon just injects the areas he will be cutting on with a little Lidocaine, to numb up the area for the patient. After the minisurgery, the patient will be given a prescription for pain medication, which hopefully, they will have filled before the numbing medicine wears off. Of course, Anesthesia is not involved in office surgeries, so we are cut out of the loop and make no money on these cases.

I get a call on my cell phone. "Doctor Deluna, there are 2 ASA class 3 patients to be seen in the Anesthesia Clinic," the Nurse tells me. The Anesthesia Clinic is where patients come in, several days before their surgery is scheduled, to get interviewed by a CRNA to make sure the Surgeon has ordered all the tests necessary to work the patient up properly for surgery, and to identify any potential Anesthesia problems in advance. These Nurses sure were notified about the new policy quickly, I am thinking. "I am tied up, busy in the OR, I can't make it over there right now," I tell her. "All right, thank you," she says to me, then hangs up. It is very easy to get around Hospital policies if you have M.D. after your name. If the Nurses fill out the volumes of paperwork required to lodge an official complaint, it will eventually go to the Medical Practice Committee, which I head. Ha, ha. Problem solved, work avoided, and there isn't a damn thing they can do about it. Boy, I'm good.

Chapter Eight

Nap Time

Walking around the OR to look into my 4 rooms and checking on the progress of these cases, I am getting sleepy. It takes no time at all to check on my 4 rooms. The CRNAs manage all the work involved in the cases 99% of the time without a hitch, and there really isn't much for me to do usually. Every room I go into I ask "Everything going okay?" and about the only answer I ever get is "Fine, everything is going okay." I go to the OR where Jim started the tubal ligation for me so that I can sign the Anesthesia Record and so bill and collect for the case. Everything is going fine with that case also. I could lapse into a coma and everything in this OR would continue to go along perfectly fine without me. The main reason that I am here and important, is that the Hospital gets a much better reimbursement for surgeries that are supervised by an Anesthesiologist. This provides a big boost to the bottom line of a Hospital, and so, makes me important.

In fact, I think I will go to my office and kick back on the sofa and lapse into a brief coma right now. The dip in my blood sugar after eating lunch plus the rough night I had are beginning to tell on me and I am tired and sleepy. I walk into my office and lock the door. I have taken many a nap in the middle of the day on the sofa in my office; it is a very comfortable piece of furniture. Plopping down on the sofa, I swing my feet up onto the ottoman and lean back to rest my head on the back of the sofa. Aah, boy does it feel good to kick back, relax and close my eyes; I didn't get much rest last night. In less than 5 minutes, I am sound asleep. I sleep so soundly that I don't have any dreams; I am just dead to the world.

Suddenly, I am startled to wakefulness. I was so deeply asleep that it takes me a minute to realize what the noise was that woke me. My cell phone is going off; that's what woke me up from a sound sleep. I hit the answer button while shaking my head to try to clear the cobwebs. "Ready for you in OR 6 Doctor Deluna," the cheerful Circulator Nurse says to me. "I'll be right there, tell the CRNA to go ahead and start," I say into the phone. After hanging up the phone, I glance at my watch, wow! It is 2 P.M. I have been asleep for about 1 ½ hours on my sofa. Still tired and groggy from sleep, I am only ½ awake as I stumble out of my office and slowly head to OR 6.

Walking into OR 6, I say "Turn down that music and warm it up in here, it's too cold." Never let them forget who's the boss. I look over at Bob, the CRNA, and ask "What are we doing here?" Nobody in this OR knows that I have been asleep for the past 1 ½ hours. For all they know, I have been busy working in other parts of the Hospital. "Total hip replacement on an 80 year old woman with bad COPD (Chronic Obstructive Pulmonary Disease) and a history of A-fib (Atrial Fibrillation—a heart condition where the atria and the ventricles are not working together as a synchronized pump. This is very common in patients 70 years old and older)," Bob replies. "Any problems on induction?" I ask. Bob says "Her blood pressure bottomed out on induction; typical hypovolemic (low blood volume) little old lady. I had to give her some Neo (Neosynephrine, a drug which constricts the blood vessels and so raises blood pressure when given IV) to get it up until I could give her sufficient IV fluids to fill up her blood vessels. She's doing fine now, blood pressure is 90."

Elderly people (80+ years old) seldom eat properly or drink enough water and other fluids, so about 99% of them are chronically dehydrated. They also don't walk so well, (because they are weak and out of balance) and frequently fall and break their hips because their bones are brittle. Dropping your blood pressure after induction of Anesthesia is a normal reaction with this patient population. Bob knows this well, and handled the situation perfectly, as usual.

I walk over to the Anesthesia Machine and sign the Anesthesia Record, so that I can bill Medicare for the case. "Good job," I say to Bob, and then I walk out of OR 6, into the hallway. Immediately, I recoil and back flat up against the door to OR 6 because someone is yelling at me "Watch out Doctor Deluna, we are coming through in a hurry!" It is Elizabeth, the CRNA. She and the Circulator Nurse are pushing a stretcher with a patient quickly down the hallway to PACU (Post Anesthesia Care

Unit—what used to be called Recovery Room). "You need to sign the Record," (the Anesthesia Record) Elizabeth says as she speeds past me. "I'll do it in PACU," I say loudly after her.

I walk to PACU to catch up with Elizabeth, who is telling the PACU Nurse to put oxygen on the patient, and look at the Anesthesia Record. The case was a hernia repair. From start to finish, it took just under 2 hours OR time. Now I remember them calling me to the OR just before I settled down for my nap in my office. "Go ahead and start, I'll be there," I told them. Oh well, I didn't make it. I was tired and sleepy and I took a nap instead. No one will dare say a word to me about it any case, because I am Doctor Jerry Deluna, Chief of Anesthesia. Who really cares anyway?

This patient looks old as dirt I think as I glance over at them. "Any problems?" I ask Elizabeth, as a reflex. "No problems at all, everything went smoothly," she says to me (the usual response). "Good," I say as I lean over to sign the Anesthesia Record. Looking at the record, I see that this patient is only 56 years old. It's kind of amazing how old this guy looks. Just then, I look over at him, and he opens his eyes, looks at me and asks "Can I have a beer?" I can't believe this. "No you can't have a beer, this is a hospital for God's sake," I say to him. Turning back to sign the record, I am having to blink my eyes like crazy to even be able to focus on the line I'm supposed to sign on, and I know where this line is located on the Record, as I have signed there 10s of thousands of times over the years. As soon as I sign my name, I turn and walk out of the PACU like I'm in a hurry and have somewhere important to go. It's not good to spend too much time in here; someone might ask me another crazy question, or a question requiring me to think right now because my brain is not working too well at present.

As I am walking in the OR hallway, I get a cell phone call "Ready for you in OR 5 Doctor Deluna." "I'll be right there," I reply. OR 5 is right next to OR 6, where my hip replacement case is going right now. Joe is the CRNA in OR 5. As I walk into OR 5, I look around and see immediately that it is one of those vascular stenting cases. The latest and biggest money maker (for the Surgeon and the Hospital) in Medicine these days is the vascular stenting procedure.

Let me explain. We have an aging baby-boomer population in the U.S. these days. They are living longer than their parents. Many of them used to be heavy smokers in the 1950's continuing through to present times, and as a result, they have really bad blood vessels. The bad shape of their blood vessels is primarily due to advanced age, long smoking history, and unlucky genetics. These patients have poor circulation to their feet (cold feet) and leg pain (called claudication) from poor circulation. Many of their arteries have narrowed areas (called stenosis), preventing blood from getting to the areas of their bodies farthest from the heart.

They go to see their regular Doctor about this problem, who refers them to a Vascular Surgeon. The Vascular Surgeon then performs a revascularization procedure (opening up the arteries to get more blood flow to the legs and feet) on them. This procedure is done in the Operating Room. It involves snaking a long wire down a stenosed (narrowed) artery, then snaking a special catheter with a small balloon at the end over the wire previously threaded. The balloon is inflated to open up the narrowed portion of artery, after which a stent is placed to keep the vessel open and thus restore blood flow to the feet and legs of the patient.

All this is done to try to prevent amputating the foot or leg when blood flow gets too poor to keep the extremity alive. This is the theory behind the recent surge in these procedures in this country. The procedures take from 1 to 5 hours of OR time (at $100 per minute), depending on the skill and luck of the Vascular Surgeon. Also, the specialized wires, balloon catheters, and stents are extremely expensive. It is not uncommon for a Vascular Surgeon to use between $15,000 and $25,000 worth of equipment to do just one of these procedures. That's Hospital cost; the patient charge for this equipment will be $100,000 and up. The Surgeon's get to charge a lot of money for doing these cases as well. All this is paid for by Medicare.

This might be all well and good if the procedure actually prevented the patient from having to have an amputation. It might be the case, even if it wasn't driving Medicare broke because these cases cost from $200,000 to$400,000 a pop. But, many of these procedures fail because of the patient population and they have to have an amputation any way, many within 72 hours of going through all that pain and expense. The vast majority don't make it 1 year even, before they have to get their foot or leg amputated anyway. This, of course, costs Medicare another big chunk of money and causes the patient a lot of pain and anguish, again.

This type of Healthcare abuse happens over and over again, when a new technology comes around that promises to relieve misery. And ignorant, desperate people and stupid Medicare jump on it over and over again; they never learn. Between the Surgeon's fees, the Anesthesia fees, the Hospital charges, the equipment required to do revascularization procedure, the extra medications, and the following amputation, you are looking at upwards of ½ million dollars spent in a year per patient with circulation problems. And there are more than 10 million people in the U.S. with circulation problems, most of whom are over 70 years old. The sad part of this is that more than half the people that sign up for this song and dance end up dead, stroked out, or amputated any way within a year. If they would have just stayed their ass at home, they would be better off a year later 95% of the time. And people wonder why Healthcare costs are spiraling out of control???

Any way, I look over and see that Joe already has the patient asleep and the Circulator Nurse is prepping the patient's legs and groin with betadine. This betadine prep is done to kill germs on the patient's skin. I walk over to the Anesthesia Machine to sign the Anesthesia Record and ask "Everything going okay?" "So far, so good," Joe replies. I reply "Well, that's good because nothing has happened yet." "That's true," Joe says back to me and laughs loudly. I laugh also; yeah we have a weird sense of humor.

After I walk out of OR 5, I think I will walk back to the Surgeon's Lounge and grab a cup of coffee. That might help clear the fog from my brain and help me wake up. Caffeine is a wonderful thing; it really helps me make it through the day a lot of times. I walk into the Surgeon's Lounge and go up to the fancy gourmet coffee maker that makes one cup at a time of any of a dozen choices of coffees. Today I think it'll be Columbian coffee, that shit is loaded with caffeine and really packs a punch. In about one minute I have a steaming cup of Columbian coffee, freshly brewed. Man, I love this stuff, even though it's not quite as good as my coffee and brandy at home.

After putting a little half and half in the coffee to smooth it out and cool it down, I turn around and see 2 teenage children, sitting on the sofa, reading books. How is it that I didn't see them when I walked into the lounge at first? What is it with this shit?!? I just can't believe these Doctors, leaving their kids in here like the Hospital is their personal emergency day care option. Oh well. I stare at them and ask "How are you doing?" "Fine sir," they both say to me. "Whose children are you?" I ask. "Doctor Hall (Michael Hall, General Surgeon) is our dad," they reply. They add "He is tending to a patient problem, and he'll soon be done and then he'll bring us home." "Where is your mom?" I ask. "Oh she's out of town for a few days," they answer.

This Michael Hall is one goofy Surgeon. Last Saturday, he had the entire OR call team hang around for more than 2 hours while he brought his dog to the Veterinarian. He was busy, doing surgery in the morning, and then he got a call from his wife about 10 A.M., while he was in the middle of a surgery. She told him that their dog was sick and needed to go to the Vet. Even though he was busy doing surgery, she told him that he had to bring the dog in because the kids were upset and she had to stay with them. After he finished the surgery he was doing at the time, he told the entire OR call team to hang around and not go anywhere until he got back because he had a gallbladder to do when he returned. He told them that he would be back in less than 1 hour; he returned in 2 hours 15 minutes. This, of course, really pissed off the entire call team. But he didn't give a shit. I tell you, this Surgeon has an ego second to none. It did not matter to him one bit that his patient had to wait to have their gallbladder removed.

This guy got kicked out of his first Surgical Residency. He had an old man patient who wanted to watch some pornography before he died. The old man talked Doctor Michael Hall (he was a Doctor when he finished Medical School, before his Surgical Residency) into personally taking him to a triple-X movie theater. He wrote a Doctor's Order for the old man to have an afternoon pass to leave the Hospital, then packed him up and brought him to the theater to watch porn and eat popcorn for a few hours. The Chairman of the Surgical Department was a very religious man who was not amused at this adventure. As a result of this, Michael was fired from his Surgical Residency and had to go to an inferior program for his surgical training. This shows in the quality of his surgical work to this day.

Many times, other Surgeons are called to his room to help and bail him out of a situation that he just can't handle on his own. Doctor Michael Hall is a very smooth talker however, and his patients never know about this, and they all love him. As a result of his silver tongue and good bedside manner, he is one of the busiest Surgeons in this town. Even though he isn't worth a crap. Crazy, huh?? Patients absolutely have no possible way to know the skill level of their Surgeon. The only way they could possibly find out about how good a Surgeon is would be to talk to someone in Anesthesia. But, to protect our brother Doctors, the odds of us revealing the sub-par skills of a Surgeon to someone are exceedingly remote. So, the patient just has to roll the dice and hope for luck when choosing a Surgeon.

Just then, Doctor Michael Hall comes into the Surgeon's Lounge, picks up his kids, and off they all go in a big hustle and bustle. This is just so damn crazy, I can hardly believe this shit is happening, but I'm living it, so I can't deny it. Oh well, I can't do anything about it. I would never bring this up at a Medical Practice Committee meeting to try to get it stopped, because it would anger the Surgeon's who are abusing the system and doing it, and I rely on them for my work and money. Surgeon's can be very vindictive. They are much like spoiled children. I just settle back into a recliner to watch the news on the television and enjoy my coffee. The news is all depressing shit. Murder here, rape there, kidnapped children. The latest way that the government is failing the people and pissing away our tax dollars on some fungus or minnow, or just plain robbing us blind. I can't stand to watch this shit for very long. The world is just so damn crazy.

Chapter Nine

Trauma Time

The loud ringing of my cell phone wakes me up and startles me. I must have dozed off after sipping a few sips of coffee and watching the news. Looking at my watch, I see that it is 4:30 P.M. Wow, another hour nap, great! The Nurse who runs the assignment board tells me that we have a trauma coming in. "What CRNA is assigned to the case?" I ask. "Bob," she replies. "He's done with the other case?" I ask. "It finished about 15 minutes ago," she says. "What kind of trauma is this?" I inquire. "MVA (Motor Vehicle Accident), a drunken crack addict stepped in front of a city bus. He probably didn't see it coming because he was so shit-faced drunk," she says. "Great, this will probably be another multimillion dollar law suit against the city," I say. "I'm sure the Lawyer is chasing the ambulance to the Hospital as we speak," she replies. What a crazy world we live in. If he dies, the family will probably sue the city of Ashburg and the Hospital. Heaven forbid that the drunk takes any responsibility for his actions.

I reach over to the table next to my recliner and pick up my cup of Columbian coffee to take a sip. Wow, it is still a little warm in the styrofoam cup. Still good coffee. After taking a few swallows, I get up and wander out into the hallway. My brain is not as foggy now as it was after my first nap. Walking over to the assignment board, I ask the Nurse who is the board runner "What OR is the trauma coming to?" "6" she says. OR 6 is a large Operating Room, which is good for all the equipment you need to have to be able to do a big trauma case. "Is Bob setting up for it?" I ask. "I think he's in there now," she replies.

Walking over to OR 6, I am thinking that I am very happy to be on call with Bob today because he can handle this type of case with ease. He has done this type of case many times. I walk into OR 6 and see Bob setting up 2 IV fluid warmers and an art-line (arterial line). When you have to give a lot of blood in a surgical case, you have to run it through a fluid warmer because the blood is cold when it arrives from the Blood Bank, and the IV fluid is room temperature (70 degrees). If you run too much cool IV fluid or blood into a patient without warming it, it will cool the patient down, which will make them bleed more. Bleeding more after or during surgery is not desirable. An art-line is a pressure measuring device which will be attached to an IV catheter placed in an artery (usually the radial artery, in the wrist). This will allow us to see the blood pressure changes with every beat of the heart.

"Do you have a central line kit handy?" I ask. Bob looks up from his work and says "Oh, high Dr. Deluna, (he was so busy working that he didn't see me walk in) I have an introducer kit in the room and I'm going to set up 3 IV blood sets." Blood sets are special IV tubing sets with a filter through which you give blood to patients. An introducer kit is a very large bore IV that is known as a central line. You can place these into the internal jugular vein or the subclavian vein (large veins known as the central circulation), and you can really give large amounts of blood or IV fluids very quickly to patients with these in place. Bob says "The EMS (Emergency Medical Services) guys placed 2-18 gauge IVs in the guy, and they intubated him in the field. So, if those 2 IVs are functional, all we have to do is put him on the ventilator, put in a central line and an art-line, and we are in business."

"Call a PACU Nurse to come in here and pump blood when the patient arrives. Also, do you know the extent of his injuries?" I ask. Bob says "He got hit pretty hard by the bus, lots of broken bones and probably lots of internal injuries as well." He continues, "Once we get him stable, 2 Orthopedic Surgeons will start working on his broken arms and legs, and then a General Surgeon will open up his belly to work on the internal injuries. We have 5 units of uncrossmatched blood ready in the Blood Bank ready to go until we can send them a sample to type and crossmatch." "Very good Bob, you have been a busy boy. What is the expected time of arrival of this train wreck?" I ask. Bob replies "Any second now."

As if on cue, the doors to OR 6 swing open and a patient on an EMS (Emergency Medical Services) stretcher with 2 Nurses pushing and a

3rd giving oxygen through the ET tube via an ambu bag comes in and interrupts our quiet time. I see that there are 2 units of blood going right now on this patient; they are hanging on the stretcher IV pole. "What's the story?" I ask loudly. One of the stretcher-pushing Nurses says loudly "This guy reeks of alcohol, shit, and body odor, has a big time history of crack abuse, and of course, he is unemployed. I don't know if he shit himself before or after the accident. He stepped out in front of a city bus and got nailed real good. One of Ashburg's finest." "Thanks for the present," I say. "You're welcome," she replies. Medical and especially, OR people, have a peculiar sense of humor.

We move the EMS stretcher next to the OR table so that we can hook up his ET tube to our breathing circuit going to the Anesthesia ventilator and thereby give him oxygen automatically. This will free up the Nurse who has been manning the ambu bag to give him oxygen. Then, we move him over to the OR table and very quickly, we hook up a blood pressure cuff, pulse oximeter, and EKG. Looking at the EKG while the blood pressure is taking, we can see that he is in a sinus rhythm. A sinus rhythm means that there is a P wave before every QRS wave, which generally means that the heart is working properly as a synchronized pump. This is normal; this is good. Next, we look to the pulse oximeter, and see a wave (which means that he has a blood pressure of at least 70) and a reading of 98%, which is good. This means that air/oxygen is getting through his lungs, into his blood stream. The blood pressure cuff has finally done its work, and it shows a pressure of 176/97, which is high, but a good pressure to maintain life for now. We will worry about getting it down to a normal range (120/80) later.

Because he has a decent blood pressure, we can turn on a little Anesthesia gas (which will keep his brain asleep), paralyze him, and get his IVs sorted out. Anesthesia people organize the patient this way so that we can put in the central line and the art-line. This will enable us to give him massive amounts of warmed blood and IV fluids very quickly and monitor his blood pressure closely at the same time. Within 10 minutes I have inserted the right internal jugular introducer, to which a PACU Nurse named Nancy (adrenalin junky, who came voluntarily into this mess to be of assistance) hooks up to a blood set going through a fluid warmer. At the same time, Bob has placed the art-line in the patient's right radial artery, and we see an arterial waveform on our monitor with a reading of 156/88. This is pretty close to the blood pressure cuff reading we got earlier, and still a very good blood pressure for this situation.

The Anesthesia gas hasn't knocked his blood pressure down too much. Anesthesia gas relaxes the whole person, and also their blood vessels (vasodilates). If a patient is hypovolemic (low on blood volume) from bleeding, the gas can really drop a blood pressure.

The 2 Circulator Nurses can now strip the remainder of his clothes off and paint his body with betadine to get some of the filth off of him, kill the germs on his skin and sterilize it. A patient like this will have blood, dirt, gravel, glass, and other debris all over him. Scrubbing this off with betadine will help prevent post-operative infections. This takes about 5 minutes, and during this time, a General Surgeon and 2 Orthopedic Surgeons have come into the OR. They have washed their hands with a germicidal soap. After drying their hands, they will get gowned, gloved, and ready to drape the patient and begin the process of trying to patch him back together and save his life. If all of this surgical care were not done for this patient, he would be dead within the hour.

This patient has a left broken humerus, radius and ulna; all 3 bones in the left arm. This resulted from the impact of the city bus on his left side. He also has a right broken humerus from impacting on the pavement after getting hit by the bus. Also, he has a broken femur (upper leg bone) and crushed hip on his left side from the impact of the bus on his body. He also has some internal injuries in his abdomen and chest from the impact, but we won't know what all has been damaged until the General Surgeon opens up his abdomen and looks over all his organs in person.

The 2 Orthopedic Surgeons each start operating on an arm, because these injuries will be the easiest and quickest to repair. Bob has placed a warming blanket on the patient's lower body to help keep him warm during surgery. The bone Doctors have to approximate the bones (put the bones back together) as close as they can to the position the bones were in before the accident. Then, they apply screws and metal plates to hold everything in place. After this, they sew up the tissue they had to cut through to get to the bones, and then finally, sew up the skin. Once they finish putting the patient's arms back together, they will take a break. Bob will then put a warming blanket over the patient's head, shoulders and arms to help keep him warm, because the lower body blanket will eventually have to come off so that the Orthopedic Surgeons can operate on the lower half. They will have to wait on the General Surgeon to do his work, so that he will be out of their way when they tackle the left leg and hip.

Many times in traumas like this, the patient dies from injury to his internal organs (those in the chest and belly). The General Surgeon and the Orthopedic Surgeons all started doing surgery on this patient at the same time. This is because while working on his broken arms, they were not in the way of the General Surgeon, who was working in the patient's belly. The patient will not usually die from broken bones, but they will die from damage to the internal organs, which will cause them to bleed to death internally. For blood to do its normal work, it needs to be in the blood vessels. If internal organs are crushed, torn, or mangled, they bleed, a lot. This blood falls out of the blood vessels, and therefore, the patient bleeds to death because there is not enough blood left in the blood vessels to keep the other parts of the body alive. This is why the General Surgeon will operate first, to perform life-saving surgery. Other Surgeons will come to do their work after the bleeding is under control and as many of the patient's body parts as possible have been salvaged. Of course Medicine has a ridiculously large term to describe this, achieving hemodynamic control or stability.

The General Surgeon has to make a 2 foot long incision down the middle of the patient's abdomen to gain access to the internal organs. After he makes this long incision, he places a retractor clamp to hold apart the skin, fat, and muscle. This will enable him to look over the liver, spleen, kidneys, stomach, bowel, and other organs and structures. The General Surgeon on call today who has the bad luck to draw this train wreck is Brett Smith. I have known him for many years, and his wife, Cindy, is a good friend of my wife, Shirley.

He makes an incision from the bottom of the patient's sternum down to just into his pubic hair in 2 seconds flat. Brett has, unfortunately, made this type of incision many times because of the many motor vehicle accident (abbreviated MVA) and other trauma patients he has operated on over the years. The bleeding from this incision is not a lot, but he dries up the bleeding vessels by touching them with the electric cautery. After this, he proceeds to work his way quickly through the fat and muscles of the abdomen to get to the good stuff underneath. There is quite a lot of damage to the organs and tissues in this patient's belly. Getting hit by a bus going 45 miles per hour will cause quite an impact on a human body. This patient's spleen and liver are both bleeding, a lot.

Brett has suctioned about 2 quarts of blood out of this guy's belly while trying to put clamps over the bleeding areas so as to slow it down. When he suctions, he can see the areas where the bleeding is coming from. After he puts clamps on the bleeders, and the torrent of bleeding is stopped, he will suture up these areas. He has some luck, and after 10 minutes or so, he has reduced the patient's bleeding to a trickle. This patient is still behind however, in replacing all the blood that he has lost. But now that the bleeding has slowed, we will be able to catch up by replacing the lost blood with units of blood bank blood. We can give this blood very quickly through fluid warmers, and thus keep the patient normothermic.

During this time, the PACU Nurse, Nancy, has been pumping blood with pressure bags applied to the plastic bags of blood bank blood as fast as she can. She has done a very good job, and has given the patient 5 units of blood in less than 30 minutes. The patient however, is still behind on blood volume. She will continue to pump blood into this patient at a good pace, but the patient's blood pressure is now 115/72. The drop in blood pressure since he arrived in the OR means that he is losing blood faster than we are giving it to him. You have to be careful when giving massive amounts of IV fluids or blood to a patient, however. With several large bore IVs, you can actually pump blood into a patient so fast that you overwhelm the heart's ability to handle the shear volume. This is not a good thing to do.

Bob has drawn blood to send to the lab from the art line he placed earlier. We will want to see a hemoglobin and hematocrit, so that we can determine how much bleeding has occurred. Hemoglobin molecules are the cells that haul oxygen around the body, and you need a certain number of these, or else the body isn't happy, but hypoxic. We also want to see a blood chemistry, which will tell us the sodium, potassium, blood urea nitrogen (BUN), creatinine, and blood glucose of this patient. The sodium and BUN will tell us how dehydrated or low on volume he is. The creatinine will tell us if he has any kidney failure. Glucose will tell us if he is a diabetic and how out of whack his blood sugar is. Last, but certainly not least, potassium is very important for heart function and conduction. Sometimes, bad alcoholics wash out their sodium and potassium, which messes up their heart function and throws all the chemical processes in the body out of kilter. Giving large amounts of blood bank blood will raise the potassium, possibly to dangerous levels. Too high a potassium, and the heart will block down and stop. Keeping all these variables in a happy range is the dance of Anesthesia in traumas.

I am tired from the 30 minutes or so of activity and thinking that I have just done. The patient is stable now, with a blood pressure of 110/56, and an oxygen saturation reading of 98%. You just can't kill a drunk until he is ready to die. I say to Bob, "This guy's pretty stable now;

you can slow down on giving more blood. I'm going to step out for a bit and check on my other rooms, but I'll have my phone on in case you need me." Bob replies "Yeah, he is stable, and besides, I have Nancy (the PACU Nurse) to pump blood and help out. She is a great help." Bob likes Nancy for more than just her help, which is very good. He likes just looking at her because she is very pretty. Nothing wrong with that in my book.

Walking out into the OR hallway, I am feeling pretty woozy. I'm not used to this much work. I hate it, and I try to avoid it as much as I possibly can, but every once in a while, you just get hit with a big pile of shit like this patient in OR 6. There is no upside to anyone in this case. If he dies, you'll be making some deposition to the suing family's Lawyer in 6 months. If he lives, he'll generate a $1 million plus medical bill, plus the cost of his disability, which the taxpayers will have to eat. This guy and his entire family will never contribute $1 million to society in their combined lives, but we are just stuck with the situation.

This patient is not unique; today there will be a thousand more just like him in Hospitals all over the entire country. You add them all up and you come up with a staggering amount of money pissed away on people, who contribute nothing, but are just playing the game and sucking everything they can from society their entire lives. And this happens every day, 24/7/365 in this country. It's amazing the healthcare system hasn't collapsed under the weight of this insanity.

The only money any of the Doctors involved with this case will get for all their hard work is the Call money ($1,000 per day of call), and this type of patient is usually the most time consuming and demanding of all. They will suck time and energy out of you like a giant mosquito, because that is all they do in their regular lives. This, of course, will take time and energy away from your regular patients, those who work, pay taxes, and buy insurance, giving them the short end of the stick. In our noble attempt to be fair to the unfortunate people in our society, we end up screwing over all the hard working people who try to play the game correctly and do the right thing.

Convicted criminals (murderers and rapists) have better health care than the Nurses and Doctors working in the Hospitals of this country. Health care is free to the criminal, but society is punished several times by the criminal. Society is punished first by the crime of the criminal, then has to pay for the courts and trials, pay for incarcerating the criminals, and pay for their education and health care??? Who in the hell came up with this shit?? Our country is ass backwards and upside down, thank you Lawyers.

Anyway, I walk over to the board runner, Nurse Genie, which gives me time to catch my breath and compose myself. "Hey Genie," I ask, "What's going on?" "You have the trauma in 6, a hernia repair going in OR 4, and a C-section going upstairs," she replies. "Damn, I've been tied up with that crack head, wino in OR 6 for a while, I didn't realize these other cases were going on," I say to her. I then ask her "Who's doing those cases?" "Joe is doing the C-section and Elizabeth is doing the hernia repair," she returns. "Thanks Genie," I say politely. Genie is one of those Nurses who can make you life heaven or hell, depending on whether she likes you or not. She likes me, thank God.

I walk over to OR 4 to see how the hernia repair is going. Walking through the door to the OR, I can see that they are in the middle of the case. Elizabeth is watching the EKG monitor and talking about her recent vacation to Alaska to the Surgeon while he is cutting and sewing. After you have seen and done 100 hernia repairs, they are all the same, so you have all sorts of conversations during surgery. You usually listen to music during surgeries as well. The EKG monitors on Anesthesia machines display not only EKG rhythm, but blood pressure and oxygen saturation, as well.

"Is everything going okay?" I ask the usual question. "Oh high Doctor Deluna, yes, everything's going just fine. We've got the hernia repaired and we'll be closing in a few minutes," Elizabeth replies. "Great," I reply as I walk over to sign the Anesthesia Record. Elizabeth says to me "I hear we have another fine, upstanding citizen all tore up in OR 6." "Yes, we have another leach on society suddenly in need of emergency medical care," I say and continue, "Isn't it great to see our tax dollars at work?" "Boy, is that a crock," Elizabeth says back to me. We have a chuckle at this before I turn to leave OR 4. The vast amount of OR staff feel this way, and probably the majority of Americans feel that this is just not right as well.

As I walk out into the hallway, I can see Joe (the CRNA who has been doing the C-section) coming up the hall toward me. "The section's all done and I'm next to leave," he says when he gets close. "Okay Joe, have a good afternoon," I say to him as I sign the Anesthesia Record on the hallway wall. "Thanks; see you tomorrow," Joe says as he turns to go file the paperwork for the C-section he just finished. He is in a hurry to get out of here. Joe was supposed to leave about an hour ago, but I stuck him with the C-section because there was no one else available to do it. He just happened to draw the short straw on this one.

Hospitals tend to staff CRNAs with as few as possible to get the work done because they are expensive. Between salary and benefits, an average CRNA costs this Hospital about $250,000 a year. Every once in a while, the work piles up quicker than usual, and someone gets stuck staying late to finish it up. Once a Nurse is assigned to a case, they cannot leave because they would be fired for abandoning the patient. The Hospital and its' managers are not penalized for abusing their staff and making Nurses work excessively long hours, or working while exhausted. Administrators are never in trouble for making their Nurses work while sleep-deprived from working too many long shifts. Only the Nursing staff is punished if they ever make a mistake.

This type of thing also happens to Nurses in ICUs (intensive care units). There is just a certain amount of mandatory overtime built into the jobs of CRNAs and ICU Nurses. This type of thing makes for burned-out and resentful staff, but there isn't a damn thing the CRNAs or ICU Nurses can do about it. It is just part of their job to get screwed every once in a while. If you feel like you are getting screwed over too often, you change jobs, just like every one else in Nursing. This is one of the major factors causing burn out and staff turnover in the Nursing profession.

From a business standpoint, this practice is good for the Hospital administrators because they can get by with fewer Nurses by squeezing more and more work out of the staff they have. It simply doesn't matter to them that it is dangerous to the patient to squeeze too much work out of the Nursing staff. It doesn't matter, that is, until a patient dies or is severely injured because of this practice. Only then, does this situation become a problem, and then, only sometimes, do they try to address the problem appropriately. Many times, administration will still try some quick fix, rather than hiring enough Nursing staff, or taking measures to keep the staff they have from leaving.

Generally, in today's healthcare environment, patient concerns take a distant back seat to Hospital financial concerns. After Hospital financial concerns, and pleasing the Doctor concerns, patient concerns come in 3rd or maybe 4th in importance, in today's healthcare systems. In some Hospitals, patient concerns rank far lower in importance; although the Hospitals are obligated to publicly say that patients' concerns are always number 1. It would be business suicide for a Hospital to do otherwise.

Chapter Ten

Time For a Break

    Well, I'm glad I'm caught up on all that, I think to myself. The trauma in OR 6 is going well, or at least, Bob hasn't called with any emergency for me to handle. Thank God. Right now, I am feeling a little shaky, my nerves are on edge. Looking at my watch, I see that it is now 6:15 P.M., and the only game in town is that trauma in OR 6. I think I'll head back to my office for a little nip. I keep a bottle of scotch, a cup, and a tin of breath mints in a locked drawer in the desk in my office. Locking the door after I enter my office, I fumble in my pocket for my keys. Unlocking the drawer in my desk, I pull out the bottle of scotch and cup. My hands are trembling a little. After pouring 2 fingers of scotch into a glass, I knock it down in one gulp. Boy that feels good. I then take 2 breath mints out and pop them into my mouth. Yes, that sure settled my nerves; I think as I kick back on my sofa and put my feet up. Playing with the strong breath mints in my mouth, using my tongue, relaxes me. The peppermints seem to open up my lungs and make it easier to breathe. I think I'll just close my eyes for a minute and relax a bit.

    Once again, I am jolted from a deep sleep by my damn cell phone going off. I answer the call and it is Bob calling me for an update on the train wreck in OR 6. Looking at my watch, I see that it is now 8:30 P.M., wow. It is so easy to catch a few cat naps at work when you have your own office. This is a wonderful thing, especially on long days at the Hospital, like today. Besides, most of my job at this Hospital is just going from room to room and signing my name. Rarely am I ever forced into doing actual patient care work.

"What's up Bob," I say. Bob reports "Well, we've got both of his arms put back together, plated and screwed. The Orthopedic Surgeons have left, but when they come back, they will put casts on his arms, then start working on his hip and leg. However, the General Surgeon has been busy. He's had to remove the guy's spleen, repair a lacerated liver that won't quit bleeding, repair injured bowel, and he is now repairing a leaking tear in the guy's abdominal aorta. We have given this guy 112 units of blood, and the Director of the Red Cross has called directly into the Operating Room to tell the Surgeon that this case has consumed so much blood products that it is putting the entire state population at risk of running out of blood if there is a large need someplace else. (People only have the equivalent of 5-10 units of blood in their bodies normally, depending on their size). The Surgeon told him to have a blood drive; he's not stopping this surgery!" He asks me "Can you believe this guy?" He continues with "I simply cannot believe this Surgeon would put the entire state's population at risk of running out of blood to continue operating on this scumbag. Doesn't he have any judgment?"

I reply "Bob, he is not allowed to have any judgment. He is committed once he began the surgery. If he doesn't do everything in his power to repair this broken patient and keep him alive, then he will be crucified in a court of law afterwards by the bloodthirsty Lawyers." "Yeah, I know you're right, it just drives me crazy sometimes how upside down the system is," Bob says. "Just keep giving blood, platelets, and FFP (fresh frozen plasma, which contains clotting factors) as you have to so that the Surgeon can keep going. Just keep the patient's heart beating until he gets out of the Operating Room, and don't forget to draw labs every hour as well," I say to him. "I won't," Bob says.

I hang up the phone after this conversation with Bob and breathe a sigh of relief that I am on call with him. A new CRNA just out of training probably wouldn't be able to handle such a complex nightmare of a case as this one without a lot of help, and I don't like to provide a lot of help. But Bob, he can handle anything. This won't even strain his talents. He has done many, many bad traumas, some nearly identical to this one, some much worse.

It is now nearly 9 P.M. and I don't have anything to do. I guess I'll go to the Surgeon's Lounge and read the newspaper for a while or maybe watch TV. Or maybe I'll just kick back on this sofa and go back to sleep. Tomorrow the crack-head wino in OR 6 will be in the newspapers. It will be interesting to see how the newspaper spins the story and find out some other details about the accident. It's about a 90% chance that he'll die from pulmonary edema in PACU within a few hours of leaving the Operating Room. That's if his heart doesn't stop beating first. The human body doesn't like to receive a big, blunt impact, like for example, getting whumped by a bus.

When a person falls from a building or gets any big, blunt trauma like this guy, they will do okay for a while, but bad chemicals are released in the body. It may take a few hours or as many as 8 hours later, but changes in the body occur which pour fluid into the lungs, along with blood. The result is a pink, frothy fluid (pulmonary edema) filling up the lungs, which goes up the ET (endotracheal tube) and ventilator tubing, making it readily visible. This is an ominous sign, when you see it. I have never seen any blunt trauma victim survive this. If we can just get this patient off the OR table and have him die in PACU or ICU, it will look better on the Operating Room statistics. An intraoperative death makes all kinds of people in Administration jump up and down and get excited. If he dies a few hours later in PACU or ICU, it is not as big a deal to the bean counters (Administrators). Crazy huh?

I am so bored that I decide to walk down the hall to the Surgeon's Lounge, just to look at something new. I decide to sit back in a recliner in the Surgeon's Lounge and watch the 24 hour news channel on the TV for a while. It's nice to be up on current events. It makes you seem intelligent, when you can discuss current news topics. After about an hour, I have seen all the current news I can stand, twice. It is now 10:15 P.M. and there isn't really anyone around to talk to and nothing to do. Most of the people here at work I don't care to talk to very much anyway. I don't want to drink anymore coffee this late at night. Maybe I'll go to OR 6 and see if Bob wants a break to get something to eat or go to the bathroom; after all, he has been working for more than 5 hours straight. You have to have the bladder capacity of a camel to be able to do Anesthesia. Also, there are very few hypoglycemics (people who have to eat frequently because they develop low blood sugar, if they don't) in this profession.

Operating Room 6 is some distance from the Surgeon's Lounge (about 60 feet) and the one thing I notice walking down the hallway this time of night is that it is dead silent. The only sound I hear is my shoes on the hallway floor. As I get within 20 feet of the door to OR 6, I can begin to hear noise and people talking. Before reaching the door, I can hear the Surgeon yelling at someone. As I open the door, he is yelling "Give me that vascular clamp, aren't you paying attention to what in the hell I'm operating on here?!?" He is obviously now working on the tear in the abdominal aorta, or another large blood vessel, and trying to control bleeding. This can be tense work because a patient can bleed to death in a matter of seconds from a rip in the aorta.

Entering the OR, I can now hear the beeping of the pulse oximeter, the EKG, the Anesthesia ventilator cycling, and the sounds made by several people being very busy. There is not a lot of conversation going on. One of the main sounds that gets my attention is that of the suction. The Scrub Tech (the person right next to the Surgeon, helping him, and acting like an extra set of hands for him) is sucking out quite a lot of blood, trying to give the Surgeon a view of where the bleeding is coming from so he can get a clamp in place and get control of it. The Surgeon is not happy, gallons of blood have been lost in this case and he has been operating for more than 4 hours. One thing is certain; he will take out his frustration on the Operating Room staff. It is just part of the job. If you don't have thick skin and can't take verbal abuse, you aren't cut out for work in the Operating Room. After the surgery, the Surgeon may or may not apologize, but he will be much nicer to everyone and he will forget about everything that was said in the OR. It's just how things work in this specialty area.

Bob noticed when I opened the door and looked up at me from the chair he is sitting on. "Hey Chief, how's it going out there?" he asks. "This is the only show in town," I reply. The PACU Nurse is still pumping blood after 4 plus hours. She goes between the central line I placed and a peripheral IV in the patient's left arm; pumping up pressure bags on blood bags continuously. This makes the blood infuse very quickly through the fluid warmers. Looking around the room, it looks like a war zone. There are dozens of suction canisters lined up against the far wall, all full of blood. There is a large puddle of blood on the floor all around the operating table. Also, there is blood all over the Surgeon and the 2 Scrub Techs assisting him. They are probably soaked down to their underwear. They better pray this slime ball patient doesn't have Hepatitis-C or AIDs. He probably has both. This guy hasn't exactly been a responsible member of society.

"Bob, you want to take a break?" I ask. "Hell yes," he replies. He proceeds to give me a short report on this case: "He is stable, with a blood pressure of 90 to 110, and the blood letting has slowed down to a trickle compared to an hour ago. Nancy here (the PACU Nurse/ blood pump) has been invaluable. She has some relief coming in a few minutes. We have Levophed going at low dose, and his oxygen saturation is 98%. What's not to love?" (Levophed, also called norepinephrine, tightens up the blood vessels, and so, raises blood pressure. Levophed has also been called leave 'em dead) "You've done some good work here Bob, get you a cup of coffee in the lounge and a snack. The cafeteria is closed now," I say to him. "The first thing I'm going to do is micturate (fancy word for pee)," Bob says as he heads for the door. Bob has such a sense of humor. He makes me chuckle.

"What have you been doing in here, slaughtering hogs?" I ask Brett in a loud voice. He looks up for a second at me and says "Oh, high Jerry. It has been a mell of a hess in here. This guy had more mangled and ripped up tissue than you could shake a stick at. That bus nailed him good." "Do you think you'll be able to get him off the table?" I ask. "I hope so. I've repaired his colon, his small bowel, his liver, removed his spleen, and I just about got a handle on this leaking tear in his abdominal aorta," he says. "He'll be very lucky if he doesn't go into shock lung after all these transfused blood products we've given him," I tell him. "Yeah, you're right," he replies. Sometimes massive transfusion of blood products can cause clotting abnormalities and/or pulmonary edema. Either one of these can be deadly by themselves.

I don't talk to him anymore because he needs to focus on the task at hand, which is patching up this bum's abdominal aorta. This mosquito on society's back will probably consume more than $100,000 worth of our health care dollars today and he only has a one in a million chance that he'll live for 24 hours. If he does hit the lottery of life and live, then he'll be permanently disabled and receive a government check every month for the rest of his life while he sits on his porch and watches traffic. Society gets punished over and over again by scum bags like this one, and we just suck it up. What a burden on the backs of the people who work for a living. What a crazy world!

Brett Smith is an excellent Surgeon with 20 years experience. He has done thousands of trauma cases in his career, but the legal environment in today's world makes getting involved in cases like this one very much like sliding down the edge of a razor blade and not getting cut. Any slight oversight or missed injury, (never mind that Brett will have repaired 20 injuries in the course of this nightmare case) which results in this bum's death will come to light at autopsy. Then, with very little trouble, the blood sucking Lawyers will talk the family into suing. Then, they'll get hold of this information and do their best to ruin his career, and his reputation, and bleed him dry financially. They do not care that this Surgeon may have saved the lives of 1,000 people and improved the lives of tens of thousands more. It does not matter to them that this person has spent his entire life trying to benefit others, and that the life of this bum has been spent trying to get everything he can out of others and society, while giving nothing back. It only matters to them that there is money to be made. How sad this is. Our country is upside down. A man's contribution to his country ought to count for something. These 2 men are not equal. One has worked for decades to contribute and give back to society, while the other hasn't lifted his finger to contribute anything to society.

The work involved in this case has decreased over the course of the surgeries that have been done to this point. So much so that one of the Circulator Nurses, Stacy, can now relieve the PACU Nurse, Nancy, who has been working nonstop for 4 hours as a human blood and IV fluid pump. Jean, the other Circulator Nurse, can now manage all the work (paper work and getting things for the Surgeon) needed to facilitate the surgery at hand. Nancy is dog tired after pumping blood products, IV fluids, and running to the Blood Bank every 30 or 40 minutes to get more bags of blood, platelets, and FFP for this patient. She loves the excitement of this intensive work, but her adrenalin has worn off and she needs a break from this case. Giving 100% for 4 plus hours will drain a person's energy. The Operating Room is really a young person's game, after 20 years (or less) of this, a lot of Nurses get very burned out; Doctors too.

I just bide my time in here, watching the monitors (EKG, blood pressure, and pulse oximeter), what the other people in the room are doing, and listening to all the sounds. I don't usually offer CRNAs breaks unless they call me and ask for one, but I like Bob, and he is a hell of a mule, doing virtually all of the heavy lifting involved in these cases on a regular basis. In 10 or 15 minutes, Bob will be back and then I'll be gone. When I was young and fresh, the excitement of these types of cases was addicting. After doing about 500 trauma cases however, the thrill starts to wane. Now, I try to stay the hell away from these situations because very little good can come my way as a result of participating in them. Many times in my career, I have had to give depositions to Lawyers suing Surgeons and Hospitals after cases just like this one. This is thankless work, and it doesn't pay for shit on top of that.

Everything is going pretty smooth in this case right now. The patient's vital signs are stable and Stacy is easily able to keep up with pumping blood into him. The amount of bleeding at this point of the surgery has decreased substantially. Brett has gotten everything pretty much under control. It may take him 1 to 2 hours more work to tidy up everything, dry up the last of the small bleeders, and close this puppy up. This case is in the finishing up stage. The fact that Bob worked like a dog during the first part of the case to get everything optimized is really telling now, toward the end of the case. Because of that, this case is on cruise control now and there is not much to do, for Anesthesia anyway. The rest of the work is almost all surgical.

I ask Jean, the Circulator Nurse, "Are the Orthopods (Orthopedic Surgeons) going to come back and fix his left hip and leg tonight?" That would require another 3 to 4 hours of surgery after we get done with this part of the repair job. This would mean that this patient's surgeries would finally finish up about 3 or 4 A.M., optimistically. Jean says "I talked to Doctor May (Orthopedic Surgeon) about an hour ago and he said to call him when we start closing, then he will come in to fix this guy's hip and leg." "Damn, that means he will start operating around 11:30 P.M. or 12 midnight," I say. Jean says "That sounds about right." In my mind I am cursing at this news because it means that I will not get to leave the Hospital and go home tonight. This case will end up finishing about sunrise, or just before (10 to 12 hours of surgery).

I will surely miss snuggling up next to Shirley in my luxurious bed tonight. Instead, I'll have to make do with naps on the sofa in my office to get any rest at all, because I am stuck here. Bob will have to stay with this case until it finishes, somewhere between 4 and 6 A.M., and then lay out in the Surgeon's Lounge on a sofa or recliner to get any rest at all. At least he's the first CRNA out in the morning, and he'll be able to leave for home shortly after the troops arrive for the day's work. He'll get out of here long before I do. I'll probably have to stay until around noon before I get to vacate the premises. This type of work situation is very typical in Anesthesia; it is not for every one; it is a crazy world.

I am musing over these thoughts when the door opens and Bob returns from his break. "Did you find anything to snack on?" I ask. "Yeah, I made a cup of coffee and found some almonds and a Danish to munch on," he says. "Great," I say "I've got some bad news. After Brett finishes, the Orthopedic Surgeon is coming in to repair his left hip and broke leg." "Damn, I was afraid of that. Oh well," Bob says. "Yeah, it sucks," I reply.

I leave OR 6 knowing that Bob will finish this case, bring the patient to ICU, put him on a ventilator, and then come back downstairs to crash out for an hour or 2 on a recliner or sofa in the Surgeon's Lounge before his sleep is interrupted by the day shift coming in. This is a CRNA's lot in life. At least they make 3 or 4 times what an ordinary RN makes, hell, they make more money than ½ of Doctors.

I leave OR 6 and walk down the hallway of the OR to my office. It is drawing up to 11 P.M. There is no other case going on in the OR and therefore, nothing to do. Time to go and kick back on the sofa for another nap. It's a tough job, but somebody's got to do it. Closing and locking the door to my office, I'm contemplating whether or not to have another 2 fingers of Scotch. It is late, but it sure would help me relax quickly and get off to sleep on my sofa. I think I will.

After knocking down the Scotch in one gulp, then chewing up a breath mint, I repose myself lengthways on the sofa. The Scotch leaves a warm trail inside me all the way to my stomach. I am feeling all warm and cozy inside. My head is resting comfortably on a pillow, and I pull up a blanket that I keep just for such occasions as this over me. I glance at my watch and see that the time is now 11 P.M., and I am very cozy. Usually, I spend several hours a day looking at menus for the restaurants in this area to decide where I want Shirley and I to go for supper. This way I will know what I want to eat when I get there and I can tell Shirley what the restaurant serves before we get there.

Most of the rest of the time I spend on the computer is engaged in looking at recipes online or playing video games. I like to print up good recipes because I am quite the gourmet chef at home on occasion. Today however, I have spent no time at all on the computer. I have just been too busy. This has been an unusually busy Call day for me. Oh well, maybe tomorrow I'll check out the menu of the new Italian restaurant in town, I think as I drift off. In no time at all, I am in a deep sleep.

Ring! Ring! Goddamn that phone I think as I am roused out of my sleep once again. As I pick up the phone to answer the call, I glance at my watch to see the time. 4 A.M., wow, it sure is late. "Hello," I say loudly into the phone while trying to shake the cobwebs from my head. It's Bob. "Hey chief, I finished up that trauma and got him up to ICU about 20 minutes ago, but now we have a C-section to do," he tells me. "Is it a STAT (emergency) section?" I ask. (One where you have to put the patient to sleep, instead on doing the usual spinal Anesthesia, which is much safer) "No, just a need to do now C-section," he replies.

This means that the OB-GYN Doctor has been up all night and just wants to get this job out of the way now. This is so that he doesn't have it hanging around during the day to mess up his other activities, like sleeping or seeing patients in the office. "Okay, go ahead and start and I'll be up in a bit," I tell him. "Okay chief," Bob replies. I have no intention of going up to participate in this C-section; I'll just sign the Anesthesia record tomorrow when I am up and about. Bob has worked with me long enough to know that he will not see me again tonight. Putting the cell phone down on the ottoman next to the sofa, I pull my blanket up around my neck and settle down for a little more rest before I have to be up and at 'em for the coming day. In no time at all I am back in a deep sleep, the world around me far, far away.

Chapter Eleven

Call is Nearly Done

Ring! Ring! Ring! Ring! Damn that phone, I think as I open my eyes. Blinking my eyes rapidly, trying to focus on the phone screen to see what in the hell it is now, I see that it is now 6 A.M. Shit, time to wake up and face the new world. I have set this phone to wake me up at this time every morning when it is turned on so that I will have 30 minutes to wash my face and get some coffee in me. This way I can be fresh-faced and sane when the rest of the troops start arriving for the day at 6:30 A.M.

The OR Nurses, Scrub Techs, and CRNAs start coming in at 6:30 A.M. so that they have time to change into scrub suits and drink some coffee before they have to punch the time clock at 7 A.M. Sometimes they start getting the equipment needed to do the surgical cases organized and then go and hit the time clock at 7, because if they punch in before 7 A.M. they will be reprimanded by their superiors. All Hospitals try to keep Nursing overtime down to a minimum while piling on more and more duties and paperwork. You either love this kind of work or you don't. If you don't love it, you'll never learn to like it.

Rising up off of the sofa, I pull myself erect slowly because I am stiff all over. I leave my office and stumble slowly down the OR hallway to the Surgeon's Lounge. Going through the lounge and dressing room, I go to the bathroom so that I can get a washcloth and wipe my face down with warm water. Boy that feels good, I think as I wipe down my face and wipe the eye boogers out. After scrubbing my face down and putting on a new paper surgical cap, I almost feel human. What a rough night, I think as I walk back into the Surgeon's Lounge to make myself a cup of strong Columbian coffee.

As I walk back through the lounge, I notice a body laid out on a sofa. It's Bob; I didn't see him when I came through the first time, but I wasn't awake then. He must have crashed out after the C-section to try to get a couple of hours rest. As I make a double dose of Columbian espresso, the coffee maker's noise wakes Bob. He pulls himself up on the sofa and says "Shit, what a night." He looks over at me with unfocused eyes while I am pouring half and half into my espresso and asks "What time is it?" "It's 6:15 A.M." I reply. "Well, I only got one hour of rest, but at least I made some money yesterday," he says with a big grin on his face. Bob gets up to go to the bathroom and wash his face, after which he'll drink as much coffee as he can, so that he can function for a little while longer.

He made $100 per hour for all the overtime he did yesterday, plus the regular day's pay for his 8 hour shift preceding that, which was $640. All in all, Bob probably knocked down $1,800 or $1,900 in the past 24 hours. Not many Nurses can make that kind of money in a day. After he does one or two small cases, he will probably get out of here by 8 or 9 A.M. and then, go home and knock out a 4 or 5 hour nap. He will then wake up this afternoon, a rested and wealthier man. The fact that he has essentially been up for more that 24 hours, and is not thinking very well right now is irrelevant. He's made a lot of money and he'll be home by lunch time. What's not to love?

I kick back in a recliner to watch the 24 hour news channel and enjoy my cup of strong coffee. It is not as good as the coffee I make at home, probably because it doesn't have the added kick of the brandy, which I am sorely missing. Every few minutes a Surgeon or CRNA comes into the lounge to make themselves a cup of coffee. I greet every one of them with a "Good morning." It's good to be cordial. After watching the news on TV for awhile and drinking my strong coffee, I realize that it is 7 A.M., time to go out and make the work assignments for the day.

There is so much routine in my life, very little surprise or spontaneity these days, I think as I walk out into the hallway to make the assignments. It is 7 A.M. and the staff is ready to go into action. I rarely make these assignments this early, but what the hell. After Call, especially a Call where I have been in the Hospital all night, I am very interested in making my assignments the easy cases that will also get me out of here as quickly as possible. On mornings like this, I try to avoid the quick cases where I have to go room to room to sign the papers. It's just too much work right now. I prefer longer cases so that I am not running around as much. Oddly enough, I don't have a headache this morning after catching cat naps on the sofa in my office yesterday. That last double shot of scotch must have helped prevent that.

This morning I have given myself the C-section upstairs (so I don't have to go anywhere for that case), a TAH (total abdominal hysterectomy, which will last 1 ½ to 2 hours), a hernia repair which will last 2 hours, and a knee surgery which will last a couple of hours (on a privately insured patient, of course). These cases will keep me busy at a relaxed pace. This will allow me to drink coffee, eat a little breakfast, and watch the news on TV. I will not have to get up and down a lot, but will be able to sit around and drink coffee a lot while all this work is going on. I love Anesthesia.

With a little luck, I'll be out of here before lunch. Then, I'll go home, and if Shirley is there, I'll tell her that I've been up all night and need a nap. After a couple hours nap in my own bed at home, I'll be right as rain. Then Shirley will be amazed at how fresh I seem after only a couple hours of nap time following such a grueling night of work. I'll regal her with tales about the trauma and all the other work I did yesterday, and she will be amazed and think that I'm superman. She'll be all sweet to me and snuggle up next to me on the sofa. We'll be able to read about the city bus hitting the civilian pedestrian, and find out other details about the accident in the newspaper. We might even be able to fool around and have some afternoon delight, oh how nice that would be.

But enough of daydreaming about what will happen later on today, I have to focus on the reality at hand. All 4 of my cases this morning involve patients with private insurance so that I can maximize my reimbursement. I am a master at this game, after many years of practice. Doctor Jim Turner has privately insured patients in 3 out of his 4 rooms. Avi and Arnash have the OR rooms with the least number of privately insured patients. They take care of a lot of Medicaid, Medicare, and indigent patients in the rooms I assign to them. Somebody has to take care of these patients, even though the reimbursement is lowest for them.

My partner, Doctor Jim Turner, comes in to the lounge and greets me with "Good morning Jerry, how was your night?" "It was hell, we just finished the last case about an hour ago," I tell him. His eyes grow big, and his face has a look of surprise as he asks me "What the hell happened?" I proceed to answer his question by going into a long diatribe about the crack head, wino that got hit by the bus. I go into gory detail about all the injuries he had as a result, and all the surgeries that took place to try to save the shithead's life. If there is one thing I truly love about Anesthesia, it's telling war stories about some of my experiences. Although he may care less about all the night's adventures, Jim looks appropriately interested and amazed at what I am relating to him. During the last part of my telling him about the C-section which followed the nightmare wino crack-head case, Jim's cell phone goes off and he is summoned to start a case. He excuses himself and goes to begin his day's work. Someday, he'll be regaling some younger Anesthesiologist with some gruesome tale about his adventures in Anesthesia. History repeats itself.

Ring, ring! My cell phone goes off with the first call of the day. "Ready for you in OR 1 Doctor Deluna," the Circulator Nurse says on the other end of the phone. This is the OR with the TAH. The patient is the wife of Joe Carlson, who owns the Mercedes-Benz dealership in Ashburg. Needless to say, he and I have known each other for close to 2 decades. I get up from the recliner where I have been sitting, drinking coffee, talking, and greeting the people who come in to the Surgeon's Lounge. All the coffee that I have been drinking for the past ½ hour has got me pretty jacked up. I am quick on my feet as I walk briskly over to Operating Room 1 to start this day's work.

When you are a Doctor in a small town, you meet the upper crust of the local society, such that it is. I am a long time member of the local Country Club, and I travel in the same social circles as the local business leaders and wealthier people in this town. I guess you could say that I am well-connected in this town. Plus, I am on the Board of Directors of the Hospital, where I also rub elbows with some of the movers and shakers of this small community. As a result of all these associations, I know almost everyone who has any money in this town, and I am known to them as well. They seem to like knowing the Chief of Anesthesia at the local Hospital, like it gives them status by association or something.

Walking into OR 1, I say to the Circulator Nurse (you can probably guess by now), "Turn up that temperature, it's too cold in here!" She walks over to the thermostat to carry out my command as I walk up to the patient on the OR table. I nod to Bob, the CRNA, to start giving the induction drugs as I say to the patient, "Hello Carol, it's Jerry, I'm here and I'm going to get you off to sleep now." She looks up at me and says "High Jerry, it's so good to see you. It is cold in here. I know I don't have to worry about anything nooooww." And, just like that, she is unconscious. As I walk over to the Anesthesia machine to sign the Anesthesia Record, Bob is putting the ET tube down her throat.

I hang around for a few minutes while Bob connects the ET tube to the Anesthesia circuit, turns on the ventilator, then, the vaporizer (which supplies the Anesthesia gas, which keeps the patient's brain asleep). While he is taping the ET tube to Carol's face (so it doesn't become dislodged), I say to him "I know that you are dog-tired from the beating you received last night. When you finish this case, you are done. In a couple of hours, you are out of here and on your way home, okay?" He looks up at me with bloodshot eyes and says "Okay boss, that suits me just fine because I sure could use a nap soon." "I know that's right," I say to Bob as I turn to leave OR 1.

It does not matter to me that Bob is working so sleep deprived that he presently has the mental function of someone who is legally drunk. It only matters to me that I can squeeze one more case out of Bob, and make a little more money off of him before he leaves. Bob is a professional, and besides, he drank 2 cups of strong coffee before he started this case. A TAH is a straightforward, simple surgical case. The OB/GYN Surgeon who is doing the surgery is a very good, very experienced Surgeon. He will have no problems and there will be no drama with this surgery. Bob has done the Anesthesia for so many TAH cases, that he could do them with his eyes closed, even though I hope he doesn't close his eyes and doze off during this one since it is the wife of someone important in the community.

An experienced CRNA, like Bob, knows how to work while sleep deprived. He has done so many TAH cases in his career that he will just follow the standard procedure in his head that he has developed from doing more than a thousand of them. Also, he will go over every detail about the case during the case in his mind, over and over; mentally checking and rechecking every detail. And there will be no problems. The fact that he will be on his way home in 2 hours is the one thought that he will keep in his brain to keep him going throughout this case. It is the one thing that will keep him going until he is home, and then he will collapse from exhaustion. This kind of mindset may sound strange to some people, but this kind of thinking and practice is common among Anesthesia people. In Anesthesia, this is as common as green grass in the pasture. This is one of several reasons why the practice of Anesthesia is not for everyone, and not just anyone can do Anesthesia.

As I am walking in the OR hallway, after leaving Bob in OR 1, Doctor Jim Turner comes up to me and asks "Did you hear what just happened in the back of the Hospital?" It is midmorning and I am thinking what in the hell could possibly be happening at the Hospital now, but I can't resist. I say "Okay, what?" Jim goes into this story "Some Doctor must have really pissed off some Nurse up on the floor (of the Hospital). He left his briefcase in the Nurse's Station for a couple of days, and they didn't like it there. So this morning, the Nurse called the bomb squad and reported a strange briefcase left on the floor. The bomb squad actually came out to the Hospital, and since they couldn't get it open, they took the suspicious briefcase out to the back of the Hospital, put it in a garbage dumpster, and blew it up!!!" My jaw dropped open at the conclusion of this story. "I can't believe that the people of this town are stupid enough to do something that crazy," I say back to Jim. "It's true, I'm not making this up, I swear," he says, while laughing so hard that he can barely speak clearly. "This story really takes the cake," I tell him, "Just when I thought that I had heard it all." Is it just my imagination, or, are crazy and stupid people taking over the whole world???

I walk away from Jim shaking my head because I can hardly believe something that crazy would actually happen at a Hospital where I worked. It is so crazy that it sounds like a scene from a movie comedy or something. Are the 3 stooges running the world???

As I walk down the OR hallway toward the Surgeon's Lounge, someone stops and asks me "Hey Doctor Deluna, did you hear about them blowing up a briefcase in the back of the Hospital?" "Yeah, I just heard," I reply. The questioner walks away laughing really loudly, and saying "Can you believe it!" This is so stupid; I just hope that it doesn't make it to the local newspaper. This type of story can do the Hospital's reputation no good.

Back in the Surgeon's Lounge, I fix myself one more cup of Columbian coffee with cream. It takes the coffee-maker about 1 minute to spit out a hot cup of delicious coffee. This coffee maker only makes one cup of coffee at a time. I wonder what people used to do before coffee? Stay tired and sleepy, I guess. The Doctors and CRNAs coming and going in the lounge are talking about the briefcase affair, but also talk about a thousand other things. These are all very bright people; top of their class in school kind of people. They have busy lives and lots of interests to occupy their brains besides the stupid briefcase story. Besides, this incident is only slightly unusual.

It is now 10 A.M., and I am going to start looking to get out of here soon and head on home. Bob has already left the building, and I want to do the same. I am anxious to get home, take a nice nap, and then wake up and fix myself a good drink to start my time off from work right.

Plus, I'm looking forward to seeing my beautiful wife, Shirley. I hope we spend the afternoon relaxing, sipping on drinks, and snuggling. Also, it will be good to hear what she has been up to while I've been gone the past 24 hours or so. If I get out of here at 12 noon, I'll have been gone from home about 35 hours. This sucks, but this too is just part of working in Anesthesia. At least I'll be completely off this afternoon, while regular people are still working at their regular jobs. Maybe Shirley and I will go out for a nice, romantic dinner, and then go home and screw our brains out. That would be so nice.

I presently have 3 cases going. Right now, I am supervising another C-section, a cardioversion (where you put the patient to sleep in their Hospital room for about 5 minutes, so that you can shock their heart back into a regular rhythm), and a gallbladder. The C-section takes about 1 hour, start to finish, the cardioversion takes about 15 minutes total, and the gallbladder takes about 1 hour. Between 11 A.M. and 12 noon, all 3 of these will be finished, and then I'll hit the eject button and get out of here.

Doctor Jim Turner is on call today, so he'll be the one who shovels all the shit this afternoon and evening. I take my cup of coffee and walk out into the OR hallway to take a look at the assignment board. Looking at the work board, I can see that he'll have a busy afternoon. There are 8 add-on cases now, in addition to all the scheduled cases. You start out the day with a list of regularly scheduled surgical cases, which were put on over the past few days, to get this mornings' list of cases. Then, as the morning progresses, other surgical cases are added on to the schedule. These cases come from patients in the ER, patients up on the floor who now are in need of surgery, and patients from Doctors offices.

A Surgeon will see patients that are referred from other Doctors (who are not Surgeons) offices. Some of these will be in need of surgery urgently, so the Surgeon tells his office Nurse to call the OR and put the patient on the surgical schedule as an add-on for today. The patient will then come to the Hospital to get admitted and worked up for surgery. The patient will have a sheet of paper from the Surgeon with his orders to admit the patient and what labwork and tests he wants done to the patient to get them ready for surgery. Prior to and, during surgery, the patient's abnormal test results will be addressed and corrected. By the time the patient is finished have his surgery, he will be 'tuned up', and everything will pretty much be corrected. Sometimes, patients are so out of whack, with their hearts or labwork, that it will take a few days to address all of the problems.

As a result of pressure to save time and therefore, money, Medicare has instituted a system called DRGs. This system will only pay for a certain number of days in the Hospital for any given health problem or surgery. If the Hospital can discharge a patient 1 or 2 days earlier than the number of days paid by the patients' DRG, they are still paid for the extra days specified in the DRG. This is of course, one of many games that Hospitals play in healthcare to squeeze out more money from the federal government, and add to their bottom line. If the patient doesn't recover by the time their DRG runs out, the Hospital has to eat the cost of the extra days of hospitalization, and so, loses money on the game. The end result of all of this is that patients suffer because many of them are discharged too quickly, while they are still in need of more medical care. So, the phrase 'discharging patients quicker and sicker' in healthcare circles came about to describe this situation. Oh well.

Anyway, there are some pretty big cases on the add-on list of cases. Most of them are short cases, taking 1 to2 hours total time in the OR. But there are a couple of them that will take 3 to 4 hours to complete. One of them is a reimplantation of a penile prosthesis, and the other one is a fem-pop bypass. The penile prosthesis is going to be redone on a patient that is 84 years old so that he can have sex. Why on earth our tax money would go to a procedure such as this on a patient this old is beyond me, but it does.

This old geezer has erectile dysfunction (he can't get his penis hard to have sex), because of long standing diabetes. His wife was probably relieved when he developed this condition. Anyway, he still wanted to be able to bone the old woman, so he went to a Urologist to see what could be done about the problem. Years ago, a penile prosthesis was put into his penis. This is a fluid-filled plastic tube which is surgically placed into the penis. This tube can be filled up from a reservoir surgically placed in the lower abdomen, which he presses on to move the liquid into the penis tube, thereby causing the penis to get bigger and stiffer. It's kind of like inflating the penis. Sensation to the penis is all screwed up because of the long standing diabetes condition, and the surgical incisions required to put in the prosthesis, but the guy is able to feel like a man because he can bone the old lady once again. It's kind of sad that only by sticking his penis into the old lady's vagina can he feel manly. But this is how some men feel, how sad.

Of course, this surgery is extremely expensive, with a total cost of the surgery adding up to around $50,000. This is Surgeon's fees, equipment fees, Anesthesia fees, and Hospital fees. Apparently, the postop pain caused by the Surgeon cutting on the guy's penis doesn't really matter to him either. This redo surgery will be even more expensive, probably on the order of $75,000. The redo is being done because the old one developed a fluid leak or has a valve problem between the reservoir and the prosthesis, or whatever. The old one just doesn't work anymore, so this old man will go through all the expense and pain all over again. Medicare pays practically all the costs for this procedure. It is a shame that our tax money is misspent like this, to help maintain the sex-life of an 80 year old man. I can promise you that if Congress was populated with 95% women, instead of 95% men, the Medicare regulation paying for this shit would have never been passed.

The other long case on the add-on list is a fem-pop bypass, which will take 2-3 hours. This is done because the patient has a blocked artery, which keeps blood from reaching his lower leg and foot. If nothing is done, the lower leg and foot will die from lack of blood flow, and have to be amputated. For this surgery, the Surgeon takes a piece of blood vessel (usually saphenous vein) and sews it into the artery before and after the blockage. This is why it is called a bypass. Needless to say, the patients that have this problem are not in the best of shape, and so, many of these surgeries fail in the first day or two postop. Then, they have to have the amputation anyway. Most of these patients, because of their physical condition, don't last a year. Many are either dead, or amputated within a year of having a fem-pop bypass. Very few survive past one year. Oh, and the total costs associated with this surgery are between $100,000 and $150,000, almost all of which is paid for by our tax money. And people actually wonder why Medicare is going broke???

Anyway, it is now 11 A.M., and my cases have all just finished. I think that I will have lunch and then head on home for a nap. I always sleep better with a full stomach. Before I leave, I need to tell Jim Turner so that he will know that I am gone, and that there will only be 3 Anesthesiologists left to do the work. The work of signing the Anesthesia Records, that is. I don't know where Jim is right now, so I just call him on my cell phone. "High Jerry, what's up?" he answers. "Jim, all my cases are done, so I am going to eat lunch and then, go to the house for a nap," I tell him. He says to me "Say Jerry, can you do me a small favor before you leave?" "Sure Jim, what do you need?" I reply. I try to help Jim out as much as I can, as long as it's not too much work. "Everyone's tied up, working. Can you go to the ER and see an old lady with a broken hip before you leave? She is the latest add-on and there is no one available to go see her," he says to me. I tell him "Sure Jim, I'll go see her right now, before I have lunch." I grab an Anesthesia Record (the preop questions are on the back) and head to the ER to question the old lady. This will only take me about 5 minutes.

Entering the ER, I walk up to the secretary's desk and ask "Where's the old lady with the broken hip?" "Room 12," she says to me. I walk over to room 12 and go through the curtains at the entrance to the room. There, in front of me is a shriveled up old woman lying on the stretcher. She is nearly as pale as the white sheet that she is lying on, and looks like she weighs about 95 pounds. Her eyes are closed when I arrive. "Excuse me, ma'am, but I'm Doctor Deluna and I need to ask you some questions," I say in a loud voice. She opens her eyes, which are clear blue, and says to me "You don't have to yell at me, not all old people are deaf!" I soften my voice and say to her "I'm sorry ma'am; I'm here to ask you some questions so that we can provide safe Anesthesia for you while you get your hip fixed." "What is Anesthesia?" she asks me. "We are the people who give you medicine so that you sleep and you don't hurt while you are having surgery," I tell her. "Oh, okay," she says back to me.

I start my questioning with "Have you ever had any problems when you were put to sleep for surgery?" "I have never had any surgery before," she says to me. I am dumfounded; this woman is 84 years old and has never had surgery. This is extremely rare. I continue my questioning with "Do you have high blood pressure or any heart problems? Do you have any lung problems? Have you ever been sick?" She stops me right there by saying "Listen, Doctor, when we were young, we were too poor to be sick. We were farmers, and we didn't have money for Doctors or Hospitals." The words coming out of her mouth stun me like I was hit in the head. In this woman's day, if you got sick, you either got better or died, and that's all there was to it. "Ma'am, I still need to ask you these questions so that we can know a little bit about you," I say to try to keep the inquiry going. "Oh, all right, all right," she says impatiently to me. She answers "no" to every question that I ask her. Her mind is as sharp as a razor, and she has never been sick a day in her life. She takes no medications. She lost her balance while standing on a chair to change a burnt out light bulb in her kitchen, and fell and broke her right hip, which doesn't hurt at all right now. I am absolutely amazed at the old woman in front of me now. She says to me "Poor people can't afford to pay for all this."

I can't help myself, I tell her "Let me tell you what a poor person with no job and no car does now days. If they stub toe on the corner of their bed, they call 911 and get an ambulance to bring them to the Hospital, which costs $1,500 for the ride. They come in to the Emergency Room, which costs another $1,500 to walk through the door. They have X-rays and blood tests done, which costs another $2,000. Then, they get a shot of pain medicine and pain pills to take home with them, and they don't pay for any of it." Her jaw drops open at all that I am telling her. She is amazed at what I am telling her happens in healthcare today. She says to me "It's no wonder that the country is going broke, with all that nonsense going on. You mean to tell me that people actually do this stuff?" "Yes ma'am, it's the honest truth," I tell her. This woman is a dinosaur, a person who gets by with whatever they have. People like her just don't exist anymore. But my mother was very much like her.

I finish filling out the questions on the back of the Anesthesia Record, thank the old woman for her time, and walk out of the ER and back to the OR to put the paperwork where it goes. Even with all the stories, this whole thing took me less than 10 minutes. Now, I'll go have a free lunch and, in less than 1 hour, I'll be lying in my bed at home, taking a nap. After putting the Anesthesia Record in its folder, so that it can be found later by the CRNA who will be doing this case, I go into the dressing room to put on my street clothes. I'll have a nice lunch and then, head home.

As I am putting on my regular clothes, I am still thinking about that old woman. It's been a long time since I met anyone like her. What a tough old bird she is. Her generation took this country from horse and buggy days to jet planes and rockets to the moon. My generation accomplished improvements to the things that her generation came up with, but we didn't come up with nearly as many new things to improve the world. As for the generation following us, forget about it. They are too spoiled to inconvenience themselves for anything. About all they have come up with is rap music, what crap. With all the good musicians in the world, how is it that this shit has lasted more than 10 years. It's all our young people listen to these days. It is painfully obvious to me that our world is not improving and moving upward, but dumbing down and going down the tubes, in a hurry.

After getting dressed, I leave the dressing room and go out into the Hospital main hallway. I hang a right and head straight for the Doctor's Dining Room. After entering this dining room, the first thing that I lay my eyes on is, you guessed it, the always cheerful chef whose name I can never remember. "Well hello Doctor Deluna. My, but you are dressed sharp today," he says to me in a loud voice. It is 11:15 A.M., and there are only 4 or 5 other Doctors in this dining room, thank goodness. "Thank you. What do you have for lunch today?" I ask him. He says back to me "We have roast beef, grilled pork chops, and grilled shrimp. We have steamed asparagus, steamed carrots, and garlic mashed potatoes. What can I prepare for you today?" This guy is really good at his job. "I think I'll have the grilled shrimp and steamed asparagus," I say to him. "Very well, Doctor Deluna, I'll have it ready in 5 minutes, just have a seat," he replies.

I walk down the cafeteria-style line to get my silverware, a bottle of water, and a garden salad with which to occupy myself while I wait for the main course. After only getting a few cat naps yesterday, I am kind of spaced-out now, so I focus all of my attention on eating my salad to pass the time until the main course arrives. Just about the time I am eating my last bite of salad, the chef arrives with my meal. "Enjoy, mon capitain," he says while placing the steaming hot plate of food on the table. He must just enjoy saying that, because he does it every time.

Because I didn't get much rest yesterday, I'm kind of grumpy and I don't look around the dining room to see if there is anyone worth talking to. I just keep my head down and wolf my food down in less than 15 minutes. After I finish the last bite, I am feeling satiated and good. I get up from the table and quickly walk back out into the main hallway of the Hospital and hang a right turn to head straight to the parking deck. As I walk out of the Hospital building, I am hit in the face by a blast of hot air. Summers in South Carolina are very hot, and it is nearly high noon. I am anxious to get to my SUV and get home. After eating that great meal, I am ready for a good nap.

After climbing into my SUV, I call home to see if Shirley is there. No answer; she must still be working out at the gym, or having lunch with her friends. God, I hope she's not out shopping. That can be dangerous. Good, no answer means that I'll have the house all to myself. It'll be quiet, and I'll settle into bed for a real good nap as soon as I get there. I am really looking forward to crawling into bed and taking a nap right now. After automatically driving myself home (I don't remember anything about the drive home), I suddenly find myself pulling into the garage. Within 5 minutes of arriving at home, I have stripped out of my clothes, peed, and am crawling into my wonderful, plush bed with only my underwear on. Oh boy does this bed feel good to me right now! I am asleep in less than 5 minutes. It is 11:55 A.M., and, after 29 hours, Call is done.

Chapter Twelve

Free Time

I consider getting off work early and having the afternoon to do with as I please while everyone else is still at work, to be free time. To me, it feels luxurious to have the afternoon off to run errands, relax, or whatever. It's like a mini vacation. When I am riding around town, looking at everyone else working while I am not, it just makes me feel good. One of the perks of Anesthesia is that, after Call, you are the first person to leave work. This is true whether you work all night or not. If you don't work at all during the nighttime, and get to sleep through the night, you still get to leave work early the next day. This is one of the things I love about Anesthesia. About 1 out of 4 Calls I get to sleep at home all night; about 1 out of four Calls I have to work all night (like last night); and the other ½ of my Calls I have to work some during the night, but I get 4 to 6 hours of straight, uninterrupted sleep. Call for CRNAs is about the same, except that they have to sleep in the Hospital if they are not working. They do not get to go home and sleep in their own bed. This is Anesthesia life, it's not for everyone.

About 2:30 P.M. Shirley arrives at the house. She has spent about 2 hours having lunch with her girlfriends after working out at the gym, but she did not go shopping afterwards. Shirley sees my SUV in the garage when she pulls up in her Jag. Coming into the house, she tries to be quiet because she knows that I was on Call last night, and right now, I am probably asleep. It took her a couple years to get used to this when we first got married, but this type of schedule is very common with Anesthesia people. She is very considerate to me, and she adjusted to my work schedule. In Anesthesia, we sometimes burn the midnight oil and work during the night, but afterwards, we sleep during the daytime. After years of this work, I can take a nap at any time and any where during the day or night.

She comes into the bedroom while I'm asleep, and puts her gym bag down so quietly that I don't hear a thing. After this, she comes over to the bed and sits down next to where I am laying and starts rubbing my head gently. This, of course, wakes me up. I look up at her, blinking my eyes to clear my vision. She is smiling down at me, looking so beautiful. "Hey baby, did you work a lot last night?" she asks. "Yeah, we were busy all night," I tell her. "Are you okay, or do you need to sleep some more?" she asks me. I have actually had a good nap, so I tell her "I've slept enough, it'll just take me a few minutes to wake up good." "Oh, my poor baby," Shirley says, and leans over to give me a kiss on my head. Not only that, but she gives me a real good, tender hug.

I am in rapture, with this beautiful, blond, big-titted woman lying on top of me. She is cradling me and being so tender to me that I don't move a muscle, just lie there and enjoy all the feelings, and the moment. This is heaven. After a minute of pure bliss, I tell her "I love you Shirley." She lifts up a little so that she can look into my eyes and says "I love you too, Jerry." We both rise up and sit for a minute on the bed. What an odd-looking couple we make right now. Me, fat and pale, with mostly gray hair, dressed in my t-shirt and briefs. Shirley, dressed in a short sun dress with ample cleavage showing. She is tan as a coconut and doesn't have 1 gray hair in her blond head. Damn, but I am one lucky guy.

"Would you like a vodka and orange juice to help get you going?" Shirley asks me. This woman really knows what I need right now. I am craving a drink, but not something too heavy. A light orange juice with some Russian vodka added would just hit the spot. "That would be great honey, would you fix me one?" I ask. "I certainly will, just give me a minute," she says, and gets up from the bed and heads for the kitchen, saying "put on some pajamas," over her shoulder as she leaves me alone in the bedroom. I can hear her singing to herself as she walks to the kitchen to fix me a drink. What a wonderful wife I have.

I stand up from the bed and stretch for a minute, after which I slide my feet into my house slippers and walk to my closet to get some pajamas on. Boy, do I feel good right now, but I am craving that drink Shirley is fixing for me. Since it is summertime, I pick out a light set of green silk pajamas to put on. Last summer, when we were in San Francisco, I bought 4 sets of silk pajamas in China Town. They were cheap, but very well made by Chinese immigrants. They were working in a sweat-shop, sewing clothes to pay off their trip to the United States. So, I took advantage of the low prices for the clothes we bought and filled a suitcase with them to bring back home. That trip to San Francisco was for an Anesthesia conference, so my plane ticket, the Hotel room, and ½ of our meals was a tax write-off. Having money sure is great. And, working the system is even better.

After I put on the silk pajamas, I walk out of the bedroom, to the kitchen, where Shirley has mixed me a fresh-squeezed orange juice (no orange juice from concentrate for us) and Stolichnaya vodka drink. This is just what I need right now to start my free time off right! She hands me the drink and says "This is for my hard-working man." I take the tall tumbler from her and say "Thank you baby," then have a large swallow to quench my thirst. Man, but this drink is good! I haven't brushed my teeth since I got home earlier, so the orange juice is not a shock to my taste buds, like it would be if I had toothpaste on my tongue. Having bad breath is the reason that Shirley didn't kiss me passionately on the mouth, earlier in the bedroom, during out tender moment.

Shirley mixed this drink just right, about ¼ vodka to ¾ orange juice. The first drink of the day shouldn't be too strong, even though this Russian vodka is very smooth. "Shirley, you mix a great drink," I tell her, "Aren't you going to join me?" "No, I'm not in the mood for a mixed drink, I think I'll have a glass of white wine instead," she replies. After she pours herself a glass of wine, we both head to the living room to watch a little television on our 72 inch, high definition plasma TV. This TV is connected to a Bose surround sound system, so it really sounds great. I put the TV on a high definition movie channel, but we don't really pay much attention to it. We mostly just engage in light conversation to catch up since the last time we saw each other.

"How was you morning, dear?" I inquire. "Oh, it was nice. I had a good workout at the gym," she says, and continues "Cindy Smith and I went out to Pancho's Mexican Restaurant for lunch after the gym. We each had a large Margarita with our meal, and that's why I'm not in the mood for a mixed drink now, I guess." "Is that the new Mexican Restaurant next to the mall on the other side of town?" I ask. "Yeah, it's been open about a month I guess," she says and adds "I wanted to give it a little time to work out the kinks before I tried it out." "Yes, that's a good idea, well, how was the food?" I ask. "Really good, we both had taco salads and they were so huge that we didn't even eat half of them," she replies. She continues "The restaurant is really nice, the décor is beautiful. They had Mexican sombreros and dresses hanging up on the walls, and they even had a pretty fountain in the middle of the restaurant! They had soft Mexican music playing in the background, and the atmosphere was just great."

I have finished off my drink while we were talking about the restaurant, so I get up from the sofa to go make myself another one at the wet bar in the corner of the living room. "That sounds really nice," I tell her while pouring vodka into my glass. This next drink is going to be a little stronger I think to myself while I am preparing it. Shirley is only about halfway finished drinking her glass of white wine because she has been talking too much to drink. Plus, she is not that big a big drinker anyway. She just can't put it away like I can.

Looking at the cable TV box, I see that the time is 4:30 P.M. I have been awake for 2 hours now, and have had a very relaxing afternoon so far, but I am beginning to think about eating. I guess all this talking about restaurants and food has got me thinking about it. After I finish mixing my drink, I walk over to the sofa where Shirley is seated and say "Hey, do you want to go back to Pancho's for dinner after a while?" She says "Not really, I don't want to do Mexican twice in one day." "Do you feel like going out for dinner later, or do you want to order in or cook something?" I ask. She replies "I don't know, let me think about it for a minute." "Hey, you haven't told me anything about your Call. How was it?" she asks me. I state "It was hell." Her eyes get big and she asks "What happened?"

I proceed to tell her about some of the activities of the preceding day. I don't go into much detail, but just skim over some the things that I did, like getting my niece a job. While I am relating my Call adventures, the look on her face tells me that she is pleased by what I am telling her. All the while I am talking; I am building up to the wino story. We are having a good time, Shirley, sipping on her wine and listening; and me, with her paying me so much attention and sipping on my drink. I just love moments like this; it makes me feel so important.

About ½ way through my 2nd vodka and orange juice, I begin to tell Shirley the story about the bus hitting the crack-head wino. She is absolutely enthralled with this tale about the trauma and the things we did to keep the patient alive. The part about the Director of the Red Cross calling into the Operating Room to warn about a potential state-wide blood shortage really impressed her. She was amazed that a human sustaining all the injuries this guy did could survive at all. I tell her "You just can't kill a drunk!" This is an old Medical Truth, and I have seen it proven many times over my career. "Do you think the guy will make it?" she asks me. "I don't know. If you or I had gotten hit by that bus, we wouldn't stand a chance, we would be dead for sure, but that slime-ball might just make it," I tell her.

Shirley says "I want to see what they say about the accident in the newspaper." "You know, I'm interested to see what they have to say about it also," I add. She gets up from the sofa to go to the kitchen, where she put the newspaper when she came into the house. Before she makes 2 steps, I ask her "Would you be a dear and make me another drink?" "Sure darling, in fact, I think I'll pour myself another glass of wine while I'm in there," she says in return. I hand her the empty wine glass to go with my empty drink glass, so that she can refill them both.

I spend the 5 minutes she is gone changing the TV from the high definition movie channel to a high definition sports channel, so that I can check on baseball scores. It's good to know who won and who lost, even though I'm not much of a sports nut, so that I can converse about it at work. Doctors love to discuss sports. I guess it's because very, very few of us were actually able to be athletes. Mostly, we were the nerds in school. We were the President of the Math Club and the Chess Club in high school. And we never got laid in high school. Only the jocks did. Now, however, we Doctors are in charge and telling the former jocks what to do because we rank above them in the Medical hierarchy. I guess, in a way, Medical School is the revenge of the nerds.

Anyway, I'm kind of zoning out, not really paying any attention to the baseball scores on the TV. But, I am building up quite a thirst for my next sip of screwdriver, which Shirley should be returning with soon. And bingo, here she comes from the kitchen, holding a glass of white wine in her left hand, my drink in her right hand, and a newspaper under her arm. I take my drink gently from her hand and say "Thank you, darling," and then take a big drag from the glass. Boy, is that good. I am feeling so good and relaxed right now, it is wonderful.

Shirley bends over and puts her wine glass down on the coffee table, then sits down on the sofa. I watch her and admire her shape as she does this. Damn, but she is graceful! She unfolds the newspaper and starts scanning the front page for the article about the bus accident. "Ah hah," she exclaims when she finds it. This town doesn't have a very large daily newspaper. Shirley leans close to me and holds the paper so that I may read it at the same time. I love it when she sits close to me. This alone can get me aroused. "Wow, the guy was only 36 years old, the same age as me," she says. "Yeah, but he looks 50 and you look 26. There's a huge difference in your life style, and how you take care of yourself," I say to her.

Even though I am reading the newspaper article with her, she still reads parts of it to me anyway. "It says that he smelled of alcohol. Was he drunk when he got hit?" she asks. I reply "He was as drunk as a skunk. They just can't say that he was drunk because they don't have a blood alcohol level at the accident scene for proof. Trust me, he was way drunk." "Do you think that's why he got hit by the bus?" Shirley asks me. "I think that he had other drugs in his system, on top of a lot of alcohol, and he probably didn't even know where in the hell he was," I reply. "How sad it will be, if he dies at age 36. It's just throwing your life away," Shirley says. "That's true," I reply. Shirley says "The paper says that he had a criminal record 24 pages long." I reply "Yes, if he was awake, he was up to no good. This guy has already cost the state of South Carolina more than a million dollars in court and incarceration costs before this accident." There is no denying it. I lean over and give her a big hug. She appreciates this because she is feeling kind of sad for this slime ball. I'm doing it mostly because I love feeling her big tits pressing against me, and I know that it will make her feel that I am in touch with her sad feelings, which makes her feel better. It's all good.

It is now 5:30 in the afternoon, I've just finished my 3rd drink, and I'm kind of tired just sitting around, talking. Plus, I'm getting pretty hungry. My 11 A.M. lunch is long gone by now. I say to Shirley "Do you feel like going out to get something to eat? I'm getting kinda hungry." "Yeah, I could go for a bite, I guess," she replies. "What are you in the mood to eat?" I ask. She says "Well, I just had some taco salad for lunch, and I could go for something heavier for dinner. Do you feel like steak or Italian?" "Hm, choices, choices. I'll have to think about this for a second," I say to her. This is a tough decision, I like steaks, but Italian food is my favorite of all. I finally make a decision. "Hell, let's go to Outback Steakhouse. They have excellent steaks, plus, they squeeze the juice from the oranges right there to mix with the vodka for your drink," I say to Shirley. "Oh, that's a good idea. I just love their shrimp," she says. I say "Well, it's all set then. I just have to take a quick shower and get dressed." She says "I just have to freshen up my makeup and I want to change clothes."

In a flash, we both get up from the sofa and walk quickly to the bedroom to go to our separate closets and bathrooms. We are on a mission, because if you get to Outback very late, you have to wait quite a while for a table. The restaurant gets very busy after 8 P.M. I hope to get home fairly early so that I can get to bed early and get a good night's rest tonight; because I have not had a good night's rest in 2 days.

I step into my closet and strip out of my pajamas and underwear in seconds, throwing all my clothes on the floor (the maid will pick them up tomorrow). Quickly I walk into my bathroom and decide not to take the time to brush my teeth; I'll just gargle with some mouthwash which I can spit in the shower. That way I'll have fresh breath and Shirley will give me a passionate kiss. I jump into the shower after taking a large mouth full of mouthwash and flip on the water by pushing a button for a quick shower. This shower has 6 preprogrammed settings for different kinds of showers, from a quick, short shower, to a long, massaging shower. In 6 minutes, I am done in the shower and drying off. Then, I head back into my closet to get dressed.

After I am all dressed and ready to go, I walk out of my closet and look at the alarm clock on the night stand next to the bed. It is 5:50 P.M. and I am ready to leave the house and head to the restaurant. Shirley is ready to go as well, and boy, does she look nice. She has on a gray silk blouse which is unbuttoned a bit at the top, to show off her wonderful cleavage. In addition, she is wearing a tight-fitting pair of slacks, which show off her lovely ass perfectly.

We are out of the house before 6 P.M., and will be at the restaurant by 6:15. This is good because the restaurant opens at 5P.M., and it gets so busy so fast, that if you arrive after 7 P.M., you will probably have to wait for a while to get a table. Outback is a very popular restaurant in Ashburg, and it does a very good business. On the way to the restaurant, we talk about the upcoming weekend. We are going to leave town Friday afternoon and go to the beach house. It will be a nice, relaxing time to be lazy, have a few drinks, and eat some really good seafood. Because it is summertime, the beach will be full of people, but our house is right on the water. So we have our own piece of the beach. No one is allowed to set up a party or cookout on our section of beach, we kind of have it to ourselves because other people only walk through our section of the beach. This is a nice setup.

It is now 6:12, and we are pulling into a parking space at the restaurant. Looking around, I can see that the parking lot is nearly full already. I get out of the SUV and walk around the back of it to open Shirley's door and assist my queen out of the carriage. She is exactly the same height as me, but ½ as wide. I feel great as the 2 of us walk into the place. After we get inside, I look around and see that there are only a few tables not occupied already. We got here just before business really picks up. In 1 hour from now, this place will be full and there will be 10-20 people waiting to get a table. We follow the hostess to a booth and sit down. I like a booth at restaurants like this one; I find them cozier for just the 2 of us. It is 6:15 P.M. and we are seated in the restaurant, whew.

A cute, young girl dressed in the Outback uniform comes up to us and asks if we would like anything to drink. Shirley orders a glass of Chardonnay, and I order a Stolichnaya and orange juice. I may as well stick with what I have already been drinking today. They make these drinks really good here because they have a machine to juice the orange into your glass, fresh, and then, they add the vodka and ice cubes. There is nothing like fresh-squeezed orange juice in a drink; it's the best.

Shirley and I look over the menu while we wait for our drinks to arrive. We decide against appetizers, and just go for Caesar salads before our main course. Our waitress comes to our booth with our drinks and asks us if we have decided on what we'd like to eat. I tell her "We have." And we proceed to order 2 salads, a filet mignon for me, and coconut shrimp for Shirley. The waitress asks me "How would you like your steak sir?" "Medium well done," I reply. "Very good," she says, and picks up our menus and hurries off to place our order. This place does a high-volume business, and they won't waste a lot of time getting your food to you. This is fine with me because I am really hungry now. I hold up my glass and say to Shirley "Let's make a toast to free time off." Shirley clinks her wine glass against my glass and says "Here, here," and we both have a drink.

Shirley and I enjoy our drinks and talk about how nice it will be having walks on the beach at sunset this weekend for a few minutes before our waitress returns with a loaf of brown bread and butter. I order another drink at this time, because I am nearly finished with the first one. These things are just so good. We slice off some of the bread and paint it with butter to munch on while we drink and wait for our salads. Our waitress is really good. In the past 10 minutes, she has brought me another Stoli and OJ, and delivered our Caesar salads. This girl is going to get a good tip tonight.

I enjoy spending time with Shirley like this, having drinks, eating, and talking. She is good to talk to and so nice to look at, all at the same time. It's all good. Within 2 minutes of us finishing our salads, our waitress arrives with our meals. Shirley has 6 very large shrimp on a bed of rice on her plate, and I have a nice filet with mashed potatoes on mine. I order another drink for myself and another glass of wine for Shirley before the waitress leaves. We both pounce on our food like we have not eaten a thing all day.

We both have a good time eating and drinking and talking for about 30 minutes. And then, we are done with our meal. After this, we pay our bill and walk out of the restaurant at 7:30 P.M., not bad. In a little over an hour after walking into the place, we are done eating and drinking and walking out. This is a very efficient operation. The only problem with this restaurant is that you have to get here early, before they get too busy. The drinks were very good, and the food was very good also. All this, and we got out of here for less than $100. You can't beat that. As soon as we leave the parking lot, Shirley leans over and snuggles next to me, exclaiming "Boy, do I feel good." I reply "I feel good too, babe." This is so nice, we'll be home in about 15 minutes, but I am in heaven right now because Shirley is rubbing my penis through my pants.

After we pull into the garage, I turn off the engine and lower the garage door. And then, I walk around the SUV to open Shirley's door for her and assist her out of the Benz. She stands up, pulls me to her and gives me a very passionate kiss, squeezing my ass at the same time. I am really getting hard as she presses her body into mine. After a minute of this, she pulls her tongue out of my mouth, looks into my eyes and asks me "Hey, big boy, you want to fool around?" "Hell, yes," I reply. We break apart and hold hands as we walk quickly into the house.

Chapter Thirteen

Booty Call

After we get to the bedroom, Shirley says "I'll see you back here in a minute," and heads to her closet. I go through my closet to my bathroom, throwing my clothes on the floor as I go. Right now I am in a big hurry to pee, wipe clean, and be back in the bed, naked, as quickly as possible.

In a flash, I am naked and back in bed because I am looking forward to what is coming next. I am rock hard in anticipation. It has been a week since we have made love. The 2 lamps on the nightstands on either side of the bed are set low, so that there is just enough light in the bedroom, but not too much. The door to Shirley's closet opens and she comes out dressed in a very short, see-through nightie, and nothing else! She slinks over to the bed, pulls the covers off of me, looks at my erection, smiles, and says "Are you happy to see me?" I reply "Yes darling." She lies down next to me in the bed and we start making out like we are in heat. The temperature is very cool in this bedroom, but it is rapidly heating up in here.

While we are kissing, I am busy with one hand undoing the nightie, so that I can take it completely off her. I like seeing her in sexy outfits, but I love the feel of her bare skin against mine. My other hand is caressing her ass, kneading it gently. Shirley loves this.

Her buns are so firm; she has a perfect, tight, pecan-shaped ass. After I finally get the nightie undone and off of her, I pull her closer to fully feel her body against mine. She is holding my penis tightly between her legs while we kiss and nibble on each others' lips. After a few minutes of this, she breaks off with the kissing and leans back a little, then cups her large breast and holds it up for me, so that I can suck on her nipple.

Shirley is really getting into this. She is moaning like crazy while I suck and nibble gently on her nipple. The whole time she is busy rubbing her clit back and forth on my penis, humping it while she is holding onto it tightly between her legs. This is feeling really fantastically hot to me. All of a sudden, Shirley tightens up her body and says "Oh, oh, I'm coming." The friction on my penis is simply too much, and 2 seconds later, I am coming as well. Inside, I am cursing myself for not hanging on longer so that I could get a little deeper than the outside of her vagina. I am really pissed at myself for this premature ejaculation. Damn it.

After we catch our breath a minute, Shirley asks me "Did you come too? You must have, because I feel sticky stuff all over my leg." I reply "Yeah, I came a little sooner than I wanted to. It was just too hot for me to hold on." "Oh, my poor baby," Shirley says to me and hugs me close, her big tits pressing into me. This, of course, makes everything better. "I'm sorry for you, but I got off really good babe," she says to me. "I'm glad. I love to please you," I tell her. I really mean this, pleasing Shirley is very important to me.

We hold this tender moment for a little while, then she says "I've got to go to the bathroom and clean up this sticky stuff," "Okay babe," I say. She gives me a quick kiss on the lips, and then gets up from the bed and walks off to her bathroom to clean up. After she leaves the bed, I am thinking to myself, well, it wasn't my best performance, but the result was good for me. The release of tension did me a world of good. There is no such thing as bad sex to a man. When it comes to sex, for a man, it's all good.

I am kind of bummed out at the way things went, but the end result was satisfactory. Premature ejaculation happens to me 2 or 3 times a year. Shirley just gets me so excited that I can't hold back from time to time. I think that if we had sex more than once a week, I could hold on longer. This was not one of my better performances. Oh well. Right now, I am very tired, so I lean over to set the alarm clock, pull up the covers over me and settle into the bed to go to sleep. Tonight, I hope that I get some good rest. I really need a good night of sleep.

A few minutes later, I am almost asleep, when Shirley comes back into the bed. She has pajamas on now, and snuggles up next to me and says "I love you Jerry," and then gives me a hug. I reply "I love you too Shirley," and lean back to put my arm around her and return her hug a little. Then, I roll back over and close my eyes. What a great wife I have. I am a lucky man.

With Shirley right next to me in the bed, I'm feeling all warm and fuzzy right now. I've had a good afternoon, with plenty of time to relax and get over yesterday's Call. We went out and had a few drinks and a good meal. During the afternoon and evening, we had some good conversation and made plans for going to the beach house this weekend. That is something I will look forward to until we leave for the beach on Friday. We had some sex when we got back from the restaurant. All in all, it has been a good day.

Well, I better shut my eyes and turn off my brain so that I can go to sleep and be well-rested for Call tomorrow. One more day of Call, and then, I will be first off on Friday. That will give us an early start on leaving to go to the beach house. When the sun rises, it'll be another day.

Chapter Fourteen

6 A.M. Thursday-Call Day

Ring! Ring! Damn that alarm clock, I think as I roll over to turn the cursed thing off. Shit, it's already time to get up and go to work again. And I was sleeping so good. Oh well, duty calls. I roll out of bed and slowly hoist myself erect. Man, but it sucks getting old. Whoever said these were the golden years was a lying son-of-a-bitch. My joints are stiff and I have to struggle at first to stand upright. After a minute, I slide my feet into my house shoes and look over at Shirley. She is sleeping like a baby. How lucky she is that she doesn't have to wake up early to an alarm clock every day. She is so beautiful, lying there; it just takes my breath away.

I turn and shuffle off to the kitchen to begin my daily routine. Before I reach the kitchen door, my nose detects the smell of coffee. Boy, I hope that coffee maker never breaks down because I rely on it to do its job every morning. First, I pour myself a ¾ cup of coffee, then I turn on the TV to watch the local news while I pour a shot of brandy into the cup. Then comes the ice cube to cool it down so that I can drink it quicker. After I sit down and take a good swallow of coffee, so that I can focus on the television news program in front of me, I notice a bunch of people yelling and complaining about a city bus driver not doing his job right while he was driving.

It finally dawns on me, after a couple of sips of coffee and a few seconds. This news program was taped yesterday, and all of the people cussing and yelling about the city and the bus driver are the family of the crack-head wino who we tried to keep alive, day before yesterday. They are yelling, cursing, and complaining as fast as they can possibly speak. The city of Ashburg is responsible for their family member's death because they don't screen and train the city bus drivers properly. The bus driver is responsible because he wasn't paying attention while he was driving. The local Hospital was responsible because they didn't do everything possible to save his life. The surgeon is responsible because he missed something and didn't do what he was supposed to do to keep the guy from dying. Absolutely everyone on earth that they can think of is responsible for the death of their family member except the guy who was on drugs and drunk and stepped out in front of a bus because he didn't look first. Of course, they have a lawyer with them on TV who is trying to settle them down, unsuccessfully.

The survival skill of looking both ways before you cross the street is usually well ingrained in children by the time they are 6 years old. Mothers, since horse and buggy days, have taught this skill without fail to all children in this country. It's just one of the most basic skills to keep from dying by way of stupidity. Don't walk off of a cliff; don't run into a brick wall; look both ways before you cross the street. If you can't figure these simple things out, you are too stupid to live very long. And yet, here on my TV, is a lawyer and this bunch of idiots telling everyone about all the people they are going to sue because their family member stepped in front of a moving bus and got killed. Well, I guess the shit-head didn't make it. Even after everything we did to try to save his life. Now, we will be punished by the family's lawyer for working like dogs, trying to save the sack of shit's life. Great.

I just shake my head in disbelief at the circus on the TV in front of me as I finish off my first cup of coffee and brandy. It just proves the old adage, no good deed goes unpunished. What kind of stupid-assed shit is this anyway? If anybody in that crack-head's family had a job, they wouldn't have the time to make an ass out of themselves on TV to begin with. This crap will be on the local news for the next month. God help anyone who didn't do his job perfectly, because this family's lawyer will crucify them in the upcoming witch hunt. The idea of being thankful to those who worked hard to try to save their family member's life will never enter these people's mind. The idea of someone taking personal responsibility for not looking and stepping in front of a bus because they were on drugs and alcohol will never enter these people's mind. I swear the whole world is ass backwards and upside down.

I get up from the chair to make myself another cup of coffee and brandy while these idiots are still raving and ranting on the TV. It is a sad world that we live in, where such things as this can happen. After I put an ice cube into my coffee cup, I sit down to watch the TV and hope that something else will come on the news soon. Finally, the news switches to car wrecks and convenience stores getting robbed, the normal stuff. This kind of tragedy and disaster I can handle. Sure enough, some poor clerk got shot when the convenience store he worked in got robbed. This type of thing used to be rare, 20 years ago. But now, this stuff happens so often that Americans have gotten used to hearing about it, so much so, that many people think that it is normal to have this sort of violence in our society. If the criminals doing all this robbing and killing would be put in prison and kept in prison, this type of thing wouldn't happen very much after a while. But the courts let them off with light sentences, and most of them go right out and do the same thing again when they get out of jail.

After watching the local news for about 20 minutes, I have finished off my 2nd cup of coffee, and I can't watch any more of this crap. My temper is rising right now, and so is my blood pressure as I watch this. So, I get up and make my 3rd cup of coffee and brandy and walk out of the kitchen to go to my bathroom and start my morning ritual. As I walk through the bedroom, I look at Shirley lying there, still asleep, and still beautiful. The picture she makes, lying there, makes me sigh. I am thinking that I am one lucky guy as I walk into the bathroom for my daily shit, shave, and shower. In that order.

After finishing in the bathroom and getting dressed in a nice dress shirt and khaki pants, I come out of my walk-in closet and look at my alarm clock. Last night I slept really good; it must have been the sex. The time is 6:45 A.M. and I am feeling pretty good and well-rested and all ready to head to work. I have finished my 3rd cup of coffee, my head is clear, and I have breath mints in my SUV. All I have left to do here is put my coffee cup back in the kitchen and give Shirley a kiss before I leave. As I walk through the bedroom to go put my empty cup back in the kitchen, I glance over at Shirley. She is still in exactly the same position that I last saw her in when I came through here 30 minutes ago. Man, it must be nice to sleep that soundly.

After I put my coffee cup on the kitchen counter, I retrace my steps back to the bedroom. I never leave the house without giving Shirley a kiss. As I walk into the bedroom, I notice that she has shifted her position, just a little, since the last time I looked at her. I lean over her and give her a kiss on the lips, then move up to her ear, and softly tell her "Bye darling, I'm going to work now. I am on Call today, so I won't see you until tomorrow." She opens her eyes halfway, looks at me and says "I love you Jerry." After which she collapses back into the bed covers. "I love you too Shirley," I reply. She makes me sigh.

I walk quickly out of the house and into the garage, where my SUV is waiting for me like a faithful horse. As I slide myself into the padded leather seat, I reach out with my right hand to open the console and retrieve a breath mint. The door of this baby always shuts with a solid-sounding thunk. I hit the button to open the garage door and start up the V8 motor at the same time. Putting the transmission in reverse, I slowly begin to back out into the real world. You have to give the garage door time to open up, and it is slow. Slower than this rocket SUV, anyway. After backing out into the turn around, I put the transmission into drive and gun the engine, just a little, and this sled leaps forward as I fly down my driveway. And off I go to work.

As I drive to the Hospital this morning, I notice that there are several new fast food restaurants which have opened. I don't know why I didn't notice them before. Oh well. This morning, the drive to work takes me 10 minutes, a little quicker that usual. By 6:57, I am driving past the cross bar and entering the parking deck. This means that I will be standing in front of the assignment board at 7 A.M., on the dot. Some people will be in shock that the work assignments are made on time, for a change. Oh well, it's good to keep them on their toes, and good to keep them guessing.

After making the Anesthesia personnel work assignments, I walk back through the Surgeon's Lounge to go to the Doctor' Dressing Room so that I can take off my street clothes and dress in a scrub suit. After I have put on my scrub suit, I am hanging my regular clothes in my locker when Doctor Arnash (Hindu Indian Anesthesiologist) comes out of the bathroom. He has been washing his face in the lavatory to wake up and get ready for today's fun and games. "Good morning Jerry," he says to me. "Good morning Arnash, how was your Call?" I ask. He relates the following to me.

"Well, we finished up the surgical schedule about 6 P.M., so I got to go home and have dinner. I enjoyed some time after dinner with my family, and then, went to bed early to get some sleep at 8 P.M. About midnight, I got a call to come in for a case. The case was removal of FB (foreign body) from rectum. This guy had been having kinky sex with his girlfriend last night. She had been doing his ass with a dildo, but the dildo slid all the way into his rectum and they couldn't get it out. Neither one of these people had a car, so the guy had to get on a bicycle and ride it to the Hospital with the dildo stuck up his ass. They live 20 miles from the Hospital, so it took him a little over an hour to ride the bicycle all the way here!"

I am staring at Arnash as he is telling me this, my mouth open in disbelief. This is one hell of a story. He continues "We got the guy to sleep about 1 A.M. After he was asleep, I placed my hand on his stomach, and I could feel that vibrator. After all the kinky sex, riding the bicycle for over an hour to get here, and being put to sleep, the thing was still vibrating! They must have used good batteries! Doctor Barns was on Call, so he came in after the patient was asleep and paralyzed. He stuck his whole hand up into the guy's rectum, so he could grab it and pull it out, but it was too slippery and he couldn't get the damn thing out. He tried and he tried, but he just couldn't get it out."

This story is getting better by the minute, I am thinking. Doctor Arnash continues, "Doctor Barns had to cut the guy's belly open, cut his rectum, and pull the damn vibrator out of him that way. The thing was still vibrating! He turned it off when he finally got it out. They must have put in fresh batteries before they started with the kinky sex. This guy ended up with a big operation. He has a 6 inch incision on his belly, and he has a colostomy now."

The bowel (large and small intestine) is full of bacteria. So, in an emergency case where you have to cut it open, such as this, the patient ends up with a colostomy. After some time, the colostomy can be taken down and the hole in the belly closed up. This happens after the gut has had a chance to heal and the infection from releasing all the bacteria inside the belly has been controlled. Of course, this requires 2 separate surgeries. In between the 2 surgeries, the patient has to wear a colostomy bag on his side, which collects all his feces. This plastic bag has to be emptied, by hand, several times a day.

This patient will now have to spend several days in the Hospital to get pain medication, antibiotics, and heal up a little before he is discharged home. I almost hate to ask, but I can't help myself, "Say Arnash, does this guy happen to have insurance?" "Ha," Arnash says, and follows with "He is unemployed and does not have any insurance. But he and his girlfriend had money for the drugs and alcohol they were taking while they were having sex." "Shit," I exclaim.

The icing on this shit cake will be if she ends up pregnant from last night's sexscapades, and comes into the ER 9 months from now, in labor.

Of course, she will not have seen an OB/GYN, and will have had no prenatal care. A lot of unemployed people breed like rabbits because they have a lot of time on their hands. They also have plenty of energy for sex because they are not tired from working. Forget about going to the Health Department and getting free birth control, they can't be bothered with such an inconvenience.

Unfortunately, we see some guy with a dildo, flashlight, salt shaker, or whatever, up his ass about once a year at this Hospital. Most of the time, the FB can be removed from their rectum by hand, in the OR, without having to have abdominal surgery, like this unlucky fool. In the majority of these cases, the patient has no insurance, even if they happen to have a job. So, once again, the lucky taxpayers get to pick up the tab for this crazy shit. Why don't they at least tie a string on the end of the thing, so that they can pull it out if it slips away and goes all the way up into the rectum??

"Damn, Arnash, this didn't keep you up all night, did it?" I ask. "Oh, no, it only took a couple hours to do that case. We finished up with that about 3 A.M., but after that, we had to do a C-section. That finished up about 4:30 A.M., so I just took a nap on the sofa in the lounge until people started arriving for the day shift. Elizabeth (the CRNA on Call with him) took her nap on the recliner," he says to me. For the 2 of them, it wasn't worth going home for 1 hour or 1 ½ hours, just to have to turn around and come back in for today's work. This type of thing (work schedule hours, not the particular case) happens all the time in Anesthesia. This is another reason why a career in Anesthesia is not for everyone.

My cell phone is going off. I have lost track of time, listening to this crazy story that Arnash has been telling me. I hold up my finger to Arnash and tell him "One second." Opening the cell phone to take the call, I say "Yes," and hear the Nurse on the other end say "Ready for you in OR 5 Doctor Deluna." "I'll be there in a minute," I reply. "Thank you," she says, and then hangs up. The start of the case is a very busy time for a circulator Nurse. I tell Arnash "As soon as we can, I'll get you and Elizabeth out of here. Hopefully you'll be home before lunch time." "Okay chief," he says back to me. In the world of Anesthesia, that's the best we can do. I turn to head out of the dressing room and go to OR 5. The time is now 7:20 A.M. Let the day begin.

The case in OR 5 is a big vascular stenting case, which will get me lots of Medicare units. These cases are big money-makers for everyone involved in them. Everyone being the Hospital, the Surgeon, and the Anesthesiologist. The OR staff and the CRNAs make the same hourly wage for these cases that they would make doing a toe surgery. The work load and stress of these cases is much greater for them than a toe case, however. The pay for the Hospital OR staff doesn't rise and fall with the complexity of any case that they do. The money for the Hospital, the Surgeon, and the Anesthesiologist does, however. Greatly.

As I enter OR 5, I loudly say "Turn up that temperature, it's too cold in her." Sound familiar? I nod at Bob, to begin giving the induction drugs, and walk over to the OR table so I can look into the patient's face and say "I'm Doctor Deluna, I'm here now, and I'm going to get you off to sleep now." I told you this job is very repetitious. Within 15 seconds, the patient is unconscious. "Have you recovered from our Call the other night?" I ask Bob. "Not completely, I don't recover as quickly as I used to," he says to me. "I know what you mean. At least you are on Call only once a week," I say back to him. "And that's a good thing," he replies. Bob has such a sense of humor. As he is placing the ET tube in the patient, I walk over to the Anesthesia machine to sign the Anesthesia Record, when my cell phone goes off again. "Doctor Deluna, can I help you?" I say. "We are ready for you in OR 4," the Nurse says to me. "I'll be right there," I reply.

It takes me 3 seconds to walk out of OR 5 and walk over to OR 4, where a total knee replacement will take place. One old patient, the other day, asked me "Why do we have to get our hip joints and knee joints replaced nowadays?" I answer "Well, 100 years ago, in 1909, the life expectancy in the United States was only about 46 years. But today, the life expectancy in this country is close to 90 years, so we wear out our hearts, our knees, and our hip joints. It used to not be a problem because we didn't live long enough to wear these body parts out." The old patient responded with "Oh, that makes sense." This made sense to the old woman because it is true.

I walk into OR 4, and it feels like I walked into an oven. The heat has been turned way up in this room. Joe, the CRNA in this room, has worked here for more than 10 years. He knows my games very well. Looking over at him, I can see the grin on his face, despite the face mask he has on. "Good morning Doctor Deluna, how are you?" he asks me. "Very well, thank you," I reply. Joe says to me "Mrs. Muldoon is 90 years old and she was cold, so we turned up the temperature a little for her." I am grinning behind my mask also, because I know the game that he is playing with me. He had the circulator Nurse crank the temp way up, so that I couldn't come into the OR and tell them to make the room warmer. The 90 year old patient is happy as a clam right now because, up until now, she has been cold the entire time that she has been in this Hospital.

I walk over to Mrs. Muldoon and ask her "Are you comfortable my dear?" She replies "Oh, yes. It feels nice in here. Why do they keep the rest of this Hospital so cold?" "I just don't know," I reply. This little old lady's mind is as sharp as they come. She tells me "I've hardly ever been sick a day in my life, but I'm getting old now and my bones are giving out on me." "All right now, you're going to take a nap now, and when you wake up, you'll have a new knee," I say to her. She is already unconscious. Joe is putting the ET tube down her throat in 1 minute. After this, he connects the breathing circuit to the ET tube, turns on the ventilator to breathe for her and flips on the vaporizer to keep her asleep. Joe is so experienced, and so smooth and quick at his job, that taking the patient from awake and talking, to asleep, paralyzed, intubated, and mechanically ventilated, takes less than 3 minutes. The patient is now on cruise control. Watching the blood pressure and heart rate continuously is the main function of the CRNA from now until the end of the case.

After I sign the Anesthesia Record, I ask Joe "How are you doing?" He replies "Great, hey, how are you doing?" I tell Joe "I'm doing good." He says to me "I heard about that wino trying to stop that bus accident a couple of days ago when you were on Call. It sounded bad, I'm sure glad that I missed that one." "Yeah, that was a train-wreck, you lucked out because you weren't on Call with me that night," I say back. "Yes, thank you Jesus," Joe says, and laughs. I turn to walk out of OR 4 and run into Doctor Danny May (Orthopedic Surgeon who worked on the wino case) in the hallway. This total knee replacement is his case. He is getting ready to wash his hands at the scrub sink.

"High Danny, how are you doing?" I ask him. He replies "High Jerry, I'm doing well. What's shaking?" Danny is a very lively guy. He likes to ride his bicycle, and probably rides it 50 miles a week. I say to him "I heard the crack-head wino from the other night didn't last very long after leaving the OR." Danny says "Yeah, the poor bastard went into pulmonary edema in the ICU, and died about 4 hours after getting there." "That pulmonary edema is a real killer," I say to him. "You got that right, brother," he replies to me. "Well, you have a nice day, okay," I say. "You do the same," he says back. Danny is a real nice guy, and an excellent Surgeon. I know it bothers him to have a patient die after working like a dog most of the night trying to put him back together. The fact that he'll no doubt be included in the family's lawsuit does not bother him. He just considers it part of the job of working in medicine in this modern world.

The other cases that I am supervising this morning consist of a C-section upstairs (I don't have to do a thing for that one), and a General Surgery OR (OR 6) that has done a gallbladder and a hernia repair (on 2 different patients) so far this morning. Most of the patients in OR 6 this morning have private insurance, so I'll do alright there. Actually, I am supervising a 2nd C-section upstairs right now. Will, the CRNA who did the first C-section, did the case and brought me the Anesthesia Record to sign about 30 minutes ago. Right after he came down from doing the first one, he got a call that they needed to do another one. After he filed the paperwork for the first one, he took a little break and then, went back upstairs to do the 2nd one. What a trooper.

It is now 9:30 A.M., and things are going smoothly in the OR. The mornings are usually very busy, but things slow down after lunch time. After 3 P.M. they usually slow way down. It is rare that we have more than 2 or 3 surgical cases going on after 5 P.M. I am caught up on all my Anesthesia Record signing, so I'll go back to the Surgeon's Lounge and make a cup of coffee. If there is anyone else drinking coffee in the lounge, I'll have someone to talk to. If not, I'll just kick back in a recliner and watch the 24 hour news channel to catch up on current events. It's a tough job, but someone's got to do it.

There happens to be no one else in this lounge right now. So, after making myself a hot cup of Columbian coffee, I settle back in a recliner to watch the news. After a few minutes, Jim Turner comes into the lounge to make himself a cup of coffee. He greets me with a big smile and says "Good morning, Jerry. How's everything going?" "Everything is going just great right now," I reply. He says to me "Hey, did you hear the terrible news about what happened to that lady at the lumber yard yesterday?" I say to him, "No, tell me what happened." We are all gossip hounds.

In Ashburg, we have 1 large lumber yard. They sell many other things besides lumber. There is a large building where they sell all sorts of things like lamps, mail boxes, nails, screws, and a thousand other items. I bought a gas bar-b-Q grill there just last summer.

The place is a very big store, with an 8 acre parking lot.

Jim takes a sip of his coffee and then proceeds to tell me the story, "A middle-aged woman was in the store, looking at lamps. There was no store clerk waiting on her. She was just by herself, looking at some lamps, when she had a heart-attack and fell on the floor. One of the other customers, an old man, saw it and went to get a store clerk to get some help for her. By the time they returned, there were 3 other customers standing around, just looking at her. Nobody there knew CPR, so they didn't do anything to or for her. The store clerk went to get his manager, who just went over to look at the woman. He didn't do anything for her, just went to call 911 to get an ambulance on the way to the store for her. She had had a heart-attack, and wasn't breathing. By the time the ambulance arrived, she was as dead as a hammer from the heart-attack. She had been lying there 15-20 minutes by this time, and no one there lifted a finger to do anything for her. The EMS guy asked why nobody did CPR on her. All of them said that they were afraid of being sued, so they didn't touch her. Can you believe that? There were 7 people there, and they all just sat around and watched her die, without helping, because they were afraid of being sued!!"

As Jim is telling me this story, I am consumed by feelings of sadness. It is a sad statement about our country when someone will fall down, dying, and no one will try to help or even provide comfort to them because they are afraid of some lawyer suing them. What a sad, sad day in America. I am saddened by this story, but I am not very surprised. Things have been heading in this direction for some time in this country. I remember the first time I went to New York City, about 20 years ago. I was walking on the sidewalk, looking at all the tall buildings and sights, when I came upon someone lying on the sidewalk, not moving. The sidewalks were full of people, walking quickly in all directions, but not one person stopped to help him. They just kept on walking and went around him, like he wasn't even there. I remember seeing that scene and thinking that this would never happen in a small town in America. I remember thinking that these big city people are just cold and uncaring. Well now, thanks to the lawyers suing people to death, this type of thing has come to small town America.

After Jim finishes the story, he asks me "Can you believe something like that would happen here in Ashburg?" I reply "Unfortunately, yes. This country is going to shit. Everyone is so afraid of being sued that soon, nobody will be doing anything at all, and the whole country will come to a standstill." I continue "Just look at all the unnecessary lab work that is ordered by the Doctors here on all these patients. They are so afraid that they will miss some minute detail, that they order every test that they can possibly think of, to avoid being sued. And they still get sued." It's crazy, but it's true. Jim has a troubled look on his face and says to me "Yeah, I guess that is true. But this story troubles me, and it makes me sad that something like this would happen in our small town." "It makes me sad also Jim," I reply.

Jim Turner and I are both feeling kind of sad after talking about yesterday's tragedy, when I get a call from a Nurse in Same Day Surgery, "Good morning Doctor Deluna, this is Nancy in Same Day Surgery. We had a patient here for a cystoscopy that owed you a past due bill for $50. He is Dan Jones' father-in-law." (Dan is a scrub tech in this OR. A scrub tech is the person in the OR at the surgeon's side, who hands scalpels, suture, and instruments to the surgeon during the case) Immediately I inquire "What do you mean, had a patient?" "Well, he just left SDS for the OR," she replies. "How did he get away from there before you could call me?" I ask. She answers "Well, the new CRNA Gene, didn't know that we are supposed to hold patients that owe you a past due bill over here until they can make payment arrangements. He is quick on his feet, and he just took the patient to the OR before we knew that he was going." "Damn," I reply.

There is no better time to collect a past due bill than when a patient is in pain, or in need of surgery. We have taught the Nurses in Same Day Surgery over the years to call us as soon as they discover a patient that owes me money on a past due bill. Patients in pain or in need of surgery are highly motivated to pay you an old bill when they realize that they will not get the healthcare they need until this problem is resolved. They or their relatives will magically come up with the money, all of a sudden, to pay off an old debt to Ashburg Anesthesia Associates. Or else, they will not have the surgery that they need today.

Well, this one almost got away from me, but they didn't quite make it. I hang up with Nancy and call the Urology OR. "Do you have a patient on the OR table named James Jones?" I ask. The Nurse answers "Yes sir, we do." "Well, pack him up and bring him back to Same Day Surgery because he owes me a past due bill," I tell her. "Alright Doctor Deluna, will do," she answers back to me.

The Circulator Nurse in Urology and the CRNA will move the patient from the OR table back to the stretcher that he was on and roll him back to Same Day Surgery. Once the patient and his family realizes that he will not be able to have his procedure done today until someone pays me the past due bill, they will cough up the $50 and settle this debt.

All I have to do now is wait a little while until the magic happens. I have done this exact thing many times during my career. You don't get to live in a million dollar house by giving away free services. Over the years, I have learned that there is no better time to squeeze someone's balls than when they are over a barrel.

This type of action really screws over the patient, the patient's surgeon, and the Hospital. Not only does the patient not get the procedure that he is here for, his surgeon doesn't get to make his money from the case either. Also, the Hospital doesn't get to charge the patient for the procedure and, if hospitalization is necessary, the following hospital stay afterwards. You just can't let people get away with shit. I don't really care if this tarnishes the Hospital's reputation in this community either. This is the way that I have operated here for 2 decades, and if anyone gets pissed about it, too bad, I don't care. There is not a damn thing that anyone can do about it anyway. I own the only Anesthesia practice in this town, and I am king of this hill.

Chapter Fifteen

Lunch Time

The time is now 10:30 A.M., and I am feeling tired after all the work that I have done so far today. The work, and listening to Jim's sad story. I get up from the recliner and go to the coffee machine to make myself another cup of that wonderful, strong Columbian. In about a minute, the machine has done its job and gives me a hot, fresh brewed cup of coffee. The caffeine in this stuff really keeps me going. After adding some half-and-half to smooth it out and cool it down, I walk back to the recliner to watch the news on TV.

Even though I have been sitting in this chair for over an hour, I haven't had a chance to watch the news very much because of the constant distractions. Some Senator is on the TV talking about how the federal government is going to improve healthcare. What a crock of shit. In the past 2 plus decades that I have been in medicine, every time that the government gets involved in healthcare, 3 things have happened without fail. First, is more and more paperwork is generated; 2nd, the cost of care goes up, a lot. And 3rd, the efficiency (how fast you can get care to the people in need of it, and how much care you can deliver to the people in need of it) of the healthcare system goes down, a lot. Despite a history of this happening over and over, they are at it again. What a crazy damn world.

It is now 11 A.M., and I have long since finished my cup of coffee. I have watched all the news that I can stand, and it is time for lunch. Jim left the lounge awhile ago to go start some cases. I'll get him to watch my OR rooms while I am gone to lunch. Calling Jim Turner on my cell phone, I say "Say Jim, how about you keeping an ear open for my rooms, so that I can go eat some lunch, and when I get back, I'll do the same for you?" "Okay Jerry, I'll watch out for your rooms while you are gone," he says and continues "I still just can't get over that tragedy at the lumber yard though." "I know, that's the first time something like that has ever happened in this small town," I say to him. As I get up from the recliner and walk out of the lounge, I think poor Jim; the tragedy of this event has hit him hard. He has a soft heart and hates to see people suffer. That's why he went into medicine and Anesthesia to begin with. In Anesthesia, especially, you relieve pain and misery, quickly. We have some of the most powerful drugs in all of medicine, and we know how to use them to do this.

I walk through the lounge, through the dressing room, and out into the Hospital's main hallway. There are lots of people coming and going in both directions in this hallway. It is only about 75 feet (30 paces) from the door of the Doctor's Dressing Room to the door to the Doctor's Dining Room, but I get a dozen greetings of "Good morning Doctor Deluna," between the 2 doors. By the time I reach the door to the Doctor's Dining Room, I am tired of saying "Good morning," to all these people. There are very few of them that I know by name. It is only just 11, but I like to take my lunch early. I consider it one of the privileges of being the Chief of Anesthesia.

After punching in the number code to open the door to the Doctor's Dining Room, I quickly enter this room and close the door to escape all the 'good mornings' in that main hallway. I turn around, and the chef says to me "Good morning Doctor Deluna!" You just can't escape this shit. "Good morning," I say back to him. He then goes into his routine of listing off what is on the menu today. "We have grilled pork chops, cheese tortellini, lasagna, and smothered steak. We have steamed broccoli, garlic mashed potatoes, steamed carrots, and succotash. What'll you have today, sir?" he says to me in a loud voice. He always talks so loudly, either he must be hard of hearing, or he thinks that I am hard of hearing. I just don't know which it is, but I decide on my lunch "I'll have the grilled pork chop, tortellini, mashed potatoes, and succotash." "Yes sir, you must have worked up an appetite today," he says to me. I don't bother answering his question. Instead, I walk down the lunch line to get some yeast rolls and butter to eat while I am waiting for him to bring my food. Today I am hungrier than usual.

Walking over to a table with my yeast rolls in hand, I notice that I am the first one here today. That's good, I like being first in here. The food will be a little fresher. Plus, by the time I am finished and leaving this dining room, it will be getting busy in here. I don't like bumping elbows, crowded tables, or hustle and bustle at lunch time. A quiet, peaceful lunch time is what I prefer. I spend my time buttering my yeast rolls and eating them, enjoying the quiet break from the OR.

While I am nibbling on my yeast roll, the door opens and 2 Doctors walk into the dining room. One of them is complaining to the other, saying "That son-of-a bitch had my patient yanked off the OR table!" Just then, they both see me and stop talking. The complaining Doctor looks at me and his face gets red. I am smiling inside at this scenario; this tickles me. The Doctor who is doing the complaining is Tony Vanna, the Urologist whose case I had pulled out of the Operating Room. He is a fairly new Doctor in town, but he knows better than to give me a hard time about delaying his case. This is because of 2 reasons. First, he can't do anything to change the way things are. He doesn't have enough power. And, secondly, he knows that I could make his life here very difficult if he gets me angry. I have a lot of political clout in the Hospital Administration and within the Medical Staff here.

Doctor Tony Vanna makes $2,000 to $3,000 per hour, and I am delaying his case 1-2 hours, at least. This will also throw the rest of his day off schedule. The patients waiting to see him in his office will just have to wait until he gets there. There have been very few times when the threat of not being able to get their surgery done because of a past due bill has actually prevented a patient from getting their procedure. 99% of the time they come up with the money, and get their procedure done with only a little delay. I find it amusing that, even though Doctor Vanna is extremely angry at me and the situation that I caused, he can't say or do anything about it.

Doctor Vanna and his friend order their lunch from the chef and go to sit down at the table farthest away from me in this dining room. They do not even wish me a 'good morning'; can you believe it? Oh well. The chef delivers my food with the usual "Enjoy mon capitain." "Thank you," I reply. This stuff looks and smells wonderful. I don't bother trying to talk to the 2 angry Doctors on the far side of the room. And they certainly aren't trying to converse with me. The only thing that interests me right now is this meal in front of me. I ordered quite a lot of food, but I am extra hungry today.

After attacking my food like a starving wolf, I am finished with my meal in less than 15 minutes. Wiping my mouth after the last bite, I glance over at the 2 Doctors on the other side of the dining room. They have been huddled and talking quietly ever since they sat down. As I get up from the table, they stop talking and look over at me. I smile at them and give them a little wave before departing this room. As I walk back out into the main hallway, I am almost laughing at the situation I just experienced. It was like a scene from a movie, perfectly scripted and acted out. Yeah, I'm doing alright.

I walk back to the OR with a big grin on my face. Well, enough of fun, I say to myself. It's time to check in with Jim Turner and see what's been going on since I left the OR for lunch. As I am walking back through the Doctor's Dressing Room, I call him on my cell phone. He answers professionally "Hello, Doctor Jim Turner, how can I help you?" As I enter the Surgeon's Lounge, I see Jim and hang up my phone. I say to him "Hello Doctor Jim Turner, what's been happening since I last saw you." He sees me, hangs up his phone and says "2 of your rooms have just finished, the Total Knee and the Vascular Stent. But a 3rd C-section is about to start in a few minutes." I say "Very good, anything else?" He replies "We do have a situation in the hallway, outside OR 1." I know better, but I have to ask "What is it?"

Jim lays this pile of manure on me "In the hallway, right out there, is a black woman who is a Muslim. She had a spontaneous abortion, and needs a suction D and C (dilatation and curettage to clean out her uterus). She has a Muslim friend with her. This friend insists that she be allowed into the Operating Room with the patient for the procedure since the OB/GYN on call who will be doing the procedure is not a Muslim." I can feel a strong case of indigestion coming on as I am listening to this crap. We have no Muslin Surgeons of any kind in this town. Jim continues, "The circulator Nurse and the CRNA introduced themselves to the patient and did the preoperative questioning. The CRNA did his history and physical questioning, so he has her medical background. After he finished the Anesthesia questioning, he asked the patient if she had any questions. At this point, the Muslim friend spoke up and asked him if he or the circulator Nurse had had any 'Cultural Diversity Training'. At this point, they both said no. Then, they came to me and told me this story and asked what should be done." I ask "What did you tell them?" Jim says "I told them that you would be here to take care of this situation directly." "Gee, thanks," I say back to Jim. Jim tells me "Well Jerry, I didn't know what else to tell them. I've never had a situation like this, and I've never even heard of Cultural Diversity Training." I reply "Neither have

I." He asks me "What are we going to do about all of this?" "I'm going to tell the friend that she cannot go into the OR, that's what I'm going to do," I reply.

I have to take a minute to calm down and compose myself before I go out and talk to this asshole! Who in the hell does she think she is, to come into my Operating Room and demand to be present during a procedure because of Religious reasons? I tell you, the whole damn world is going crazy. If you had $1 left to spend on healthcare, would you rather spend it on saving a child's life, or let the child die and spend it on Cultural Diversity Training for your staff so that no one's religious beliefs would be offended??? This is just crazy! Spending our precious healthcare dollars on crap like that is one of the reasons that our healthcare system is so expensive.

After a couple minutes, I have calmed down enough to go out and deal with this jackass. I'll have to be careful with what I say to this asshole, or else we could all end up in court, getting spanked by some asshole Lawyer for racial discrimination, religious persecution, or some other nonsense he would drum up to make a buck on us.

I walk out into the OR hallway and immediately see them both, about 20 feet away, looking righteously indignant. Yes, I can smell trouble from these 2 idiots all the way from where I am standing. To these kinds of people, making their point is more important than all the healthcare we provide to the thousands of patients we take care of yearly. Well, I take a deep breath and walk up to them with a smile on my face, and say "How do you do? I'm Doctor Deluna, the Chief of Anesthesia. They tell me that you want to be present in the Operating Room during you friend's procedure. Is that correct?" The patient's friend has no expression on her face as she says to me "Yes sir. I need to be present because there will be no other Muslim's in the OR when the procedure is being done, and I will be there to make sure that her religious beliefs are not violated." "Do you have any medical or Nurses' training?" I ask her. She replies "No sir, I am just her friend. I am a professor at the local Vocational Technical School, where I teach math."

Now, this is beginning to take shape in my brain. I tell her "Yes ma'am, I understand your concern for your friend. It is very good to have a friend like you. She is lucky to have you. However, it is the policy of this Operating Room not to let any family members or friends into the OR with the patient for any reason. There are 2 reasons for this. First, we are concerned about infection. The more people there are in the OR, the greater the chance of infection. All of the people who work in the OR have to change their clothes when they come to work and wash their hands frequently and take other precautions to prevent infection. They are trained to take these precautions. Secondly, it is dangerous to you. There will be blood and unfamiliar smells and sights which could cause you to pass out and injure yourself. Years ago, we allowed a retired Nurse into the OR with her daughter for a procedure such as this. Soon after the procedure got started, she passed out, fell and hit her head against the wall and ended up dead as a result. And she was a Nurse. We don't ever want that to happen again, so now, we don't allow any noncritical people into the OR. I hope you understand our reasons for taking this position and allow us to take care of your friend. She is in need of help, and we can help her."

Damn, I'm good. I should get an Academy Award for the speech I just gave. The patient's friend had a troubled look on her face the entire time that I was talking to them. It changed to surprise at the part where the retired Nurse passed out, hit her head, and died. This was something that she had not thought of. This was new information that she suddenly had to process. And she arrives at the correct decision. "All right, I understand. We will allow her to go into the OR without me to have this procedure done, because she is bleeding badly and needs this," she says to me.

Inside, I breathe a sigh of relief. I tell her "Your friend does need this procedure. She could die if we don't help her. The Nurse will show you to the Surgical Waiting Room, and as soon as your friend gets to Recovery Room, we will go get you and allow you to sit with her in there." "Thank you. That will be good," she says to me, and even smiles a little. Her friend nods her approval and seems to be okay with this arrangement as well. "Thank you," I say, and smile before turning to walk away. Who the hell needs Cultural Diversity Training anyway?

Assholes like these come along every once in a while. You have to keep your cool and not let them drag you down to their level. They are visibly pleased when they can stop a whole Hospital from functioning and have the head of the department come and bow to them. This patient's friend is happy because she got special consideration in being allowed to come into the Recovery Room to sit with her friend after her surgery. It's all about power.

I walk over to the circulator Nurse and CRNA, who are waiting in the hallway by the assignment board. "Everything's okay, the patient can have her procedure without the friend being present in the OR, but she must be allowed to sit with her in the PACU afterwards," I tell them. They both have a look of amazement on their faces when I give them this news. "Well alright, let's get moving. Chop chop," I say to them. They immediately spring into action to bring the patient to the OR. Another Nurse will bring the patient's friend to the Surgical Waiting Room to wait until she gets to PACU.

Now that everything's okay to proceed, they will bring the patient to the OR. They will get her moved over, onto the OR table and get her hooked up to the blood pressure cuff, the pulse oximeter, and the EKG. Then, they will call the OB/GYN who is on Call and tell him that everything is okay and the patient is getting ready to go to sleep. He is right next door in my Doctor's Office Building. He will be amazed when he gets this news, and then he will come to the OR to do this patient's D & C. After they call the OB/GYN, they will call me, and I'll come to the OR and we'll get this patient off to sleep. This kind of goat-roping happens from time to time in the OR. You just have to keep your wits about you to handle these delicate situations.

After I have finished getting this Muslim patient off to sleep, and signing the Anesthesia Record, I am really tired. It must be from a combination of the work of the busy morning and the heavy lunch I ate. My other 3 cases are going well and will keep on going for another couple hours each. There is nothing else that needs my immediate attention right now, and I believe that this is a perfect time for a break.

Chapter Sixteen

Nap Time

I walk quickly to my office, hoping that no one will stop me to deal with any more bullshit before I get there. Right now, I am trying to de-stress from the preceding situation. My nerves are a little rattled at the moment. That pile of crap was a little trickier to handle than most of the things that I have to deal with around here. It took a lot of energy right out of me. Right now, I could really use a nap to recharge my battery. I look forward to taking a nap after lunch, in the middle of the day. 95% of the time, I can pull this off at work without any trouble.

After locking the door to my office, I decide to help settle my nerves with 2 fingers of scotch. That always seems to settle my nerves, which are still a little frazzled right now, after my encounter with those 2 Muslim assholes. Imagine them trying to get us to change the way we do things just to accommodate them. I unlock the drawer in my desk to get the scotch and a glass, and set them both on my desk. There are only a few shots of scotch left in this bottle, I notice before I pour a strong shot into the glass. I'll have to bring in another bottle next week, hidden in my briefcase. I swallow the 2 fingers of scotch in one swallow. Man, that feels good, going all the way down to the pit of my stomach. My nerves are already calming down as I return the glass and bottle to the drawer and lock it shut. I grab a couple of breath mints and pop them in my mouth to kill the smell of the liquor on my tongue.

It is so nice having my own office, right here in the OR. It is my little sanctuary away from my home sanctuary. I can relax in here, and shut out the hustle and bustle of the world. The digital clock on my desk says 12 noon. Now, it's time to kick back on my sofa, put my feet up on the ottoman, close my eyes, and catch a little rest. I love taking naps in here everyday, after lunch. Ring! Ring! My cell phone goes off and startles me. Goddamit, I say as I flip the damned phone open to answer the call. "Hello," I say into the phone. "Hello Jerry, this is Arnash. My rooms will be done in a few minutes, so I am about to leave for my home," he says. "Okay Arnash, have a nice day," I tell him. Whew, this phone call wasn't so bad. He was on call yesterday, so he is the first one out today. The other Anesthesiologists are supposed to call the on Call Doctor and let them know when they are leaving.

The on Call Anesthesiologist needs to know what other Anesthesiologists are here at all times. The on Call Anesthesiologist needs to be aware when the other Anesthesiologists are checking out so that they know what manpower is available in case an emergency arises. The surgical schedule today is not too bad. It is busy enough to make us a good amount of money, but not so busy that it works us to death. The afternoon doesn't look too bad today. This surgical schedule could finish early with a little luck. If it does finish early, I could go home and have dinner with Shirley. Who knows what fun and games await me later this afternoon.

Anyway, I put my feet up on the ottoman and lay my head back on the sofa. That phone call had rattled my nerves at first, but as soon as I heard Arnash's voice, I knew that it was nothing to worry about. I let out a long sigh and close my eyes. My nerves are calming down quickly, probably helped out by that shot of scotch. Also, this office has a calming effect on me. As I am resting here, it is so comfortable that I have the sensation that I am sinking deeper and deeper into the sofa. Oh yes, I am feeling relaxed now. I am sound asleep in 5 minutes.

Ring! Ring! My cell phone rouses me from a deep, deep sleep. After shaking my head a few times to clear the fog from my brain, I answer the call. "Hello," I say. "Doctor Deluna, Mr. Jones has a blood pressure of 185/99. Can I give him 10 milligrams of Labetolol (a drug to slow down the heart and relax the blood vessels)?" a PACU Nurse asks me. "Yes, that'll be okay," I reply. I don't have any idea who Mr. Jones is right now. Looking at my watch, I see that the time is 2 P.M.

It has been almost 2 hours since I closed my eyes, but I just can't shake the fog from my brain. Well, I know what will help this situation because I have done it many times. I get up from the sofa slowly because I'm not feeling very good at the moment and walk the 3 steps to my desk. A little hair of the dog will make me right as rain, I think as I unlock the desk drawer and retrieve the scotch and glass. Pouring 2 fingers of scotch into the glass, I notice that my hand is trembling a little. As I put the bottle down on my desk, I make a mental note to bring in another bottle next week because there is only about 2 inches left in this one. About a bottle a week keeps my nerves from getting too jangled here at work. I knock down the shot of scotch in one gulp. Man, that feels good all the way down, I think as I enjoy the warm feeling of the liquid going down my esophagus. That felt so good, I think I'll have another, and I do.

After the 2nd shot of scotch, I put the bottle and glass back in the drawer and lock it up. My nerves are calm now, as I chew on a couple of breath mints. There's nothing wrong with having good-smelling, minty breath. I'll finish chewing the first 2 mints, then put another one in my mouth before I leave my office. That should do just fine to cover up the scotch breath. Walking out of my office, I turn to lock the door, as I always do. I don't want any riffraff walking into my office, uninvited. The air in the hallway is cool on my face as I walk down to the assignment board to find the board runner Nurse and find out what is going on.

On my way to the assignment board, I walk past OR 7 and the door opens. Dan, the CRNA, pokes his head out and says to me "Hey Doctor Deluna, you've got to see this." I turn and walk into the OR and ask Dan "What's going on?" He says "Do you see that liquid up on the wall to your left?" "Yes," I reply. Dan tells me this "This patient is having a hemorrhoidectomy. He is an old guy, 78 years old. The Nurse on the floor didn't take out his dentures, and so we took them out after he went to sleep down here in the OR. His dentures were black with mold, because they hadn't been cleaned in forever. So Jenny (the Circulator Nurse) put them in a denture cup with some peroxide to clean up the mold. Then, she snapped the lid on the denture cup shut. Well, the pressure built up until the plastic denture cup exploded and spewed that nasty juice you see on the wall there. The old man's dentures flew 6 feet up in the air, but they didn't break. Isn't that crazy?" I am laughing uncontrollably as I hear the end of this story. "That is one hell of a story, alright Dan," I say when I can stop laughing long enough to speak.

Dan continues "The Surgeon was sitting on a stool and working between the old guy's legs when the thing exploded. It made a really loud 'pop' when it blew. You should have seen how high he jumped off that stool!" I am laughing so hard that tears are running down my face. When I can finally catch my breath, I say "Stop, please stop Dan, I can't take any more." Dan says "Jenny was talking to another Doctor on the phone when the denture cup exploded. The Doctor on the other end of the phone asked what the loud 'pop' was. He said it sounded like a shot on the phone." I barely manage to say "I can't take anymore," as I turn to walk out of OR 7. I have to lean against the wall in the hallway to steady myself because of how hard I am laughing. In back of me, I can hear the staff in the OR howling with laughter. After a couple of minutes, I manage to gather myself, dry the tears off my face, and take a couple of deep breaths. What a crazy story, I think to myself as I walk toward the assignment board. The air in the hallway is cool on my face as I walk, still giggling from that story. The hemorrhoid case in OR 7 will be done in 5 minutes.

Pearl is running the board today. I see her and ask "What is going right now?" She is not one of my favorite Nurses, and she knows it. She looks at me with a sour look on her face and says "Good afternoon Doctor Deluna. You have a total knee replacement going in OR 5, a vascular stent going in OR 6, and a C-section going upstairs. Doctor Avi just finished a C-section, and he has an I & D (incision and drainage) of a neck abscess going in OR 4, which will be done shortly. Doctor Turner is doing a knee arthroscopy in OR 2, a shoulder in OR 3, and his hysterectomy in OR 1 is just about finished." She continues "There is still a D & C, another hysterectomy, 2 gallbladders, an appendix, 2 hernia repairs, a bunion, and a broken arm left to be done."

I look at my cell phone to see why I haven't been called to start the knee, the vascular stent, and the C-section. The problem is easy to diagnose, the battery is dead. Oh, well. I just put the phone in a charger at the assignment board and walk to my 2 rooms going to sign the Anesthesia Records for the cases. In an hour, my phone will be fully charged and I'll be good to go for the rest of my Call. I'll just have to be a little more active during that hour to stay on top of my cases. Looking at my watch, I see that the time is 2:30 P.M.

These 9 cases aren't very long surgeries. The longest one will be the hysterectomy, which will last about 2 hours, start to finish. The next longest one will be the broken arm, which will take about 1 ½ hours. Most of the rest of them can be done in 30 minutes to 1 hour. With a little luck, I might actually get out of here by 5 P.M. or so. That means that I could have dinner at home with Shirley this evening. I am going to go sign in on my cases, then see about getting these other cases started as soon as possible. If I can push these cases into getting started quickly, I might just be able to do it. I don't have to do any packing for our trip to the beach house tomorrow because we have clothes and supplies already there. All we have to get for the weekend is food and drinks.

Walking into OR 5, where the total knee replacement is going, I am immediately relieved when I set eyes on Bob. For some reason, he always has a calming effect on me. "How's it going Bob?" I say to him. He looks up from the Anesthesia Record where he is writing down the patient's blood pressure and says "Oh, high Chief. Everything's going just dandy. You doing okay?" "Yeah, I'm doing okay. How long has this been going?" I inquire. Bob says "We made the incision about an hour ago, and we just cemented, so we'll be done in 30 to 40 minutes." "That's great," I tell him as I lean over to sign the Anesthesia Record. The shafts of knee replacements and hip replacements which go inside of the patient's bones are glued in place with a very strong glue that we call cement. "My cell phone went dead on me. Any problems?" I say to him. "No, no problems at all." He replies. That's why I like to work with Bob, I think as I leave OR 5.

As I walk into OR 6 to check in on the vascular stenting procedure, I can see Junius Britt tearing off his paper surgical gown. This case is done. I look over at Joe and say "My cell phone died awhile ago. Did everything go alright?" "Yes, everything went fine," he replies. I walk over to sign the Anesthesia Record, then turn to leave the OR. One of the good things about supervising multiple CRNAs doing multiple cases is that they are stuck in the OR and aren't aware of what I am doing. For all they know, I have been busy handling emergencies for the past 2 hours. Because of this, they think nothing of me coming into the room late to sign the record, or even signing it in PACU after the case is all done. The fact that I don't always come into the OR for the induction, or to sign the record at the beginning of the case doesn't bother them. Thank God they are all able to function independently without me.

After tearing off his gown and taking off his gloves, Junius sees me and says "High Jerry. Hey, can you make me a loan?" I laugh and say "Shit, Junius, you are worth more money than all of us put together." "I wish that were true my friend, I wish that that were true," he says and laughs like crazy at his own joke. Junius is a good guy and a good Surgeon. He just had a little financial setback when he divorced his first wife and married his beautiful, young office Nurse, Kelly. Thank goodness he just had to make one very large payoff to his first wife to satisfy her and her lawyer. He makes about $400,000 a year as a Vascular Surgeon, so he and his new, young bride have a nice lifestyle. They both seem to be very happy with the situation. Kelly just loves being 'the Doctor's wife', and Junius loves being seen with a hot, young babe on his arm. He tells me that he also loves the hot, hot sex. Isn't love great?

I walk out of OR 6 with Junius and ask "Hey Junius, do you still have another case to do, or are you going home to that hot little wife of yours?" Junius operates on Tuesdays and Thursdays, and I already know that he is done for the day. "Shit bo, its 3 o'clock. Its time to knock off and go home," he replies and continues "Kelly and I are going to go to that new Mexican restaurant, Pancho's, tonight. She's been dying to try it out. Do you know if the food's any good?" I tell him "Shirley had lunch there yesterday, and she said that the food is good. She also said that the place has a real nice atmosphere to it." Junius smiles and says "That sounds great. Kelly and I will eat, get toasted on Margaritas, and go home and screw our brains out." "That sounds like a perfect evening to me," I say. Junius says to me "Well, let me go and take care of a little paperwork at the office and then, I can go home and make it happen." "All right Junius, you have fun," I say to him as he walks away.

Right now, it is 3 P.M. and I need to go to the board to see what cases are left to be done. Will, the CRNA, comes up to me while I am walking toward the assignment board and presents me with the Anesthesia Record for the C-section to sign. This is great because I am now down to one room, the total knee replacement, and I can now cover 3 more new cases. I stop in the hallway as Will reaches me so that I can sign the paperwork on the wall. This case is done. "Everything go okay with the section?" I ask Will. "Yep, everything went smooth as silk. She was 5 foot 7 and only weighed 145 pounds, I couldn't believe it. I finally got a normal-sized patient for a C-section," he says to me. I reply "Well, you need a break every once in a while." Will says "Yeah, but it's been 6 months since I've seen one like her," and heads off to go file the paperwork for the case. So many women these days gain 100 pounds or more during their pregnancy. Don't they know that they'll never lose all that weight???

I absent-mindedly watch Will walk down the hallway a few steps, and then turn to go to the assignment board to see if I can get this schedule going. Right now, I am hoping for an early wrap up to the day's work. The OR staff would like to get these cases finished as quickly as possible this afternoon so that they can go home also. At 3 P.M. there is a lot of motivation to hurry up and get the work done so that we can all be home for dinner.

Chapter Seventeen

9 Cases to Go

I walk up to Pearl, the Nurse who is running the board, and ask "What's going on now Pearl?" She looks up from her paperwork at me with a sour look on her face. I swear this woman never smiles. Maybe it's just her game face. She cannot leave her job until all the cases have either been done, or are in a room, going. Once she has placed the last surgical case in an OR, she can leave for home. At this point, the RN who is on Call takes over if any other surgical case comes along. Pearl works 50 to 60 hours per week. Getting all the surgical cases done in a timely manner is not an easy job. Doctors are impatient and can give her a hard time when they are ready to operate. Every Surgeon acts as if their case is the most important one to be done; and they don't like waiting.

Pearl says to me "Doctor Turner just started the hysterectomy. The patient is a friend of his wife, so he'll stay to finish that. His shoulder is still going, but should be done soon. He also started the D & C and the bunion. The D & C will be done in 15 minutes and the bunion should be done in an hour. Doctor Avi has started one of the gallbladders, the appendix, and is getting ready to start one of the hernias. That just leaves a gallbladder, a hernia, and the broken arm, which should all be starting in the next few minutes. They should be calling you shortly." I tell her "Give me your phone to use until mine gets charged." She does so without hesitation. She'll just have to use a land line to call the Nurses and CRNAs in my ORs and let them know to call me on her phone for the next hour, until my phone is recharged.

She certainly is on top of things, I think as I listen to her rattle off the cases. Pearl continues "All of these cases should be in a room and going in the next 15 to 20 minutes, and then I'll be out of here." That's why she didn't protest about giving me her phone to use for the next hour. I look at my watch and see that the time is 3:30 P.M. That is why she is so motivated to get all the surgical cases in a room and going as quickly as possible. Doctor Avi's cases should all be done by 5, if not before. When his cases are done, he will go home. Doctor Arnash will be on Call tomorrow and the weekend. He is probably napping or taking it easy right now to rest up for his 3-day weekend of Call. Doctor Turner's shoulder, D & C, and bunion should all be finished by 4:30. His hysterectomy should be done by 5 or 5:30, and then he'll go home. It's too bad that he is requested for that case.

When a patient requests you to do the Anesthesia for their surgery, it is both an honor and a curse. If everything goes perfectly, you are a hero and the patient will tell all his friends and relatives what a great Doctor you are. If, however, things don't go well and the patient has problems, they tend to look at you as if you are part of the problem. They don't tend to look at you as a good guy, someone who is trying to make the problem better. And God help you if the patient who requests you dies during the surgery, or shortly after. You really lose style points on that one. Even if the family doesn't include you in the following lawsuit, they will probably still talk badly about you.

My phone is going off. "Hello," I say. "Doctor Deluna, we are ready for you in OR 2," the Nurse says to me. I reply "I'll be right there." I walk quickly to OR 2 because I am anxious to get these cases going and done. As I approach the OR, I see Doctor Danny May (Orthopedic Surgeon) washing his hands at the scrub sink. "Hey Danny, what's the story here?" I ask. He says "This kid is the son of Nancy (one of our PACU Nurses). He fell off his 4-wheeler and hit his forearm and broke his radius and ulna midshaft (both of the bones of the forearm). I'm just going to set the bones and put a cast on him. It shouldn't take more than 20 or 30 minutes." This is music to my ears. Not only will this case not last very long, but the patient also has insurance. A double bonus!

Walking into OR 2, I hold the door open for Doctor May to walk through and look at the patient on the OR table. It is a young man (about 16 or 17) with his right arm wrapped in a large bandage. I have to ask "Did your mom put that bandage on you?" He says "Yes sir, she drove me to the Hospital too." "Did the bones break through the skin?" I ask. The kid says "No sir, but I have a bad scrape and it really hurts." I nod to Elizabeth, the CRNA, to begin giving the induction drugs to put him to sleep. "It's alright son, I'm Doctor Deluna and I'll get you off to sleep now. Everything's going to be okay. You just pick out a nice dream," I tell him, just like I've done thousands of times before. By the time I get finished with my spiel, he is unconscious.

After the patient is asleep, Elizabeth says to John, the scrub tech, "Didn't you used to work at the Level 1 trauma center in Columbia?" John replies "Yes, I did." Elizabeth asks "Didn't they have a crazy Orthopedic Surgeon that made everyone in his room tape up the bottom pants legs of their scrubs so that they wouldn't drop pubic hair on the floor in his OR?" "Yes, they sure did. But that's one thing I didn't have to worry about," John replies and laughs (implying that he shaves his pubic hair). Doctor May pipes in with "I didn't need to know that! That's TMI (too much information)." John is laughing like crazy, and so is Elizabeth. "What was that crazy guy's name?" Elizabeth inquires. John answers "Doctor Shadluck, but he's retired now." "Thank God," Elizabeth says. "Yes, he was old when I was there, and things were getting to him," John answers back. I can hardly believe the conversation that I am listening to, but it is indeed taking place. It just goes to show that you don't have to be sane to finish Medical School. Not since my Residency have I had to work with a Surgeon as crazy as Doctor Shadluck. I walk over to sign the Anesthesia Record and leave OR 2 because my phone is going off again to tell me about another case to start.

After flipping open the phone to answer the call, I say "Hello, this is Doctor Deluna." "Ready for you in OR 3 Doctor Deluna," the OR Nurse says to me. I walk the 5 paces from OR 2 to OR 3 quickly, open the door, and say "I'll be right there," as I walk in. The Nurse on the phone looks at me with astonishment on her face, and then smiles and says "You were right outside, weren't you?" "Yes, I was," I reply, and follow with "Turn up that temperature, it's too cold in here." I look over and see that Joe, the CRNA, is pushing the induction drugs in the IV to put the patient to sleep right now. After waiting 30 seconds (until the patient is asleep), I ask him "What are we doing here?" "Gallbladder," Joe says to me. "Who is the Surgeon?" I ask. Joe replies "Jake Barns." This is good news because Jake is very quick, and this case will be done in less than an hour. I walk over to the Anesthesia machine to sign the record, and exit the room without any further conversation.

Once I am out in the hallway, I pull down my paper mask so that I can breathe better. Those things suck! The air in the OR hallway feels very cool and good on my face. Operating Rooms are usually kept very cool, with a temperature around 65 degrees, and the humidity below 50%. You get spoiled to this degree of air conditioning. After years of working in this environment, I am not able to handle heat very well. I look at my watch and see that the time is 4 P.M. All is going well right now. A noise to my left catches my attention, and I turn to see what it is. It's Bob, rolling the total knee replacement into the PACU. There is only the hernia repair left to start, and then every case will be going. This afternoon is really starting to shape up.

I follow Bob into the PACU and ask "Everything go okay, Bob?" He turns around to look at me, smiles and says "Smooth like butter chief." There is something that I want to know. I ask him "Hey Bob, are you on Call with me tonight?" "No sir, one beating per week is about all that I can take at my age these days," He replies. This means that he takes Call one day a week, and one weekend a month. This adds about $60,000 a year to his income. I laugh and say "Oh come on Bob, it wasn't all that bad." "The hell it wasn't. I just can't work like I used to," He says back to me. "Who can, who can?" I say back to him. This is not good news to me. I was hoping to be on call with Bob tonight because he can handle absolutely everything with no trouble. I have to ask, "What CRNA is on call tonight?" "Will has got the duty tonight," he says back.

Just then, Mrs. Ginn walks into the PACU. She is the woman who does our billing for Anesthesia services. When she sees me, she says "Doctor Deluna, I've got something to show you." I can't wait to see what this is about. She shows me a billing card. A billing card is filled out by the CRNA during the surgical case, so that we can use that information to generate a bill which we send to the insurance company. "Do you see anything wrong?" she asks me. I look at the procedure line on the card, and it says Incision and Debridement of Volvo. I have to read it twice to make sure that I am seeing what I am seeing. Mrs. Ginn is frowning at me while I am reading. When I am finished reading it for the second time, I just laugh and say to her "Paul (the CRNA) must have been distracted when he wrote this. I'm sure the OB/GYN on this case I & D'ed a Vulva, not a Volvo. I'll get him to correct it tomorrow." She has a look of relief on her face and says to me "Thank you Doctor Deluna." She turns and goes to pick up today's billing cards so that the money can keep on rolling in. I'm sure that this little mistake upset her a lot because she is a very religious and straight-laced woman.

So Will is on call with me tonight. Well, I guess that's not too bad. Will is a solid performer. If I can't be on Call with Bob, Will is not a bad alternative. He has nearly as much experience as Bob. I can breathe easy tonight. There are just a couple of CRNAs out of the 14 who work here that I don't care to work with very much. They just don't have as much experience. Just then, my phone goes off. I say "Hello, this is Doctor Deluna." "Ready for you in OR 6 Doctor Deluna," the Nurse says. I reply "I'll be right there." "Have a good afternoon, you lazy bum," I say to Bob. He laughs and says "Thanks, you too chief." Off to OR 6 I go to get the last case of the day started. I am excited because, in about 5 minutes, every case will be in a room and going. This is wonderful. I can see the light at the end of the tunnel.

When I get close to the door to OR 6, I see none other than my friend, Brett Smith, washing his hands at the scrub sink. "Hey Brett," I say as I walk past him. I crack the door open and see Will, the CRNA, holding the oxygen mask on the patient's face. "Go ahead," I say to him. He nods okay to me and proceeds with the induction. I turn and walk the 3 steps to the scrub sink and say "High Brett. How have you and Cindy been doing?" Brett says "When you walked past me, I thought you were mad at me because you didn't stop to talk." I laugh and say "Hell no, I just wanted to get your case going quickly." "Well, there's nothing wrong with that," he says back and continues "Cindy is doing well. She is a very solid, constant woman. I'm really glad that I have her in my life. I, on the other hand, am all over the place. Hell, I might even be working too hard." He laughs after he makes this comment. "Say it isn't so," I say to him and share a laugh with him.

Brett says to me "Hey Jerry, what time do you have?" I look at my watch and tell him "It's 4:15." He says "That's good. This is just an inguinal hernia, which will only take me 30 or 40 minutes to do. I have somewhere to be at 5:30." Operating Room people are very time conscious people. I guess it's because we measure our activities at work in minutes, all day, every day. Brett is done with the surgical scrub of his hands, so I walk in front of him and hold the door to the OR open for him to pass through. "Go get em, tiger," I say to him. He laughs as he walks over to take the sterile paper towel from the scrub tech to dry his hands. After he has dried his hands, the scrub tech will help him put on the surgical gown and sterile gloves which all Surgeons wear when doing their work. There is a very particular way that gowning and gloving a Surgeon has to be done, so that he maintains the sterility of the outside of his gown and gloves.

I walk over to the Anesthesia machine to sign the Anesthesia Record and say to Will "I hear that you are on Call with me tonight." He replies "That is correct." "Let's keep it quiet tonight, okay?" I say to him. He laughs and says to me "I'll do my best." He and I both have absolutely nothing to do with how busy we will be tonight, or not. I pull the billing card out of my pocket that has Volvo as the surgical procedure on it and show it to Will. "Do you see anything wrong with this?" I ask him. He laughs and says "Shit, let me correct this. I don't know what I was thinking when I wrote this." "I know that's right," I say back to him as I hand him the card.

He was probably distracted by someone talking to him when he wrote Volvo on the billing card. It's not part of the patient's Medical Record, so there's no harm done at all. All he has to do is draw a line through what he wrote, and write I & D of Vulva for the surgical procedure. After that, he'll just put it in the bin with all the other bills for all the other surgeries, so that Mrs. Ginn can pick it up. This is a very simple thing. Mrs. Ginn is not supposed to write on the Anesthesia billing card at all. I won't correct it myself because I don't write on the billing cards at all. I just collect the money from them. The CRNAs fill out the billing cards, and if they do it wrong, they have to correct it. It's just one of the many things that they have to do, while also doing the Anesthesia that is their main job. Oh well.

Well, that detail is taken care of. I walk out of OR 6 and head down the hall to pick up my cell phone from the charger and replace it with Pearl's. Then I walk to the Surgeon's Lounge. It's 4:30 P.M., and I'm excited at the way that this afternoon of Call is playing out. Right now, I'm going to go make me a cup of coffee, and then give Shirley a call. She'll be delighted to hear that I will be coming home in an hour or so. We might even have a nice, quiet dinner at home, and maybe a little sex afterwards. That would be so nice. With a little luck, I'll be able to sleep in my own bed tonight.

In less than 2 minutes, I have a hot cup of Columbian coffee with a little cream in it. This stuff really is delicious. I sit down in a recliner and use the remote control to turn down the volume on the television, which is tuned to the financial channel. In this lounge, the TV is almost always on the 24 hour news channel, or the financial channel. Doctors love to watch the stock market go up and down. I take another sip of coffee and dial my home number on my cell phone.

After the second ring, Shirley answers the phone and says "Hello." "Hello darling, how are you doing?" I say to her. "High Jerry, I've just got a couple of ice chests out to pack some food in when we leave for the beach house tomorrow. Maybe we could fill them with some good shrimp and fresh fish to bring back home on Sunday," she says. "That sounds like a great idea," I reply.

Our beach house is fully stocked with all the things we need to stay there, even clothes, shoes and toiletries. We just stop at a grocery store and a liquor store near the place to load up on the booze and perishable food that we need. It's very nice to have all the things we need to be comfortable, already there for us. There is a fresh seafood market just a short distance from our beach house, where we can load up on seafood just brought in from the boats. We'll go there on Saturday and put it in our freezer at the beach house so that it will be frozen solid for the trip back on Sunday. I like keeping good, fresh seafood in the house at all times. You never know when you might like some good shrimp, fish, or crab for a meal at a moment's notice.

Shirley asks me "How are things looking at work? Are you real busy? Are you going to have to stay there all night?" You never can predict how a Call will go. Sugar can turn to shit in a second, and vice versa. Poor Shirley is worried that I'll have to pull an all-nighter like I did on Tuesday. I am smiling as she pops these questions at me, one after another. She always gets excited when we go to the beach house. She loves it there. When she pauses, I reply "Things are actually looking pretty good over here. It looks like everything might be done in about an hour, and I should be home between 5:30 and 6." "Oh Jerry, that sounds great," she says, and continues "Do you want to pick up some take-out on the way home? I'll light some candles and we could have a nice, romantic dinner at home." I tell her "That sounds great babe. Hey, how about let's have Italian tonight, since we'll be eating seafood all weekend." She says "Yes, that's a great idea. You call me when you are about to leave the Hospital, and I'll call Marino's to place our order."

Shirley knows that I just love the lasagna from Marino's Italian Restaurant. This helps her because she knows that if she orders the lasagna for me, I'll be happy. The only problem for her is to decide what she wants to eat from there. She is more finicky. She likes the shrimp salad, but we'll be eating a lot of seafood at the beach. If she's really hungry, she'll probably order a steak. It's a good thing that she'll have a half hour or so to look at their menu and decide what to order.

Just then, my phone is beeping at me, telling me that I have another call coming in. I tell Shirley that I love her and have to hang up on her to answer the other call. "Hello," I say into the phone. "Hey Doctor Deluna, its Bob. The total knee is done and I have the patient in PACU. Everything's good and I'm going to get out of here now since I'm not on Call," he says to me. I tell him "That sounds good Bob. Hey, did I sign the record?" He replies "Yes sir, you signed it." "Alright Bob, you have a good evening," I tell him. That Bob is always on top of things.

I look at my watch and see that the time is 5:00 P.M. One down and three to go, I think to myself. This is looking really good. I think I'll go to my office and have a shot of scotch to celebrate my good fortune. Before I can get up from the recliner, Doctor Avi comes into the lounge with a big grin on his face and sits down in the recliner next to mine. He's looking right at me with a grin from ear to ear. I can't wait to hear this.

Doctor Avi finally stops grinning, says to me "Jerry, the gallbladder is out and they are starting to close the patient's belly. This is my last case, so I'll leave when they are in PACU." "That sounds good Avi," I reply. He has such a big grin on his face that I just know something else is coming. "Jerry, I have something else to tell you," he says. I say "What is it?"

Doctor Avi starts his story. He says to me "Jerry, do you know the freelance Anesthesiologist, Micky Johns, who has been working at Jonesboro?" "No, I have heard of him, but I don't really know him at all" I reply. I knew that the old Anesthesiologist had retired and the hospital in Jonesboro has been hiring freelance Anesthesiologists to replace him through a temporary agency for the past year. Avi says "Well, I know a CRNA who works down there and she called me an hour ago to tell me that Micky started having an affair with a Nurse from the OR there. His soon-to-be ex-wife, who lives at their home in Florida, found out about it, and now she is looking for him." I shouldn't do it, but I have to ask "Is he missing?" "Yes," Doctor Avi says, and continues, "He also interviewed at the hospital in Oldtown for a position. They gave him a $20,000 sign-on bonus to take the job. He took the money, but never showed up for work. And so, the hospital in Oldtown is looking for him now too. It appears that he and his new girlfriend, the OR Nurse from Jonesboro, took off together and no one knows where they are."

I just shake my head at this story and say "That guy is going to be in a world of pain when his wife and that hospital catch up to him." A story like this just goes to show that you don't have to be sane to finish Medical School. "He's going to be in jail when they catch up to him," Avi says. He is still grinning, and asks me "Do you want to hear another crazy story?" He never talks this much to me, but I say "Oh, why not. Go ahead." He obviously is dying to tell me another story, and I have a few minutes. Besides, I haven't heard any really good gossip in a few days.

Doctor Avi tells me "The hospital in Winterville has been having to hire freelance Anesthesiologists to fill some positions also. They hired a guy through an agency last month. He seemed alright during the job interview and the first day. But on the second day, he began to appear weak. He just slid down the hallways, holding onto the handrail as he walked, and sliding against the wall to get down the hallway to the ORs. People thought that was a bit strange. They had not seen anything yet. On the second week of work, he came to work in a wheelchair. He was too weak to walk at all, and he had to go from OR to OR in his wheelchair to sign the Anesthesia Record." "Damn Avi, what in the hell was wrong with him?" I ask. He tells me "Well, the Chief of Anesthesia made a phone call to the last hospital that he worked at and talked to the Chief of Anesthesia there to see if he could get some information. It turns out that this guy is HIV+. Apparently he and his boyfriend have been working their way down the East coast, working at hospitals along the way through a temporary agency that didn't check him out very well." In this state, if you are HIV+, you can't work in healthcare at all.

"Damn Avi. Is that true?" I ask. He replies "Yes sir, I verified it with another person I know who works down there. Both of those stories are true." I tell him "Well, that's some of the craziest stories I've ever heard in my life. Thank God that son-of-a-bitch with HIV didn't actually have to touch a patient. I know there has been an Anesthesia shortage ever since the Clintons were in the White House and screwed up healthcare in this country. But, are we really that short of Anesthesia Doctors and Nurses in this country that we would have to resort to sorry lunatics like these two Doctors for manpower?" Avi says to me "Yes sir. Two years after the Clintons were in the White House and they started to mess with healthcare, there was almost no one going into Anesthesia Residency programs. As a result of their meddling, salaries for Anesthesia went up 30% before Bill finished his first term, due to personnel shortage, and the manpower shortage they created will not be caught up in our lifetimes." "That is true," I say and continue, "I don't know what makes politicians think that they can improve the healthcare in this country. Hell, the politicians would probably do more to benefit healthcare if they made it illegal."

Just then, both our phones go off. We both answer our calls. My phone call is from Joe, the CRNA, telling me that the gallbladder is done and the patient is in the PACU. Hot damn, 2 cases to go. After Doctor Avi answers his phone call, he says to me "Jerry, my gallbladder is done and the patient is in PACU. I will be going home now. I hope that you have a good Call." As he rises from the recliner, I tell him "Have a good evening Avi." "Thank you sir," he replies as he walks away.

My phone goes off again. "Hello," I say. Elizabeth, the CRNA, says "High Doctor Deluna, this is Elizabeth. We are done with the fractured arm. The patient is in PACU. He is doing fine. I'm getting ready to head home." I reply "Okay Elizabeth, have a good afternoon." This is shaping up; the only case left is the hernia, and that should be finished soon. Checking my watch, I see that the time is 5:30 P.M. I think I'll go to my office and have that shot of scotch now to celebrate my good fortune at the way this Call is shaping up this afternoon.

I stand up from the recliner and have to struggle to steady myself for a second. Whew, I was feeling a little woozy there, for a second. The feeling of being unsteady passes quickly, thank goodness, and I head out of the lounge to go to my office. After locking the door to my office behind me, a feeling of calmness comes over me. Right now, I am in my little sanctuary, and I always feel better when I am in my office. After putting my cell phone on my desk, I unlock the desk drawer and pull out the nearly-empty bottle and the glass. I pour an inch of scotch in the glass and see that there is only one shot left in the bottle. In one gulp, I knock down the shot. My nerves are immediately soothed as the liquor warms its way down to my stomach.

My phone goes off and I answer the call. I am hopeful that this is the word on the last case, the hernia repair. It is. Will, the CRNA, says to me "High Doctor Deluna, this is Will. The hernia is done. We'll be leaving the OR in less than 5 minutes." I tell him "That's great Will. Did everything go okay?" "Yes sir, the patient was a little slow to come back breathing on their own, but they are doing great now and we are putting the dressing on as we speak." "Alright, good job Will," I reply.

This is great; the hernia will be in PACU in 10 minutes, or less. I'll just make a pass through the PACU to look in on the patients, show a little face time, so to speak, and then I'll be out of here. Oh happy day. To celebrate, I pour the last shot out of the bottle of scotch into the glass. After that, I pack the empty bottle into my briefcase so I can through it in the trashcan in the parking deck when I leave. I knock down the last shot in one gulp. Man, but that was good! My nerves are calm as can be.

After putting a couple of breath mints into my mouth, I give Shirley a call to tell her the good news that I'll be out of here in 15 minutes. I look at my watch and see that the time is 5:45. She picks up the phone on the second ring and says "Hello." "Hello darling, I'll be out of here in 15 minutes," I say to her. She replies "That's wonderful Jerry. Do you want me to order some lasagna from Marino's for you for dinner?" "That will be perfect dear, thank you," I say to her. She says "Jerry this is great, I am excited about going to the beach house tomorrow. It's been more than a month since we've been there. We'll have a nice, cozy little Italian dinner at home. And with a little luck, you won't be called back tonight, so you will be rested for our trip to the beach tomorrow." "That's what I'm hoping for dear," I say to her, and continue "Well, let me go check on a few patients in recovery room, and then I'll get dressed and come home." Shirley says "That sounds good. I'll call in our order to Marino's so that it'll be ready when you get there." "That sounds good. Love you," I reply. "Love you," she says and hangs up.

That Shirley is a good wife. And she is so hot-looking. I feel lucky to have her. Well, here we go. I grab my briefcase and lock up my office for the day. Next Monday I'll bring in another bottle of scotch to put into my desk drawer. All I have to do is swing through PACU briefly, and then get dressed in my street clothes and head to Marino's to pick up our food before I go home. That sounds like a good plan.

I spend less than 5 minutes in recovery room, mostly just double-checking that I signed the Anesthesia Record on each case. Before I leave PACU, I say to Will "I hope I don't see you anymore tonight." He laughs and says "I hope I don't see you either." This is our way of saying that we both hope that we don't have any more cases tonight. Will gets paid just for being on Call, even when he just sits around the lounge or sleeps. And I would rather sleep in my own bed tonight, rather than come in and make money doing more Anesthesia.

I pick up my briefcase before I leave PACU and walk quickly to the dressing room to change into my regular clothes. When I glanced at all the patients in the PACU, I could see that they were all doing well by the vital signs on their monitors. A couple of them were even sitting up and looking around. In less than 1 hour, they will all be in their regular hospital rooms. In less than 5 minutes, I am in my street clothes and walking out of the dressing room with my briefcase in hand. Walking briskly down the hallway, I glance at my watch and see that the time is 6 P.M., perfect. As I walk out of the building and into the parking deck, I look around to see if anyone else is around. There is no one else in this deck, so I walk over to a trashcan and deposit the empty scotch bottle into it. I'm glad that's done. After this, I go to my SUV and jump into the glove-soft leather seat. I fire up the big V8, man but I love the sound of this engine, I think as I rev it up a little. Putting the transmission into reverse, I prepare to haul-ass out of this parking deck. I am ready to get my food and get home.

Chapter Eighteen

Call is Almost Done

As I pull out of the parking deck, I see that it is raining a light summer rain. I sure hope that it doesn't rain the entire time we are at the beach. Off to Marino's Italian Restaurant I go to pick up our to-go order. Shirley called it in about 15 minutes ago and it will take me 10 minutes to get there, so it should be ready when I get there. Driving in the rain is always a little stressful because people around here nut up when it rains. I am chewing on another breath mint because I want to have sweet breath when I get home and kiss Shirley. She'll appreciate it, I hope.

After a few minutes of driving cautiously in the rain, I pull into the parking lot of Marino's. There is to-go parking right in front of the restaurant, near the front door. The light rain has eased up so that I hardly get wet going the 20 feet from my car door to the front door of the restaurant. As soon as I enter the door, Mr. Marino, who is manning the cash register, says "Doctor Deluna, how are you? Not getting too wet outside, I hope." He has known me for years. "Not too bad, the rain is easing up," I say to him and add "I have a to-go order to pick up." "I'll have the girl bring it right up," Mr. Marino says. He makes a phone call and 1 minute later, a waitress arrives, carrying a large bag. Mr. Marino says "I put some extra bruschetta in there for you." "Thanks, I appreciate it. What do I owe you?" I say to him. Without hesitation, he says "$39.50." Wow, I think to myself, Shirley must have gone all out on this order. I slap 2 twenties on the counter and tell him "Keep the change." He laughs and says "Alright, big spender." "Take care," I tell him as I turn and walk outside.

Shirley and I have gone to this restaurant many times, and I like to joke around with Mr. Marino. He likes to joke around too. The rain has completely let up now. I put the bag of food on the passenger floor board and buckle up for the ride home. Another 10 minute ride and I'll be home. I can't wait, this food smells so good. The aroma of tomato sauce and garlic is filling up the car.

On my way home, I see a wreck. These idiots just can't drive in the rain. Hell, they can't drive when it's not raining. They can't figure out that they need to slow down because you just can't stop as fast as normal. I speed past the accident scene as soon as I am able to, because I never stop at wrecks to see if I can be of help. It just isn't worth it. Financially, it's not even worth it to do trauma in the Operating Room because they almost never have insurance. Plus, I'm in a hurry.

In no time, I'm pulling into my driveway and opening the garage door. I just pull up, shut the garage door, and turn off the engine. Aah, a calmness comes over me as the garage door shuts. This always happens to me when I come home. I grab the bag with the to-go order and get out of the SUV to see Shirley smiling at me from the door. Man, that's a welcome sight. "Honey, I'm home," I say to her with a big smile on my face. She steps up and gives me a hug and a kiss when I get close. I can only hug her back with one arm because the other one is carrying our food. "I'm so glad things finished up early and you are home," she says to me. "So am I," I reply.

Shirley turns and holds the door open for me to pass through. We walk into the kitchen, where I set the bag of Italian food down on a counter. "That sure smells good," she says. "Well, let's eat," I say back to her. I am really hungry. She asks me "Would you like a glass of Chianti with dinner?" I tell her "I sure would." Nothing is better with Italian food than a good Chianti. We both get busy, preparing for dinner. Shirley opens a bottle of wine, and I open the to-go containers. We move everything to a small table in the corner of the kitchen, where we sometimes eat breakfast, or a cozy dinner like this.

I just love the lasagna from Marino's, and they always give you a large serving. Shirley ordered veal marsala for herself, and salads for us both. She also ordered fried ravioli for our appetizer. The woman went all out this time. We end up drinking, talking, and eating for nearly 2 hours. During this time, we drink 2 bottles of Chianti. The time is now 9:00 P.M., and we are both feeling full and lazy. Shirley has had a busy day getting a few things ready for our trip to the beach house tomorrow. She has also packed us some snack food for the 2 hour drive. And I have had a busy day at work.

Shirley stretches her arms to the ceiling and says "Boy, am I tired. What do you say we call it an early night so we can be rested for our trip tomorrow." "That sounds like a good idea to me. Besides, I might get called and have to go in and work later tonight," I reply. My Call ends at 7 A.M. "Don't say it. Let's think positively," she says. "Alright, alright," I say back to her. I hope to God that I don't get called back to the Hospital tonight for something.

We leave our empty wine bottles and the empty to-go containers on the table where we ate, and head to the bedroom. The maid will clean it up tomorrow. Within 15 minutes we are both in our pajamas, lying next to each other in bed. You have to brush your teeth really good after Italian food, or else you'll have garlic breath. Shirley says "That was really a good meal. I feel so good. I'm going to sleep like a baby tonight. I love you Jerry." She snuggles a little closer to me to settle in. I tell her that I love her too and give her a kiss on the head. Right now, I'm feeling really good also, between the good Italian food, the good Italian wine, and having Shirley snuggled up close to me. Life is good. We are both asleep in no time.

Ring! Ring! It takes me a few seconds to realize that my cell phone is going off. Shit, I hope this is nothing important, I think as I shake my head to try to clear the cobwebs. I sit up in bed and answer the call. This just better not be anything serious. "Hello," I say. The clock on the nightstand says 11:00 P.M. Will, the CRNA, says "Hello Doctor Deluna, sorry to call you this late, but we have a C-section to do." "Can you handle it by yourself?" I ask. "Sure, no problem," he says to me. "Alright then, call me if you have any problems," I reply. "I'll be okay," he says. "Alright," I say and hang up the phone and lie back down in bed. He will be okay. Will has done thousands of C-sections without an Anesthesiologist present. I'll just sign the Anesthesia Record for this case on Monday, when I am back at work. That way, I can collect ½ the Anesthesia fees for the case. I sure am relieved that it was not any big surgical case, because I would have to get dressed and go to the Hospital for that. Even though all I would have to do for that is sign the record, and then go to my office and sleep on the sofa. This way, I'll get to sleep in my own bed tonight. That is always better for a good night's rest.

I sure am glad that I have experienced CRNAs like Will at work, who can handle little things like this on their own. It gives me peace of mind. I can hear the sound of Shirley breathing after I snuggle back into my pillow. In less than 10 minutes after I have hung up the phone, I am back in a deep, deep sleep. The world is a million miles away.

Chapter Nineteen

My Weekend Starts

My eyes open to see Shirley holding a large glass of what looks like orange juice out to me and saying "Good morning darling. Here is a mimosa to get you going." Wow, what a woman! "What time is it?" I ask, as I sit up in bed and take the drink from her hand. She leans over and gives me a kiss and says "Why it's 7:30 in the morning, and your Call is done." "Yeah!" I say back to her, and take a big swallow of the champagne and orange juice. Wow, that's good. What a great way to start my weekend. Shirley says to me "I already have the SUV packed for the trip, with 2 empty ice chests in the back and a picnic bag of snacks in the front. I heated up some cinnamon rolls for breakfast if you are hungry. I bought them at the bakery yesterday." I take another big swallow of my drink, and say "Hell yes, that sounds great for breakfast!" I love cinnamon rolls, and I love mimosas in the morning. This is great; we'll be at the beach house and have time for a walk in the sand before lunchtime. We just have to stop at the liquor store for supplies, and the grocery store for perishables on the way.

After 2 cinnamon rolls and 2 more mimosas, I am good and awake. I quickly get dressed in a T-shirt, shorts, and sandals. 30 minutes after I have opened my eyes, we are in the SUV and backing out of the garage. It's off for a weekend at the beach house for us. Party time.

Conclusion

I have been wanting to write this book for a long time. Over the years, I have seen things that made me think, what would people say if they knew that things like this happened in Medicine. Well, I finally sat down and pulled a few of the stories in my memory together for this book. There are many stories which simply would not be good for public consumption. These will stay tucked away in permanent storage.

In the Operating Room, I have seen miracles worked. There is one thing that Lawyers and nonmedical people will never understand. When you help a person do things that they are unable to do for themselves, there is a spiritual component which transcends this world we live in. You cannot put a dollar value on this. Most Surgeons, Nurses, and Anesthesiologists are working like dogs every day to take care of patients in a system that they did not create. A system which is becoming more and more oppressive over time. Healthcare is so over-regulated now that it is sad. This is a major factor causing inefficiency and high cost. But there is no end in site.

I have seen true wizards doing Medicine and Nursing. They are magical and awesome to behold when they perform patient care. Many Nurses and Doctors touch not only the patient's body, but their soul as well. I hope the bureaucrats don't kill them off with overregulation. They inspire the regular, more normal of us to do better and greater things. Medicine (and Nursing) is still a place where you can truly touch another person's soul when doing your job. There is nothing like it. I hope it always keeps a little bit of this.

Edwards Brothers,Inc!
Thorofare, NJ 08086
14 September, 2010
BA2010257